Fang Chronicles: Book II
Emily's Story

By
D'Elen McClain

Copyright 2012 D'Elen McClain

All rights reserved including the right to reproduce this book or portions thereof in any form.

This is a work of fiction. ALL characters are derived from the author's imagination.

No person, brand, or corporation mentioned in this Book should be taken to have endorsed this Book nor should the events surrounding them be considered in any way factual.

Chapter 1

Nineteen years ago…

The soft patter of rain beating against the rooftop did not mask the sound of breaking glass coming from the first floor of Carolynn's home or diminish the ire at having her sleep disturbed. Living in a rural community was usually peaceful. Wild animals sometimes crashed through windows but crime was virtually nonexistent.

She grabbed the Glock from the nightstand drawer. In the event the intruder was a large predator the shotgun would have been a better choice but it waited uselessly downstairs in the gun cabinet. The 9mm would do.

Even though silence crept up the dark steps meeting her descent, she knew she would never get back to sleep if she didn't check the house. The damage a raccoon could do by morning was unbelievable.

Slowly she made her way downstairs, peering into the looming darkness, wondering if she should turn on a light, dreading what she might find. Her feelings of unease grew but she had no one to face the darkness in her stead. Taking a deep breath to steady her nerves, she walked the final steps to the first floor.

The porch light outside cast a soft welcoming glow into the front room. She turned and silently moved toward the kitchen.

Suddenly, a soft noise whispered through the darkness and she spun toward the sound.

A naked man stood ten feet away almost concealed by the dark shadows of the room.

In one swift movement she lifted the gun and took a short inward breath. She had a split second to notice the man do the oddest thing. He smiled.

The hard trigger clicked and the gun jerked. The explosion thundered throughout the house as his body slammed into hers.

Her back hit the hard unforgiving floor and the gun flew from her hand. Pinned beneath the intruder, she could only watch as the gun slide out of reach.

Instinct took over and Carolynn fought. Her arms flailed and her legs kicked while her fingers gouged at unyielding flesh.

She never had a chance.

Her pleas did not change the course of events that occurred over the next hour.

The stranger never uttered a word. He walked out the front door when he was finished.

She could only stare at the dark bloody smears that trailed across the floor and her skin from the bullet wound to his arm. Despite the shock to her mind and body, his smell was the one thing Carolynn would never forget. It was the pungent odor of a wet dog.

She cried at the injustice. Her skin turned raw under the scalding spray of the shower as the force of a stiff prickly brush covered in soap scrubbed her flesh again and again. She wasn't young or beautiful. Until tonight, she had only been with one man in her life. Her husband Dale died three years before. She was too young for widowhood and she thought, too old for savage rape.

That night became her tormented secret. She refused to speak more than clipped sentences to anyone in her congregation and finally stopped going to church.

She and Dale never had a baby and it was three months before she discovered her body held the horror of what happened. Her hatred blossomed when she felt the first flutters of the tiny being within her stomach. Suicide was a mortal sin but she welcomed eternity in hell over giving birth to the monster's seed.

Thoughts of killing herself and the child drove her crazy but she never took that final step.

When the first cramps of labor began, she decided she would drown the hell spawn before its first breath.

No one heard her screams of pain and seven hours later the small body slipped from her womb while Carolynn lay on the bathroom floor. Cold water filled the bathtub and waited to close around the infant who would never know more than a few seconds of life.

Half crouching, half standing, Carolynn scooped up the bloody wet newborn and carried it to the tub.

Carolynn tried not to look at what she held but her eyes lowered. The baby made not a sound but stark blue eyes, just like her own, locked on hers and pulled her into their depth. They would not release their hold. Carolynn collapsed to the floor, tears rolling down her face. She brought the softness of the baby's cheek to her breast.

Emily was granted life.

A small spark of love began to grow within Carolynn's heart but extinguished when Emily was two weeks old. The baby became a monster even more real than her rapist.

Carolynn placed the wolf-child in a cage. The prison existed for nineteen years. During those years, her mother's instinct fought the need to kill the demon in the basement.

***

Emily's entire universe was the caged room in the cellar. She knew little kindness and received only enough food to stay alive. She understood nothing of the world above stairs. She would have died in the room of her childhood, but her world changed the day she could take no more. Her life began the day she killed her mother.

Chapter 2

Current day...

    The quietly opening door at the top of the stairs jarred Emily from her stupor. She scrambled to her feet and tensed, sniffing the air. She listened to the routine sounds with a growing sense of dread. No food. Her stomach clenched tightly with hunger and fear. She listened to the clicking steps as her mother made her way down into the darkness. A light went on in the outer room and glowed under the heavy wooden door. The outside bar lifted and the hinges creaked when it slid open. Emily squinted at the sudden brightness. Her heart sank when her eyes confirmed what her nose had known; through the bars she could see Carolynn's empty hands. No food.

    Her mother grabbed the hose rod and though this normally caused terror, today was different. Something was going on within Emily's body. She was on fire and she was burning up from the inside. It had been this way for several weeks, but the feeling was now more intense. Despite the lack of food, she felt stronger. She wasn't sure what had changed, but she almost welcomed the pain from the pounding icy spray biting into her skin. Bringing her head up though closing her eyes against the full force of the water, Emily knew what Carolynn wanted. Fighting her inner rebellion she slowly shuffled into a smaller cage made of iron.

    The water stopped. Carolynn released the nozzle's trigger and used a key to unlock the outer bars of the basement prison. Grunts escaped her lips as she dragged the hose into the cell with her.

    Emily knew this was a bad sign and sudden fear invaded her awareness. Trained to sit quietly and stay away from the cage door, she made not a sound or dared to move even an inch. Carolynn came closer and Emily could smell the sour odor emitting from her body. Oily hair hung limp and covered part of her mother's stern features.

    Carolynn's voice cracked with hatred and spittle. "The devil's child will not defy me. The Lord named me guardian to see this world was saved from your evil."

    The monotony of the words, said many times before, spat from Carolynn's mouth as her hands reached to the wall where Emily's drawings hung. The sound of the first tear drew her eyes to the color filled images. Carolynn destroyed one after the other. Emily stared in horror and her mother's angry words became muted.

Emily's rage grew and the heat within her body became unbearable.

The last pieces floated silently to the wet floor but Carolyn didn't stop. Crayons, pencils, and blank paper from the small desk were next. They flew through the door to the outer prison before resting in front of the cellar steps.

Blinding intense fury consumed Emily while flashes of images were running through her mind; Carolyn reading children's bible stories and showing her the pictures, small fingers drawing painstakingly from memory and bright colors adding small joys to her cellar room. Her rage boiled. More flashes; God's vengeance preached from a black leather bible, her mother's voice screaming in anger, hateful words; devil, demon, hell spawn, Satan's offspring. They blended one into the other. The foggy scenes continued and she became blind to her mother's movements.

Reaching into the pocket of her dress, Carolynn pulled out the hypodermic syringe. Sweat ran down her face and dampened her oily hairline as she approached the bars. Her speech demanded compliance, "Place the devil's arm outside the cage."

Through a haze, Emily glared into her mother's hate filled eyes.

Carolynn screamed, "Give me your arm."

Emily didn't move and again the full force of water burned her skin. Turning her head, she protected her eyes from the spray and used her hands and arms to take the punishing assault. The water suddenly shut off.

"Put-your-arm-outside-the-cage." Carolynn's voice was now low, succinct, and laced with loathing.

Emily's chest rumbled and her skin seemed to catch fire. Red mist rolled over her eyes and demon hands grabbed the cage bars. The metal bent and slowly separated.

A white beast snarled, launching itself through the bars at Carolynn. Blood sprayed over the walls.

Screaming and fighting, Carolynn managed to ram the needle into the beast's side. A moment of satisfaction was all she felt before the monster's fangs tore open her throat.

Frenzied teeth continued to rip through flesh, muscle, and bone before the crazed wolf became sluggish. Bloodied paws faded to blood covered hands. The drugs flowed throughout Emily's system and the red mist turned black.

***

Blood caked skin, growing colder on the icy concrete floor, caused Emily to open her eyes. Moving her head, she took in the blood coated walls and thick congealed mess covering the floor. It was all that remained of Carolynn. Placing her hands beneath her body, she pushed upwards looking at what was left of her mother. Sadness, self-loathing, and bewilderment fought within her mind. But, even with all these bewildering thoughts, when she contemplated what lay beyond the door she had never before walked through, terror froze her movements.

Eventually, two days without food caused unrelenting hunger. Not sure how long she remained crouching in the bloodied room, the heavy grumbling noise from her belly made her take that first hesitant step.

One step followed another and her trembling feet traveled the stairs into the unknown. Grabbing the knob of the door at the top of the stairs she slowly pushed it outwards. Sunshine washed over her bare bloodied body. Countertops partially surrounded the room and Emily's gaze zeroed in on bananas hanging from a strange contraption a short distance away. Her stomach overrode her fear and she walked swiftly to the fruit and devoured all three without taking time to peel them.

After swallowing the last bite, she looked up and stared out at sunshine, trees, and mountains. Straightening her arm she reached for the light but her hand connected with a transparent barrier. She looked with longing and fear at what lay on the other side. Shades of greens and browns painted the outside world.

With the slight edge taken off her hunger, she realized her fingers and skin were sticky with Carolynn's blood. Using the kitchen sink to wash herself, she cupped her hands in the water then emptied them over her head. Over and over she poured the fresh water down her body allowing pink rivulets of water to cover the floor.

When the last of the blood flowed from her skin, she gazed more closely at her surroundings. One by one she opened the drawers and doors of the cabinets. Not understanding what she found inside, her hands skimmed the strange contents and continued their exploration. The last cabinet, like the ones before, held nothing she could eat. Looking around, another door caught her attention and she walked slowly in its direction. Her feet sloshed through the pink water covering the now slippery floor. Reaching her hand to the door's handle she twisted and opened it.

Several boxes of cereal sat on a shelf. She had never seen the boxes before but her nose recognized the smell. She hooked her arms around the stash and carried them to a table in a small room beside the kitchen where the strong odor of Carolynn's blood was not as prevalent. The boxes tore easily and Emily devoured the dry food inside while looking at her surroundings in fascination. Slowly, the hunger pains faded from her belly.

Her blue frightened eyes took in the surroundings and her curiosity propelled her up another flight of stairs. White walls changed to pale blue at the top. The first room smelled faintly of her mother but except for a small bed the room was bare. The next room held a more condensed odor of Carolynn and Emily knew it was where her mother slept. Entering, she skimmed her fingers over the bed coverings and along the walls. Her fingers grasped the knob on another door and pulled it open. Several brown dresses hung from a long pole across one side of the small room. They were her mother's clothing. Three pairs of brown shoes sat on the floor lined up neatly below the hanging garments. Emily's fingers touched the colorless shrouds but she didn't remove them. In the back corner she saw faded blue material and reaching over she pulled it out. Her fingers glided softly over the texture, its feel was different than the dresses her and her mother wore. Staring at the strange apparel, it took her several minutes to figure out how it could cover her legs. She continued her search, found soft white shirts, and pulled one over her head to complete her new outfit. She didn't put on Carolynn's shoes. Every step she took was a different sensation for her feet and toes and she liked it.

The lower floor beckoned and she made her way back to the translucent barrier. Yearning to touch the colors beyond, her fingers traveled over the smooth surface. Apprehension held her back. Taking deep breaths, she pulled herself away and explored some more, putting names to the words her mother used and described.

Heaviness descended over her body and she grew lethargic. Finally, she sat on a long soft bed with sides where she could see the world beyond. Slowly her body slid sideways and her knees met her stomach. Sleep took over.

"Carolynn." Thump, thump, "Carolynn, are you all right?"

The loud pounding and gruff voice woke Emily and she quickly slipped to the floor and lay still. The red haze slid back over her eyes. If the person entered the house she would let the demon have them.

The knocking and voice finally stopped. Taking a hesitant glance outside, she saw a large blue object rumbling away. She noticed the light shining into the room wasn't as bright. Resisting the other side of the barrier was getting harder.

Again, rumbles came from her stomach and she turned away and made her way to search for more to eat. She discovered a cabinet filled with cold food and devoured everything her stomach could hold. When she finished eating, the last rays of sunlight were leaving the sky. Dark shadows enveloped the room and Emily could no longer fight the needs of her beast. Her fingers played with the front door lock until it swung open and the scent of the wild filled the room.

Emily was no longer afraid.

Chapter 3

Dying during a challenge for alpha wasn't Brandt's original plan. But the fight continued and he realized it would solve his biggest problem; his lack of a desire to live.

Cheri, his clan leader and the vampire who could help him heal from death injuries, was in Europe working to bring the overseas clans into the 21st century. So far her success was minimal.

Brandt knew she would be one pissed off vampire when she returned and found him dead. Not that it mattered because he wouldn't be around to feel her wrath. And, she would have no choice but to accept Clem if he won the challenge for alpha. Pack rules dictated that if Clem killed him, he deserved the alpha title. Unfortunately, the pack did not deserve Clem.

Brandt's blood flowed and his life essence slowly faded. Over five-hundred years old, three-hundred of those years spent being leader of his pack, and a young barely two-hundred year old pup was getting the best of him. He could feel his broken ribs grinding and he knew they presented the biggest danger. He would not survive if one pierced his heart.

Clem's insanity had shown for years and Brandt should have killed him long before this, but it was too late to go back now.

The large fist landed slightly to the side of Brandt's midsection and the sensitive wolf ears surrounding the ring heard the grating cracks. His pack had quieted to a hush of uneasy realization.

Clem changed from man to wolf. He came in close for the death strike and his large teeth had one target, Brandt's throat.

"You fucking wolf, if you die I'll follow you into the afterlife and kick your ass again." Loud and clear, Cheri's voice entered his mind and Brandt felt her presence like a beacon of energy.

She could come to his aid in healing if he won, but according to pack law she couldn't help him fight.

Brandt's internal sadness had rarely left him during the past year. He was tired of his life, but in that instant he decided that Clem would not be the one to take it.

Brandt had no time to seek out the eyes of his queen. At the sound of her voice, he decided today was not a good day to die. Wrenching his head away, he avoided the yellow foam covered teeth attempting to tear out his jugular. Brandt's body flowed seamlessly into his wolf form and twisted. The clang of vicious fangs missing purchase on his neck was satisfyingly sweet. In the next instant fur, flesh, and muscle from his shoulder tore in a savage twist by his enemy's jaws. The pain caused him to focus.

Brandt's arms and legs changed to their human form.

He grabbed Clem and brought the wolf's neck to his elongated fangs. In one savage bite Clem's life was no more. He threw the body to the ground and then changed to full wolf.

Unsteady aching legs carried him from the ring into the surrounding woods and hills. His wolf form was pitch black in color and the night swallowed him leaving his queen behind.

Brandt knew his injuries were life threatening, but he continued to run until his paws gave out and he lost too much blood to rise again. He lay on the leaves of the overgrown forest and allowed his breathing to slow. He embraced the pain, hoping for death.

Her voice was exasperated, "What are you doing Brandt? Do you really think I would let you die? Even across an ocean, I can feel the turmoil in your stupid brain. You were once my lover and are now my friend. I'm not willing to lose you this way."

He heard soft footsteps approach and felt her strong arms lift him slightly. His world went black but his last thought was that death would not be his today, maybe tomorrow.

***

The cool cloth brought him back to consciousness. Cheri used it to wipe the blood and sweat from his nude body. He knew this room but hadn't been there in far too many years. She was aware that he was awake, but he didn't speak. She continued her attention to his bare human skin.

Her long brown hair fell forward and the smell of strawberry wine touched his nostrils. Dark lush eyelashes swept over large emerald eyes and softened the defined lines of her high cheekbones. Her alabaster skin untouched by the sun felt like rose petals. She was five foot eight, tall for a woman, but the sway of her body when she moved showed controlled grace and confidence born from hundreds of years of life. Her hands were silk but like a spider's web, their strength impossible to escape once they trapped you in their steel grip.

His strong masculine fingers finally grasped hers knowing he didn't have the power to stop their movement. "You should have let me go. I'm ready; this life has nothing for me."

She looked into his gaze. Chocolate brown pain-filled stared from his perfectly sculptured face. His body, a mass of defined muscles flowed one into the other and quivered beneath her touch. Every inch of him a honed fighting machine that reeked of sullen unforgiving alpha power. A human or werewolf would be afraid but she was vampire and spoke to him like she would a child, "You're selfish, and you can't stop thinking with your dick. I should let you suffer slowly and heal your own injuries. You think I would allow you to die just because you're too spoiled to grow up? Besides, do you really think that jackass Clem could lead my people? I would have killed him myself."

His arm flexed and muscles stood out, punishingly he squeezed her fingers. He couldn't physically hurt her but his anguish was apparent in the demanding pressure, "I know, but I wouldn't have been around to care."

Her tone softened, "I don't understand what you need Brandt. I would give you anything in my power."

Her words hurt him more than his injuries. He loved her and shared a far too short time in her bed. Her heart craved another and the knowledge killed him slowly. His pack did not need a weak, lovesick alpha. He died a little more each day from desiring her for his mate. His heart had chosen and this life was not worth living. Anger coursed through his blood. Anger at her and hatred for the man she loved.

Brandt was the strongest wolf she had ever known; fierce, loyal, and loving with his pack. She had reduced him to this and her blood cringed with his next words.

"I can't live this way. It's killing me slowly each day. I no longer want to watch the sun rise. You are my queen your responsibility is to put the clan first and give me peace. Hatred and jealousy are eating me alive and I'm attracting death to my pack. It is my brothers I kill. They cannot help but challenge my position with this uncertainty weighing me down. My reign as alpha is over and only you can release my soul to the afterlife. Do your duty." The words carried all the hurt and fury he contained just below the surface of his human form.

She could also hear his desolation. Sharp fangs again entered his jugular to give him a short time of peace. Her heart ached because she loved him but knew he wanted more. She had cut off their affair many years before. His body, love making, and passion were *almost* the most incredible she ever felt, but she could not give him the ultimate gift; her heart. After the breakup their friendship suffered for years but finally returned. During these past months she sensed his sadness. She couldn't change the cause and it had grown worse after his return from the Central Clan's cub naming ceremony in Arizona. Her trip to Europe was a short term solution to give him space.

She stood and left the room giving instructions for Dominique, a pack she-wolf, to stay by his side. Closing the door softly she vanished, only to reappear in a cabin far from the main house.

Strong loving arms wrapped around her as she wearily climbed onto the high bed. He wasn't alpha nor was he one of the dominant wolves of his pack, but this was where she belonged. His greatest strength lay in his character and his love for her and his family. Killing was not in his nature though he killed for the pack when necessary. His gentleness was what attracted her. She had been part of incredible violence during her early years of being vampire. She was dangerous and deadly but the arms around her brought soothing warmth and the promise of passion.

"He lives but something must be done." She said with a soft sigh in his ear.

"I couldn't bring myself to attend the challenge and the longer I stayed in this house the more I sensed he would die." His arms tightened around the woman he loved. "Thank you for coming to my call and for saving my son."

Chapter 4

Brandt's wounds healed quickly from the enzymes in Cheri's bites. However, his despair didn't lessen. He knew his father sent the distress call to their queen. He also knew the two loved one another and both deserved the love they found together.

Knowing this didn't make it any easier for Brandt's heart to accept. He needed a reason to live.

A soft knock on his door signaled an unwelcome guest. That, the individual could block their mind signature from him, the Alpha of the pack, immediately told Brandt who was knocking and that he couldn't deny him entry.

With a resigned sigh, Brandt told his father to come in.

Pausing just inside the room, Thomas took a deep breath. He raised his son with pride and honor and tried to keep violence away from him, but early on it was apparent Brandt would one day lead the pack. To do so, Brandt had to kill Thomas' best friend. It was the way of beastkind. Thomas grieved and missed his friend, but he loved his son more than anyone, except Cheri. He had delayed the inevitable long enough. He took the remaining steps to his son's side.

Staring with deadly intent Brandt met his father's eyes. He might behave badly where his feelings for Cheri were concerned, but he was alpha and did not back down from anyone. Just seeing the look on his father's face, Brandt knew Thomas planned to bring the situation into the open. His dad had not held long eye contact with him since Brandt became alpha but now he would not look away. His words were short and clipped rumbling with a low growl, "I know dad. I've known for a long time but I'm not discussing it. You shouldn't be near me."

Thomas placed his hand on his son's shoulder but Brandt twisted. In an instant, he was off the bed. Thomas' body flew across the room landing against the far wall. Brandt followed with quick strides and his hand circled his father's throat cutting off his air. "I want you dead. I want to feel your bones crush beneath my hands and I want to hear the last breath you ever take. This is what you have done to me. Tell your lover to end my life or I will end yours."

The punishing grip relaxed and Brandt was out of the room with wolf-like speed.

Thomas flinched when his sensitive hearing picked up the sound of the front door crashing against the large house. Knowing there was only one thing left for him to do, he wiped the single tear from his face and made the decision which might save his son but would bring lasting pain to many.

That afternoon, Cheri sent the call to Brandt and his wolves. They swiftly arrived at the clearing reserved for challenges and clan business. Cheri's fury rolled from her body in thick waves. The scent of her rage floated throughout the area. Deadly wrath consumed her features and amber eyes stared out at her assembled clan.

Turmoil had besieged the wolves for many months due to Brandt's disinterest. The lupines had animal natures. Unrest caused them to become unstable. Many of them were angry with Brandt while others saw the opening they needed to become the next alpha wolf for their pack. If Brandt continued on his present course of destruction, the past hundred years of work to civilize the pack would be for nothing. Not only did Cheri not agree with the solution Thomas proposed, but she knew there was a high chance she would kill Brandt herself in the end.

Standing to the side, Thomas knew another challenge was only a matter of time and he would do what he must to save his son. The wolves began to quiet waiting for Cheri to speak. He didn't give her an opportunity nor did he give another wolf a chance to threaten Brandt. Steady legs carried him forward, turning to his son who was standing next to the woman he loved, he didn't hesitate "I challenge for alpha."

For three heartbeat, no one said a word but then Brandt swore, "You fucking-idiot old man. What the hell do you think you're doing? I warned you."

"I delivered my challenge before the pack. This is a challenge to the death. You have no choice Brandt. You chose to be alpha; you fought for the right by being the strongest among us. You killed one of my oldest friends for the title. I challenge!" Resolve, sorrow, and anger spilled from Thomas' pores. He knew speaking of their old pack leader would goad his son into action.

Brandt looked at Cheri, her amber eyes promised death. He knew she was capable of killing him at that moment. He also knew he couldn't kill his father and only his father could back down from the challenge. Unfortunately, his alpha blood had other thoughts and his inner wolf raged against any love he felt. Just keeping his human form from shifting was difficult. His teeth desired purchase on flesh. His entire being desired his father's blood.

"Tomorrow night." His voice came through elongated teeth and with his wolf barely kept in check, Brandt turned and walked away.

Thomas' arms circled Cheri's shoulders, pulling her close.

She was stunned and unable to relax into his warmth. They had never shown their feelings for each other to the clan.

"If I die tomorrow, everyone should know that you're mine." His powerful embrace tightened and the wolves slowly faded into the surrounding area.

Passionate lips came down on hers. She couldn't believe he was claiming her now when he would die the following day. Pulling away and turning to her lover, she looked into his eyes. "I love you. Don't do this. If he kills you, I will end his life. Please don't make me lose both of you."

"You will not end his life. The Goddess will decide the outcome and you will let her guide our clan through the next hundred years."

"You will die. I know you won't kill him. Even if you wanted to, you wouldn't have a chance. He knows about us and he might love you but he wants your blood to flow. His actions have not been sane for many months."

"He needs a mate and he needs to know it will never be you. You are mine and even with my death, he will not have you. The bond between the two of you is only in his heart and not in his blood. A true wolf claim cannot be broken. This false assertion of his can, but he will die if he doesn't figure that out."

"What will he do after he kills you Thomas? Will the challenges never end? Don't leave me." There was desperation in her voice.

The night was warm and smelled faintly of a summer storm that had yet to make an appearance. He pulled her body securely against his and lifted her against his chest. Purposeful strides took them to his cabin. If he only had tonight, he would make it perfect for them both.

***

The clan gathered the next evening at midnight. For six months, challenges and bloodshed swept through the pack. Tonight would be difficult for them all. Brandt was strong. He held his position with brains, brute force, blood, and death. The recent challenges came because his uncertainty enveloped them all. The pack respected Thomas. He ran the majority of business enterprises that kept the clan wealthy and they needed his calm strength to counter his son's alpha nature. There was no chance Thomas could win a physical challenge and the death song would ring through the trees the following night when they lay him to rest.

Brandt looked wild; his short brown hair unruly, and his eyes barren. His breathing labored in and out. He barely held back his need to provide death to the challenging wolf.

With a strong resolve, Thomas looked to his son. "I love you and have supported you always. I cannot help loving Cheri and the mate bond is sealed. She has promised not to kill you after I'm dead. I don't know if I believe her." His eyes met Cheri's and his next words were for her, "I love you and in front of my pack, your clan, I claim you. Even in death the bond will continue. You will be able to seek love in other arms but no wolf will claim your true heart and we will see each other again in the afterlife. I'm sorry my love. Forgive me."

Cheri turned away sharply her eyes meeting Brandt's. "He is your father. I love him. I can't love you the same way. Step down as alpha and walk away from the pack. Thomas will not back down, I have tried everything. He's willing to give his life over this stupid mate bond you think is between us. Thomas and I are bonded, I cannot merge with you. I'm begging you not to do this." Anguish colored her words. She thought he would turn away, she had prayed since last night that he would heed her plea. Looking into dead eyes and deep into his black soul, she realized Thomas would die. Her tormented scream sent shivers through the pack as a power surge swept her hair in gusty strands up and around her shoulders.

Ignoring everything but his need for his father's blood, Brandt removed his clothing without a word. His father followed suit and the clearing grew quiet. The two men looked at one another. One was a legend for his fighting skills. Dark closely cropped hair, olive toned skin, and arms bulging with muscle only added to the hot energy he exuded. His chest and back showed the definition of a body builder and his legs held the power of the pack's strongest. Thomas was muscular but did not have a fighter's build. He could beat half the pack wolves and any human but did not have a chance against his son. And, if by some miracle Thomas won, there would be an immediate challenge from another wolf. Thomas would not leave the ring alive and Cheri's heart would never recover.

The air grew thick with the cloying pressure from their clan vampire and their alpha. The pack waited for Brandt to make the first move. His eyes traveled around the circle and then with barely a breath, he attacked. Man shifted to beast and huge paws launched from the ground. Two hundred pounds of wrath hit Thomas and followed him to the dirt. Thomas's change to wolf followed. He managed to roll from under the powerful jaws of his son. Deadly werewolf claws raked Brandt's back, going through fur and skin but doing little damage.

Brandt twisted from the hold with little effort. He was stronger, faster, and deadlier. He hadn't hurt his father and before his next attack, a small ray of sanity came through the red haze consuming his senses. He shifted to human form. "Give up old man and walk away, leave Cheri behind."

The angry wolf facing his son hurled through the air with deadly intent.

Brandt again shifted to wolf and sidestepped, launching himself on top of his father. Sharp, pointed teeth bit deep into the back of Thomas' neck. The jugular was his primary goal but ripping out the spinal cord would be deadly too. Bloody fangs bit down, past fur, skin, and muscle.

Suddenly his grip eased and he looked to the road.

Thinking this was the dumbest move his son had ever made, Thomas rolled on his back and came within a half inch of closing his own jaws around Brandt's throat. The sound of a distant vehicle stopped his teeth from descending into their target.

A truck sped toward them and rounded the last bend in the road coming to a stop with screeching breaks, throwing dust and rocks, while gasoline fumes punctuated the air. Clan energy tapered down a notch when they recognized the occupant of the vehicle. It was driven by one of the few humans that knew their secrets.

Both Brandt and Thomas put their pants on though neither bothered with shirts. Deputy Charles McNabb jumped out, not realizing the mood of the wolves or his danger. Humans were stupid. The clan accepted this one because his aunt mated with one of their wolves many years before. Stella was now dead because human life was but a blink in the eyes of the clan.

The deputy's breathing was fast and inconsistent with driving the truck. "There's been a murder three hundred miles from here. It was a woman. She kept something in her basement. The authorities aren't sure if it was a person, animal, or one of each. They called in hounds to search for the killer and the other possible victim." Charles took another deep breath and looked around the clearing, "I think the murderer was a werewolf."

Chapter 5

"Let's get back to the house." Cheri's voice held relief. A little time might change the course of events that Thomas' challenge set in motion. She needed time. Taking a swift look at her mate, he waved her on. She flashed from the site.

The relieved wolves began to disperse and return to their homes.

Brandt jumped in the passenger side of the truck to get more of the story.

Charles drove slowly allowing time for the entire rundown of events. "I was called to hold the scene last night and only told it was a violent murder. It wasn't until a few hours ago that I helped remove the remains and spoke to the investigator. The victim was in her sixties. The basement where they found her was a blood bath."

His breathing remained harsh and clenched fingers tightened on the steering wheel, "It was a prison. There were female clothes for various stages of growth from infant to adult. Someone was in there for years. There was also a heavy-duty dog kennel inside, horse tranquilizers sitting on a table outside the basement prison, and an empty syringe lying in the mangled body parts. It was a bloodbath. They think whatever was kept in the kennel killed the woman and tore her limb from limb." He took another deep breath and went on, "The body was disemboweled too, but none of it appears to have been eaten. The investigator thinks that whatever was in the cage killed the woman and possibly the girl that she kept in the room. A set of bloody bare footprints were on the stairway leading to the first floor of the house. The old woman that owned the home never had children and was a recluse that had little interaction with others. Apparently someone from her church made monthly visits and when he didn't get an answer at the door, he requested my office do a welfare check. I have no doubt that it was a werewolf kill. I think the beastkind was imprisoned for years and I'm worried she will kill anyone she encounters." Charles glanced sideways at Brandt seeing how he took the news. He should have known better, Brandt had "blank expression" down better than anyone Charles knew. He looked back at the road and saw the vampire's house in the distance.

"No one was home when I arrived here so I headed to the circle. I'm sorry, but I thought this was more important than anything you had going on tonight." There was relief in Charles' voice. He had passed his information up the chain of command. The wolves took care of their own problems and he could relax now. He refused to be curious about the blood on Brandt's face and chest. That was wolf business and he was human so it was none of his.

Brandt's gut told him they had a feral werewolf on their hands. It didn't matter that it was female; putting her down was in the best interest of the pack.

Cheri met them at the front door and escorted them to a meeting room where several of the dominant wolves waited. Brandt relayed what he knew then gave orders to assemble the teams that would be part of the hunt. They would take twelve wolves, three of whom were his best trackers.

Charles drove away after he ate a quick meal. He would not participate in the hunt or the feral werewolf's death.

Killing was part of an alpha's life. It bothered Brandt little that it was a female. He understood that male werewolves outnumbered the females two to one but he would do what was best for his pack.

Fifteen minutes later three black sports utility vehicles arrived at the front of the house and the three teams got in. Cheri would only come if they needed her aid. Vampire talents did not include tracking so she would not get involved in locating the feral wolf. Her assistance might be required if they had trouble taking it down; otherwise the tracking and kill would most likely take place in daylight and Cheri had to limit her sun exposure.

Taking Thomas' hand she walked to the waiting vehicles and gave little thought to Brandt's displeasure.

His eyes traveled from their joined fingers to her gaze. Thomas would not be a part of the teams. This wasn't his kind of work.

She met Brandt's angry stare with unfeeling eyes. "Do you think this is one of Malcolm's?"

Controlling his voice he answered, "I'm almost sure of it."

Cheri nodded her head and stepped away from the SUV. The three vehicles sped from the house.

Seeing Cheri's smaller hand enveloped by his father's caused pain to lance through Brandt's chest. With deep even breathing he brought his simmering rage under control and mentally reviewed the problems Malcolm's actions caused. Almost twenty years before,

Malcolm, one of their own, sexually assaulted an unknown number of human women. He was trying to impregnate the females and they only knew he succeeded twice. Against the advice of Samson his second in charge, Brandt gave the serial rapist a fair fight. He knew his wolves would take care of Malcolm if he didn't win. Werewolves did not force females, wolf, or human. Malcolm died and Brandt made sure it wasn't a pretty ending. He played with the blood-covered wolf and made sure Malcolm suffered before he breathed his last. A side benefit was the lesson his wolves learned about the punishment given to those who broke pack law. Brandt was a wolf; it was his nature and pleasure to relish the memory of wrapping his jaws around the serial rapist's throat.

The location of the woman's murder was in the same county as one of Malcolm's other rapes. If the escaped prisoner was indeed a feral werewolf then the serial rapist was the only possibility as the father. It would mean the she-wolf was approximately twenty years old. Brandt could not imagine what she suffered in her life. Caged werewolves lost their sanity. If she had grown up in the pack, she would be with her parents for at least another year. Some females stayed for closer to thirty. Their adolescence tended to be less volatile than that of males. The women controlled their anger and aggression better. They could be far deadlier but didn't need to be sent away to fight in foreign wars to get the killing rage out of their systems.

An hour later, the distance finally separated Brandt's internal awareness from Cheri and his father. His mind raced. He knew he needed to leave the pack. He had been seconds from killing his father and was having no luck in controlling his inner chaos.

He received news a few weeks before that his friend Ivan had lost his mate Alba. Ivan left his pack to his oldest son and then disappeared. Brandt hoped his friend would seek out a vampire in the next few months. Werewolves were beastkind and their longevity tied to vampires. The strongest vampires controlled the strongest clans. Beastkind lived as long as their vampire clan leader. There was something in the vampire saliva that tied them by blood and gave beastkind lasting life and the ability to mind read within the clan over long distances. The two, beastkind and vampire, had once been enemies but their blood alliances were now hundreds of years old and served both well.

The vehicles sped to their destination. Brandt knew he needed sleep but was unable to get his spinning thoughts calmed. The other men in the vehicle didn't speak. He realized even in the small confines of the SUV his wolves were giving him space.

When had his control of the pack, become so damaged? He realized Cheri's words about the mate bond were true but his heart would not stop feeling the connection to her. After killing the feral wolf he needed to step down. He had no son to leave his pack to and didn't know if his second in command was capable of holding it without courting the constant threat of death from challenges. He was alpha, the leader of his pack and his disinterest in the day-to-day lives of his brothers was now attracting them to death. He had to get control of himself for the sake of his wolves.

Another hour passed before they arrived within fifty miles of their target location. The last of the three vehicles stopped and prepared to hunt. They would cover the surrounding area in case the she-wolf slipped by the other two teams. If they detected the feral scent, they would all converge. A wild werewolf was a killing machine and must die.

Chapter 6

The next two groups separated twenty miles later, with Brandt's group heading to the house where they knew they could locate the scent. It was risky but they hoped to remain undetected. In their last communication with Charles, he said there was a delay in getting the bloodhounds and the police wouldn't begin the forest search until later in the morning. It was now three a.m. and the night was dark with only a quarter moon showing. The wolves had perfect night vision so no moon would have been preferable if they were to remain unseen, but you take what you get.

They removed their clothes, folded them, and stowed them neatly inside black duffle bags in the back of the vehicle. If someone found the SUV, they didn't want anyone thinking they had four naked men running around in the area.

"Move the vehicle into the trees and let's get this done." Brandt was wasting no time.

Dense pine trees shadowed the forest floor and the needles crunched beneath their bare feet and then beneath paws.

The scent was easy to locate. There were no other beastkind scents to follow and now Brandt was sure it was Malcolm's get and not a lone cat. Beastkind cats were the sworn enemies of werewolves. The death he would dish out would have been more satisfying if the killer was a cat, but since it wasn't, he hoped this would be the last time he had to think of Malcolm and his vicious crimes or deal with their repercussions.

She-wolf scent blazed a path through the trees and powerful werewolf legs followed in quick pursuit.

Brandt notified the other team they were on the trail. Samson, his second in command, and friend, ran beside him. Samson was a dominant but so far, resisted challenging Brandt during his turmoil. He was playing it smart by staying away from his alpha. If Brandt decided to leave, he considered Samson the best choice for pack leader. Samson's dominant nature might be capable of handling challenges until the other wolves accepted his authority.

Brandt would give serious consideration on how he could help that along after the hunt.

About a mile from the house, they scented where the she-wolf stopped and discarded her clothing and then changed to wolf. A smell of illness was often associated with a feral but not always and this one did not smell sick. It didn't matter though because killing humans was unacceptable and her death was inevitable.

Another hour passed. Brandt and his wolves could hear the second team in the distance. His group changed to human. She had not gotten past them so they knew they were closing in. Brandt put his hand up and everyone froze. Up ahead he caught the first sight of his target and astonishingly her fur was pure white. The color was rare and it was a shame she would die. She was looking away from them but suddenly her head turned in their direction and a split second later she took off.

Brandt gave chase, shifting to wolf and giving commands for the others to change and spread out around her.

Her running gait was uncoordinated and awkward. Brandt assumed it was due to her time in a cage. Within sixty seconds, he ate up the distance between them and launched up and forward. The female sensed him somehow and dodged to the left at the last moment. He managed to sink his teeth into the flank and a pain filled howl escaped her throat. Brandt clamped down hard, drawing blood, and tearing into muscle. She was down and he meant to finish it quickly.

Sweet tangy blood rapidly absorbed into the pores of his mouth. His killing drive was slower to catch up and scrambling up her body his deadly jaws found purchase on her throat. At the same instant her taste reached his brain. His jaws stopped their powerful pressure and she stopped struggling.

The two wolf teams closed in and Brandt's eyes traveled away from his captive. A low growl emitted from his throat and his pack mates back away, not sure what was happening.

The rich and powerful scent of her blood hit Samson's nostrils. Never smelling it before from a female he nonetheless knew what it was. The she-wolf was an alpha.

Shaking his head to dispel her odor, Samson spoke telepathically, "Shit Brandt, it doesn't make a difference. It only means she's more dangerous than a feral."

Brandt's jaws slowly released as energy from her blood pounded through his system fastening to every cell. Unbearable heat built and caused a suffocating effect. Each painful breath caused her alpha power to mesh with his. He fought for control and spread his muscled legs into a fighting stance. Killing Samson and the other wolves surrounding him would be easy. Shaking his head, the buzz coursing along his nerve endings faded enough for him to growl out, "I claim her as mate."

Silence descended. But then, with a low snarl, Samson found his voice, "Fuck, you can't be serious. What's happened? You're out of your mind. She'll kill you if given a chance and she poses too much danger to the pack." Large deadly paws took two steps in Brant's direction.

"You challenge?" Vehemence filled Brandt's eyes and he was a split second from killing his friend. His vicious growls became louder. The feel of his mate's body rolling and trying to escape stopped him. He placed his back paw solidly on the she-wolf's side hoping her injury kept her down. His lethal eyes promised death if anyone came closer.

Samson lowered his gaze, quieted his voice and fought the need to challenge, "No my friend, I backed you for a long time and have been trying to give you the chance to get your head on straight. I think this makes you appear crazier than ever. I'll still follow you, but I'll kill her myself if she harms anyone."

Brandt's heart raced. He was prepared to kill every wolf who defied him. After a few deep breaths, controlling his beast became easier and he managed to remove some of the ferocity from his voice, "She is one of ours. I've claimed her and I'll make sure she's safe to the pack. If anyone goes against me they will die. Samson you have my back." With a rumbling low growl, Brandt turned to his captive. He sent out the call for Cheri and seconds later she was standing in front of him.

She expected to fight but the sight of Brandt guarding the female wolf gave her pause. Brandt's large fangs bared in her direction, the fool. Giving her another reason to separate his head from his body only made her smile in anticipation. Killing him would solve her biggest problem but unfortunately, she didn't think Thomas would forgive her. She stood her ground and waited.

Brandt's body transformed to human. He took his foot from the female's side. "I need your help. I mate claimed her but she's hurt and we must get her to the ranch. I could carry her but I'm afraid I'd be chewed to bits by the time we reached the car."

Cheri knew she misunderstood his words. "She's feral. You can't mate claim her." Shock was evident in her voice.

"She's not feral and I don't have a choice. Her blood is now part of mine."

This was not the moment to crack a joke but it was next to impossible not to send him flying into the next week with one well-placed fist. His claim for her was over in a heartbeat because he bloodied a strange she-wolf. She glanced into the same eyes which promised death to Thomas only hours before. They were barely sane but gave truth to his words. This female might be the answer to the clan's problems. Then again she could be the beginning of bigger ones. Cheri straightened from her fighting stance and nodded her head in acquiescence. "Okay, I'll render her unconscious but you'll need to move out of my way.

He trusted Cheri implicitly but the compulsion to protect his injured mate was overriding any good sense he had left. A low whine of pain came from the wolf at his feet and he was able to step aside and allow Cheri to work her magic.

The vampire was standing five feet away and then she had the injured wolf in her arms. Glancing up at Brandt, she gentled her voice. "You know I hate fur in my teeth." Her fangs entered the wolf's throat. Several minutes later, the body she was holding transformed into a human female. She was beautiful even with matted hair and blood coating her lower extremities. Her leg began healing immediately and no scar would remain after a few days. She would sleep for hours and in the meantime they must decide how to ensure the pack's safety. Stepping aside without another word, Cheri flashed home to discuss the complications with her own mate.

Pulling her thin nude body into his arms, Brandt carried her for miles through the woods and back to the vehicle. Using a soft blanket from the trunk, he covered her fragile body and pulled her close. He sat in the back of the SUV where her scent continued to combine with his. The mate bond intensified. Samson drove but the other two wolves, with them at the beginning of their quest, squeezed into the accompanying vehicles.

Brandt's thoughts were chaotic and he agreed with Samson on this one. He was insane and his current situation only proved it. Though amazing and seemingly impossible, this unknown female was part of him. The gut wrenching knowledge was exhilarating and terrifying all at once. There was no comparison between his feelings for Cheri and the woman he now held in his arms. His thoughts drifted to his friend Ivan from the Central Clan. He realized Ivan would die if he hadn't already. He didn't think anyone could lose this connection and survive.

He couldn't help but touch her and his large rough hands gently glided over her unclothed body learning the velvety texture of her skin. Removing his hands and covering her again with the blanket caused his chest to tighten. After an hour, with her body drawn securely to his chest, he managed to relax enough to sleep. The vehicle jerked slightly startling him awake. Looking out the window he could see the familiar landmarks of the clan property. He turned his head and his eyes caught Samson's in the mirror.

The voice from the driver's seat was intense, "I stayed away from you so I wouldn't challenge."

"I know."

"What you don't know is that every fiber of my being feels the compulsion to take your position. I don't know how much longer I can withstand the desire to kill you. Get your shit together and take back your full alpha status. If not, I'll leave. I don't want you to kill me."

"Do you think I could?"

"Until recently, I never doubted it. It's what keeps our drive to be leader down. You were always the strongest among us and we need you to take your place again."

"For the first time in months, I feel at peace with being alpha and I don't think anyone can take it from me." Brandt pushed a small bit of his power up from his center and allowed it to leak from his pores so his second would know he was back in control.

Samson felt the cloying weight of alpha wolf and the stiffness in his shoulders eased for the first time in months. With a deriding snort and another glance into the rearview mirror he murmured, "Hell Brandt, she's going to kill you before anyone else has a chance. She's an untamed wolf who has never been in a pack. She's crazy and she killed her own mother. What makes you think if she could do that, she won't tear your throat out the first chance she gets? Your first mating will be a war. Please give me a docile she-wolf any day."

Brandt's eyes held a smile and he felt relief that his friend would not leave or worse die. He glanced to his mate and the smile grew. He was up for any battle she would bring his way.

They pulled up to the house. His father and Cheri came out but didn't get close. Taking the stairs two at a time, Brandt carried his bundle to his bedroom on the second floor. Kicking the door closed behind him, he laid his burden on the high bed. Blood stained her skin and he could smell its rancid odor. Getting her clean before she woke was the first item on his agenda. He sent a mental message to Dominique telling her what items to bring from the lower floor. Her submissive behavior kept her from entering the room but with a soft knock Dominique let him know the things he needed were outside the room.

Even after a lifetime of being caged, he didn't think the woman on the bed had a submissive bone in her body.

A firmer knock sounded at the door and Cheri walked in. Drawn to the bed she looked down at the small slip of a woman lying pale and unresponsive. Not sure what Brandt saw in her she tried to keep the feelings of doubt from her tone. "I can help if you need me. My biggest concern is keeping the clan safe from your mate. Right now you feel volatile. Your dad explained this to me. He enlightened me about why he felt the need to challenge you. I still don't quite understand but I think you have enough dead wolves on your hands and you pose almost the same danger as she does."

"If the pack avoids getting between me and my mate they are safe. Once the mating is complete and our blood settles, the clan will heal and I plan on being around to see to it. You need have no further fear I will attack my father."

She knew this was the only apology she would receive so she got to the reason for her visit. "Before I returned home, I went to the murdered woman's house. The werewolf scent is only a thin trail around the inside of the house and then leads outside unless you go to the basement. Evidence suggests she lived there since her birth but she's the only one with complete answers. There was a toilet, small sink, a hard bar of soap, and a single towel. Clothes of various sizes filled a large plastic bin. It held several pairs of white undergarments and plain brown smocks. Cheri glanced at the woman in Brandt's arms and her heart melted slightly. "There was a power washer outside the cell with the hose inside. It was one of the ways the woman controlled her. The other was tranquilizers. She's wild Brandt. I hope you know what you're doing."

He didn't acknowledge any of her statements with more than a low growl but said, "This woman is mine. I don't understand why or how it happened. Maybe the Goddess my dad always speaks of is out there and has a plan. I can smell my father's mate bond on you. It feels comfortable to me."

Cheri held back tears. She loved Brandt though she loved his father more. She had seen blood and death over many lifetimes, and dealt death to hundreds. She always thought her heart would go to the strongest but she'd been wrong. She was more powerful than anyone around and she needed a tender touch to counteract her violent nature. An incredibly gentle man loved her. Looking back at the woman on the bed she spoke, "You are going to need help with her. I'll come when you call. I know it seems hard but I think she might be safer in one of the cages in the basement."

A deep growl came from Brandt and fire sparked in his eyes.

"Hear me out, damn it. She's a danger to herself and my clan. You will need to sleep sometime. Your father will help too, but he may be unable to control her and I don't want him dead. When you first recognized her blood, you knew what was happening and I'm sure even then it was hard to process. She knows none of our ways. She will not understand what is going on in her body and someone could die. I need to be sure everyone is safe."

Brandt's heart rate dropped slowly. The need to protect his mate from Cheri eased. "Move my father into the house and I'll have the wolves ready his cabin. We can bar the windows and secure the doors. She needs to see outside. She's been imprisoned down in a basement, how much sunlight has she seen in her life?"

A minute went by while Cheri silently communicated her needs to Thomas. "It's done. Your father will organize the pack and have the cabin ready in a few hours. They will weld the bars quickly. Do you want a cage inside?"

"God no, the bars on the windows will be enough. I'll make sure the pack knows to stay away after the work is complete. Thank you."

"Thank me after you have her under control."

A slight chuckle escaped him, "Hell, she's alpha, I may never have control again."

Chapter 7

Running the warm washcloth over her body, he memorized every curve. He replaced the cloth with his callused fingers and learned the feel of her skin. His nose followed his hands. Her essence soaked into his pores and continued to make his heart thrum. She was malnourished and each rib protruded under her tissue-like silky skin. Her hair was a mess and saturating it with conditioner would be the only way to get the snarls out but it could wait. Even dirty the strands were such a light color; almost white like her fur. It would be a shame to cut it. She continued to sleep through his ministrations.

An hour later, the tensing of her body told him she was awake and then unsurprisingly her unclothed body shifted to wolf. Low growls came from her throat. He waited patiently just watching her. Without warning, lethal sharp teeth tried to eat him. Her snapping jaws were a hair's breadth from his face and it took all his strength to hold her down. He stayed in human form and spoke soothingly, "You're safe here. No harm will come to you. Relax and control your breathing."

It was obvious his words had little effect and she continued to fight. With both arms straining, he managed to keep her on the bed. He racked his brain for some way to calm her. A far off memory of his father holding him when he was a young child filtered through his mind. The humming melody of Somewhere Over The Rainbow vibrated from his vocal cords and filled the large room with the melody. He knew the wolves in the house could hear him but he didn't have a chance to feel uncomfortable because her heart rate slowed and her limbs relaxed. Finally, loosening his grip, he rolled to the side and gazed into her terror stricken blue eyes.

Human skin replaced white fur, her breathing became more erratic. Her eyes flashed around the room and he knew she was looking for a way to escape. Calculating the distance to the door, she looked at him and back at the closet. He knew laughter was not a good idea but his lip quirked slightly. He could interpret every expression on her face while she deliberated her options.

Then, horrified eyes looked downward. Seeing her nude body she closed her eyes tightly. He expected her to revert to wolf form but she didn't. Tears fell leaving damp trails down her cheeks but other than loud breathing she made not a sound. After the quick moment of reprieve, she kicked out and then her fingers scored his face. Having no choice, he rolled over and pressed her into the mattress. His hands clasped hers and brought them above her head.

She growled using her human vocal cords. His heavier body strained to keep her down. "Please give me cover." Her voice was horse and unused.

Communication was a good sign and Brandt felt relief that she could speak. Her nakedness should be the least of her problems under the circumstances but he was game for whatever helped calm her. "I'll put the blanket over you if you'll stop fighting. I'm not going to hurt you but I don't need your claws damaging my pretty face more than they already have."

Slowly, the tension eased from her body. Releasing his grip, he rolled to the side. Her eyes were open again and he calmly reached for the blanket and pulled it over her. Her knees immediately came up to her chest and she turned her face into the bed. The trembling of her body shown from under the covers and he wasn't sure what to do next. Remaining quiet seemed like his best course of action.

Several minutes later, his father sent him a message that his cabin was ready. This caused another dilemma. He didn't move and his voice came out barely a whisper, "We must change locations. I have a place with windows so you can see outside." She didn't move and he looked around the room at the heavy rolling shutters that electronically closed during daylight hours and darkened his room. He spent very little time here except to sleep so it never bothered him. If his mate was going to be happy, she needed sunlight and a taste of freedom.

Trying again, he released a small amount of his alpha energy trying to coax her into feeling safe. "I need to carry you but you can stay inside the blanket with your eyes closed if that will help." His whispered words neither calmed nor seemed to startle her.

With no verbal response or movement from under the shroud except for her shaking, he sent a mental message back to his father to check on food for the cabin.

"Everything is in place."

"I'm moving her." he responded, "Clear everyone from the trail and tell them to stay away from the cabin until I say otherwise."

A moment later his reply came, "It's done. Cheri is sleeping. Do you think you should wait for Cheri's help when the sun goes down?"

"No, I want my mate to see the sun and trees. It's important."

There was no further communication. Moving to his knees he looked at the lump beneath the blanket. "I will carry you. You're safe. There are clothes at the cabin and you will be able to shower and dress. He moved to scoop her into his arms feeling her body tense. He began humming the same melody from before and she allowed him to pick her up. With her head buried in the blanket, he carried her straight downstairs and out the front door. The cabin was more than a mile away. He walked the thick wooded path with swift strides. Her body tensed immediately before she changed shape and her wolf form struggled out of the blanket twisting from his arms and leaping to the ground. He prepared for this earlier by changing into sweatpants and a t-shirt. He quickly shed his clothes while watching her run. She wasn't fast and her strides were awkward, but she was beautiful and she was his. Dark fur covered his body and four legs swiftly gave chase.

Emily ran. This was the second time she intentionally called her demon and it cooperated by charging through the trees just wanting to get away. Suddenly her body froze. A young child was in front of her. She was tiny, beautiful, and miraculous. Lowering her demon's body to the ground so she wouldn't cause fright, Emily looked at the child with reverence. Two green eyes sparkled and met Emily's.

A sing-song voice came from the tiny human, "Oh, do you want to play?" The dress lifted over her head and nakedness swiftly changed to a small brown monster.

Heart stopping panic seized Brandt when his mate's screams shattered the quiet afternoon. Kinsee, one of the few cubs in the pack was standing in wolf form, her large eyes stricken with terror. Immediately he shifted to human, ready to tackle his mate.

Suddenly, she backed up and made to scramble away. He caught her in an iron grip. She changed into her human form and fought savagely to get away.

"Demon, demon!" She screamed, her hands pummeling Brandt.

A terrified and crying Kinsee ran off.

He tried to stop the thrashing of arms and legs and using his greater strength, pulled her back hard against his chest. It didn't stop her struggles so he did the only thing he knew to subdue an out of control she-wolf. His teeth took hold of her neck where her smooth skin joined her shoulder. He didn't draw blood but his mouth was firm enough to make her freeze. He groaned. His growing erection was becoming uncomfortable and impossible to hold back. Having her body this close with naked flesh to naked flesh was unbearable.

Emily sensed his distraction. Twisting, she broke his grip and brought her knee between his legs allowing her to get away.

"Oomph," the air left his lungs. His arms released her going to his damaged manhood.

Cheri appeared in front of his panicked mate. Her fangs flashed and the screams of demon began again. Brandt, breathing hard, walked gingerly forward. Cheri lunged and caught the girl in an unbreakable grip. Her fangs sank into the soft neck and quickly gave much needed oblivion. The vampire laughed while shading her eyes with one hand, blocking the sun to look at Brandt.

"If you need help with healing your injury, come to the house after the sun goes down."

Cheri flashed away and he reached out for his mate, barely catching the deadweight of her body before she hit the ground. He picked her up and began walking to the cabin once more. His gait was tentative but he no longer had to worry about his body's sexual response. He gave a soft chuckle but then the smile disappeared. What had gone on in her prison for all those years? She thought a child a demon. He understood her reaction to the vampire, but Kinsee had turned into a werewolf. It should have brought about fascination, not terror.

Seeing the cabin ahead, he grimaced at the bars on the windows. Sadness and rage twisted inside him but he knew they had to keep her contained. He also needed her name if she had one. Calling her mate worked for him but he doubted she would like the sound of it if she knew what it meant. He entered the small structure and went to his father's bedroom. His dad's and Cheri's scents permeated the room. Before today, it would have destroyed him but now he only noticed in passing. Thankfully, the sheets were clean and smelled of fabric softener so he pulled the top one back and laid her on the bed. He was hungry and knew she must be starving. His eyes again took in the sight of her defined ribs. It was easy to detect in her scent that she hadn't had enough meat in her diet. Werewolves could survive with little meat, but it made them weak. The twinge between his legs reminded him that he should be happy she was not at full strength. But, it angered him that she was deprived of the food her body craved and needed most.

Using the time while she slept, he cooked. It wasn't something he normally did but he was capable of cooking up a steak when required. He grilled two large steaks and baked some potatoes. While they heated, his thoughts drifted to hunting and hoped she could be by his side the next time he let his wild run free. She needed to feel the thrill of the hot blood of a kill and understand what she was. They had a long way to go but he had no doubt they would make it.

The sun was going down when he heard her roll over in the bed. He left the kitchen and walked to the bedroom. Damn it, he needed a name. Looking into the room he saw her startling blue eyes were open.

Emily's mind slowly made its way back from unconsciousness and she found herself in another strange room. She took long deep breaths while her eyes took in her surroundings. A noise made her look toward the door. He was standing there, large, his shoulders nearly reaching the width of the door and he was so different from her, so…something. She didn't understand why she was grateful to see him again when she knew she had to get away. His penetrating eyes met hers and his deep voice sent an unexpected ripple through her body.

"We're at your new home. I'm cooking dinner and it's almost ready. There are clothes on the dresser. They're only sweats but with your change happening so often, it's for the best." He backed away and returned to the kitchen.

She looked around the room again and gingerly got to her feet. She saw the clothes he spoke of and quickly put them on. Glancing around, she could see a shadowed opening opposite the door with a cloth covering. Walking to the possible escape route, she pushed away the cloth but met resistance beneath. She could see the other side. *Bars.* Her hand came up to her chest and her breaths became agitated and the room swam around in front of her eyes. A cage was once again her world and her demon needed to kill again.

He heard the rustling of clothing and began placing the food on the table. The small wood cabin had two bedrooms, an office, small living area, kitchen/dining room and one bathroom. There was a loft that looked out over the den with a large arcadia window that led out to a balcony. He had checked the bars on the large glass door. They would be the first he removed when she was ready. He heard a noise at the bedroom door and looked down the short hall.

The words were soft and hesitant. "I need privacy."

Her head was down, which surprised him. It was hard for an alpha to look down and even if she was being submissive, he could feel the raw and volatile power she was radiating. He had to shake himself from the subconscious pull to surround her body with his scent and mark her again. With a blink he realized her problem. He walked over and opened the door to the bathroom. "What you need is in here." He knew she wouldn't approach while he was standing so close. "You can use the sink to wash up before dinner. I left towels out. We'll tackle a shower after we eat." He walked back into the kitchen. He heard the bathroom door close and minutes later the unmistakable sound of the toilet flushing. He smiled when he heard the water turn on in the sink. After it shut off, there was no additional noise from the bathroom but she didn't come out for several minutes.

The toilet was like the one she grew up with and she let the cool water run over her hands after she did her business. The looking glass was new to her though she saw one in her mother's home when she went up the stairs. The same face looked back at her. Her eyes were blue and she smiled, she loved blue. Moving her head side to side, she thought about the man. His scent was different than her mother and it reminded her of her own odor. She wanted to stay in the small room where she felt safer but the smell of food and the need to kill the man in the other room drew her out. Her anger spiked but terror also made her weary. Peeking down the hallway she could see him. Blue eyes blazed into his. "Are the demons here?"

Chapter 8

She wasn't dropping her gaze now and her alpha's scent rolled from her body in waves. He shook his head slightly to recover from the effects of her power and the sexual attraction he was feeling.

"There are no demons here. Kinsee is a young child and she's precious to us. Cheri, with the teeth, is a vampire and she is our queen. I know this doesn't make sense but I won't let anyone harm you." Her face betrayed she had little understanding of what he was saying. She was his mate and he opened his link with her mind not sure if it would work.

Blood, there will be more blood when I kill him.

Her thoughts flooded his mind. Feeding her would probably be a good idea right now. He would save the worry about his death until after dinner, though he would keep a close eye on the knife she would need to cut her steak. Backing slowly to the table, he pulled out a chair for her and sat down in the one next to hers. She didn't come closer. Using his fork, he placed a steak on his plate and then picked up his knife making the first cut. Bringing the meat to his mouth, he watched her while chewing his food.

Her eyes followed ever movement he made, then stopped, and fastened on his mouth. Yearning to eat what caused the incredible odor and making her mouth water, overcame her fear. Thoughts of tearing his body apart and escaping her new prison diminished and the need to fill her empty stomach took its place. She pulled the chair out further and sat down. Picking up the plate, she scratched her fingernail against the hard surface. It was strange and she put it down. Keeping her eyes on the plate and using her fingers, she swiftly grabbed the meat, transferring it to her place setting. Blood drip across the table and surrounded the meat. Panic seized her when she noticed the messy trail she left on the table. The man lay down the instruments he was holding. She tensed ready to attack if he took her food.

Misunderstanding her body language his voice was soft, "You're hungry, and the eating utensils will only be frustrating. Eat like this." He picked up his meat with both hands and took a large bite from the side. The bloody juice dripped onto his plate.

She didn't hesitate. Her teeth flashed and sank deeply into the meat. Her eyes partially closed and she barely chewed before swallowing. The tension left her body with the first bite. He wasn't going to take her food. She took another bite after seeing him do the same and began eating without reservation. His hand startled her when it moved the rest of his meat onto her plate. She glanced up, not understanding why he would give up his food but then her stomach overruled her curiosity.

Brandt knew he could make more if she needed it. He began fixing a potato, first adding butter, and chives. He then cut it into quarters and added them to her plate before making his own. He also cut his into quarters and then ate with his fingers. When the steak was gone she started on the potato finishing it quickly.

"Do you want more?" Intense eyes just stared at him. He linked with her mind.

Yes, yes, yes.

She took a deep breath, "No." She spoke but looked away from him.

"I have a surprise for you, give me a minute." Rising, he walked to the kitchen, taking their dirty dishes with him. Aware she watched his every move; he removed two small plates from a cabinet and then opened the oven pulling out a warm pan of brownies. "I thought of baking a cake but the brownies were faster and I believe easier. I'm not the world's greatest cook but I doubt you will complain. If you're like most of us you'll love anything chocolate." Carrying their dessert to the table, he placed a plate in front of her. Sitting down, he picked up the brownie from his own plate and using his fingers, he took a bite.

She watched and then her hand brought the brown square to her lips. Before she took a bite she breathed in. Her eyes shot to his then down to the brown square in her hand. A nibble, and then a bigger one, it was gone in four large bites. Laughter came from the man and then he got up and returned bringing more brown food with him. He grabbed a brownie and sat back down. Lifting her hand she placed it on another warm square and brought it to her mouth again. It was so good and she wanted more. She began eating another.

His eyes didn't leave her mouth. She ate and his chewing slowed. He watched the look on her face. It was carnal and she was turning him on again. His groin no longer ached from her well placed knee and he wouldn't need to visit a laughing Cheri.

He was so caught up in the bliss of watching her eat he almost missed the fact her knife was gone. *Hide the knives*, the thought made him smile and startled at his grin, her fingers stopped their ascent to her mouth. His voice was low, "Go ahead and eat, I'm full."

She quickly consumed each bite.

Her stomach felt good and her thoughts became focused on the man again. He'd given her food. He caged her. He was in the cage with her. His smell was intriguing. What would his blood taste like? Her finger smoothed over the long pointed eating utensil she hid beneath the table. She might not need her demon to kill him. With a shaking hand, she kept it on her lap and waited.

Rising, Brandt picked up the plates, walking close to her. He was ready.

Her left arm rose quickly and she lunged.

Dropped the plates to the wood floor, he made to grab her hand but wasn't fast enough and the sharp edge sliced a burning path across his arm. He managed to grab her fingers which held tightly to her weapon. Blood welled from the cut though it wasn't deep. She was struggling but he only used one arm to secure her and with the other, he tossed the knife across the room for a perfect landing in the sink. Grabbing her other hand in a punishing grip, he twisted her around so her back was to him. Using his uninjured arm, he held both of her hands in one of his. He kept his voice stern and softly rebuked her, "Not a good idea. I'm not easy to kill and I don't want to hurt you. Keeping you prisoner is not the way I want your life here to start, but if I can't trust you, you'll be trapped inside the cabin." With his other hand, he wiped blood from his wound onto his finger and brought it to her tightly shut lips. His finger smeared, leaving a trail across her soft lower lip, "This is what my blood tastes like. It is the blood of your mate. He pulled his finger back before she could bite it but slowly noticed the effect his blood had on her and began to scent the chemical change in her body. Her breathing deepened and he knew she had no idea what was happening. Her wolf, wild and untamed recognized his.

"I would really love to know your name." The words were little more than a warm whispered breath in her ear.

Burning heat traveled from her mouth throughout her body. Sparks were running along her skin and mostly, she craved more. More blood, more him. She needed to taste, smell, and roll into his flesh, soaking the scent into her skin. The feelings were so strong, almost flashes of pain but mostly, uncontrollable need.

He knew exactly what her body wanted and needed but she didn't answer his inquiry about her name and he wasn't giving an inch even if his own desire drove him crazy. He held on tight for a few more minutes feeling her alpha's electric charge increase. Their courtship would be volatile and bloody. Controlling his own wolf was difficult, controlling his erection was impossible. Deep breaths, he needed deep breaths. Closing his eyes he relaxed his muscles and let his scent change marginally to help her control what she was feeling. Her body became pliant. Slowly his arms loosened and he released her and stepped away. Picking the broken dishes up from the floor, he took deep controlled breaths and acted like nothing happened. He ignored her trembling body, her scent and her wanting eyes. His mate tried to kill him. He wasn't angry but every fiber of his being wanted to sink into her body. He knew even with sharing his blood she wouldn't understand. Hell, he didn't understand though his wolf did.

She didn't move and her wary eyes followed him. After cleaning the table and kitchen, he entered the bathroom, turning on the shower, and running his hands beneath the water. Maybe she wouldn't want to kill him if she was clean. When the water temperature met his requirements, he walked out of the small room. Her feet slowly backed away. The room contained a new strong bitter scent and her frozen face held absolute terror.

The power washer, he was incredibly stupid.

Punishment. The water spray meant pain and humiliation. Images of Carolynn holding the spray flashed through her mind; her fight to remain standing, icy water hitting her arms and legs, and tears. Tears caused by her mother's hatred. And finally escape. She looked around backing away from the sound. More thoughts flooded her brain; his blood, the taste, her need. They continued; his smile, his voice, food, his food offered to her. Her thoughts were jumbled confusion. The panic receded and she tried to gain control. Looking up his intense gaze stared back.

He turned away and walked back into the bathroom, shut off the shower, and let the bathtub slowly fill. From the corner of his eye he saw the tail end of her shadow move past the bathroom door. He'd created a mess and spiked her fear. Turning both knobs off, he walked to the bedroom. Not seeing her he let his nose lead him to the closet. Hidden and hunched down toward the back, her arms clasped her knees to her chest. She was small and vulnerable. He crouched down bringing his eyes level with hers.

"This is my fault. I don't mean to scare you. I turned the water off and stopped the spray. I washed your body earlier while you slept but a bath will make you feel even better. Your hair is tangled and I don't want to cut it. I'll show you what to do and I'll help." Bringing his hand forward, he waited. They had reached their quota of accomplishments for the day and this was up to her.

Delicate fingers unfolded and her arms released her knees. She brought her eyes up. He smelled so good. He was so beautiful. Placing her hands on the floor, she pushed up not taking his extended hand. She wouldn't touch. She couldn't. His body straightened and he stepped backwards giving her room. He turned away and left the room. She no longer heard the sound of water spraying. Slowly she followed and stopped outside the water room.

He didn't look at the door but knew she was there. He ran his hand through the water while sitting on the side of the tub. "These knobs control the temperature, just like a sink. I'll leave the room and give you privacy. The shampoo and conditioner go on your hair, shampoo first, and then rinse it out with water. You may need to use a lot of the conditioner to get the tangles out but we'll see how it goes." He glanced up to see if she was following what he said. Her gaze stared into the mirror and her fingers traveled over her face. He realized this must have held her up in the bathroom earlier. He didn't know if she had ever seen herself. Walking past her, she followed his movements in the mirror. The door closed with a gentle click.

Her eyes went to the water and she walked over and sat down where she saw him sit. Fingers tentatively lowered. Warmth spread on her skin. Her hands went to her clothes and she couldn't get them off fast enough. Her bare leg lifted and settled in the water and then her other one followed. Slowly she melted and submerged herself. Stretching back, she felt the silky liquid cover her limbs and she drifted fully into the water. Her eyes closed and her muscles relaxed. Peace settled and she let out a slow breath drifting into a world of dreams.

He refused to worry. Ten minutes turned into thirty. What if she drowned? Did she remove her clothes? Now he was being stupid but that was only one of the feelings she brought out. Another was hot, feral, desire. The thought of water soaking over her naked body was driving him crazy. He wanted to feel the soap on his palm sliding over her curves and making their way to her breasts, her thighs. "Damn it!" He exclaimed out loud. This was torture and he could take no more. Even knowing he shouldn't his legs had a mind of their own and his hand clasped the bathroom door knob and pushed gently.

Her nose and the tips of her breasts were the only thing sticking out of the water. Bubbles, he would have bubble bath delivered tomorrow. He could think of nothing at this moment that would be more erotic. Stepping back, he silently closed the door.

Fifteen minutes later, she came out wearing flannel pajama bottoms and a soft cotton t-shirt he'd left on the bathroom counter, dripping hair, bare feet, and large blue eyes. Exquisite. He left her standing in the living area and walked to the bathroom grabbing another towel and a comb from a drawer. The smell of the comb made him smile. Cheri. But not for long if his mate would cooperate. Holding the towel toward her, he patiently waited until her hand reached out and took it. "Follow me." He walked to the couch expecting her to follow. "Sit here and I'll dry your hair a little more and get the tangles out."

Her lack of hesitation surprised him. She kneeled down and then sat at his feet, facing away from him. Wrapping the towel around the wet ends of her hair, he couldn't help but lean forward and inhale. Her smell was magnificent. Reaching for the comb, he gently began untangling the wet strands. Her fists clenched tightly and her shoulders remained tense but finally, with gentle patience, her platinum blonde hair slid smoothly through his fingers. Placing the comb on the couch beside him, he rested his hands on her shoulders and gradually, with exquisite care, soothed her muscles. She flinched ever so slightly with each aching touch. He thought she might run but she stayed seated. He worked his fingers into her neck, shoulders, and back. Her muscles finally loosened and her body, with a mind of its own, swayed back against his legs.

Brandt's lips were a hairs breadth from her ear, his voice gentle and coaxing, "Of everything you missed in your life, touch is what wolves need most. To be part of a pack is to be loved, cherished, and nurtured. We crave the closeness of our kind and sharing our scent connects our family's lineage and enhances the bond." Brandt's hands lightly skimmed her neck and the underside of her jaw. "Touch is everything." Gently, his lips touched the top of her head.

A single tear slid down her cheek. Her body unresistingly melted further into his.

Her chin rubbed against his hand and he smiled. She sat silently allowing his touch, her wolf craving his closeness. Finally, she released a gentle snore causing him to smile fully and then lift her to his lap. Her body remained lax and she didn't stir. Holding her close, he let another hour pass just to saver the scent of his mate.

His insides, knotted and tense from months of strain were slowly untying, turmoil giving way to protectiveness and love. He gave her one last kiss on the cheek before carrying her to bed. He shed his clothes needing her scent to blend with his. Closing his eyes he allowed the sense of peace to wash over him. Drawing her more firmly to his body, he fell asleep with his nose in her hair and a last thought before darkness closed around him. *What is her name?*

Terrifying screams jolted him from the bed. Deadly wolf eyes searched for danger but there was none. She was sitting up with her eyes staring straight ahead and trapped in a nightmare. Climbing back on the bed, he moved to her side. "Shhhh, you're okay." He kept his voice soft and melodic and gently touched her arm. The screaming stopped suddenly but uncontrollable tremors racked her body. Holding her close, his hands traveled up and down her arms giving what comfort he could. Finally, her muscles went slack, her breathing slowed, and her body calmed. His alpha's rage intensified because there was no one to kill.

Chapter 9

Bright sunlight and strong arms holding her close brought Emily awake. She was on her side and sprawled half on top of his warmth with her cheek against his chest. His eyes closed and his face peaceful, she inhaled deeply. Bringing her hand up, she touched one finger to the skin beside her cheek. Soft but hard she allowed her hand, with a feather touch, to glide over his chest and then travel higher.

The whisper of a touch brought him awake. Not opening his eyes, her smell enveloped him. Incredibly soft fingers trail from his chest to his neck. The soft caress became a gentle poke and he couldn't help but smile. Her hand jerked away. He peered between his eyelids. Her eyes were downcast and using his hand he tilted her face to his gaze. His voice, gruff with sleep whispered, "I need touch like you. My body is different, hard where yours is soft." Taking her hand he placed it back on his chest. Her fingers balled into a fist and didn't move. Connecting with her mind, he couldn't help it and laughed out loud at her thoughts.

He's a sin.

Exhaling with a low sigh over his self-imposed and momentary lack of wickedness, he got out of bed, and reached for his sweatpants. She had no idea how sinful he could be. "We need food, I'm starved." Turning, he walked to the bathroom and closed the door behind him.

Her erect profile sitting at the table greeted him when he came out. "I don't mind cooking and feeding you but you might enjoy learning. I'm in the mood for bacon and pancakes; you can help if you wish." He passed close and she gave him an inquisitive look when he entered the kitchen and began gathering bowls and pans. Over the clatter, he heard the soft click of the bathroom door.

Closing the door behind her, she sank to the cool floor. Quiet tears turned into muffled sobs. Her hands covered her face. So much want, so much need; his touch most of all. She didn't know what was happening to her. When her tears slowed, she cautiously removed her clothing. She shifted to the demon she hated and the monster looked back through the looking glass. Bringing her front paws up to rest on the countertop, she stared. Human eyes peered back but nothing else was the same. Cocking her head to the side, she examined herself. Without thinking, her muscles tensed and she lunged upwards.

The loud clatter rang through the house. It sounded like several items fell off the bathroom counter. His heart pounding, he opened the door and saw a scrambling white wolf trying to right herself on the floor moving away to the back of the small room. His eyes took in the scattered accessories from the counter and with relief he realized she tried to jump on top in wolf form. Not taking his eyes from the she-wolf in front of him, he sent a mental message to Dominique to have a large free standing mirror sent over in an hour. His mental telepathy caused him to miss the deadly quick change in her demeanor.

Complete panic at the thought of punishment caused the red haze to fall over her eyes. Anger; intense, deadly, and focused on Brandt took over. With a loud rumbling growl, her wolf body flew across the small space.

Brandt, in the process of backing up slowly, knew what was about to happen. His wolf senses registered the danger before his human brain. His wide shoulders barely passed through the doorframe when white fur and large extended teeth launched. He flew backwards and smashed against the hallway wall when her body collided with his. His arms strained to keep her snapping jaws from his face. Her back legs found purchase and raked down his upper thigh, the sharp nails slicing deeply into his skin. Grabbing her upper wolf's body and using his greater strength, he tossed her hard against the wall beside the bathroom door. The jarring impact made a loud thud and a slight whine escaped her throat. She immediately shifted to human. Sinking to the floor, she curled into a tight ball and tremors ravaged her body.

Bending forward, he grasped her arm tightly. Using his other hand, he tilted her face so her eyes looked into his. A low growl left his throat before he spoke. He battled with his alpha's need for blood, her blood. "Babe, if you want a fight I'll give it to you." His eyes burned. "I'm stronger and deadlier. Right now you can't win. The last thing I want is to hurt you but I won't hesitate if you challenge me. Get dressed and meet me in the kitchen." His dominant voice left no room for argument.

Dressed, but with resentment radiating from her pores, she appeared in the kitchen a few minutes later.

His anger had lessoned to disgruntlement though his thigh burned and blood soaked through his pants. He looked up and struggled not to laugh. She was no docile she-wolf but somehow she managed to control her irritation and keep her gaze down though her scent betrayed her. Their alphas needed to play and he couldn't help but chuckle while picturing the blood spattered walls of their playground when it happened.

For a few moments he let her stand there. He assembled flour, eggs, and the other ingredients needed to prepare pancakes. Two pounds of bacon were sizzling in a large frying pan. Her nose twitched and he noticed her inhale. Spooning flour into a measuring cup, he walked over and used his body to gently nudge her toward the counter. The scent of her anger kindled but she moved.

He continued to press his luck and placed the cup in her tense fingers, squeezing slightly so she would hold on. "I'm hungry and I know you are too. We can fight or make pancakes."

After a moment's hesitation she calmed.

Food might be his saving grace and he would remember to use it. "Now, pour the flour into this bowl." He pushed the bowl in front of her and guided her hand, showing her what he wanted. Filling the cup again with flour, he repeated the process three more times. Next were the eggs and using the same slow movements he showed her what to do. Sugar, baking powder, and milk joined the other ingredients and then he handed her a whisk. Following his hand motions she began mixing the batter. The pan was ready and he added butter. Looking sideways, he could see her in deep concentration while she stirred. Taking a step closer, he heard her heartbeat accelerate when he looked over her shoulder and into the bowl. It was time. Ignoring her slight scent of distress, he again took her hand in his placing a large spoon in her fingers and them scooping the creamy mixture and dropping a dollop onto the greased pan.

He left her watching the first batch cook and walked into the living room. His father loved soothing instrumental music. It wasn't Brandt's favorite but somehow he knew she would enjoy it. He chose Carter Burwell's "Honor Inflamed". It was a powerful piece with haunting flute and violins. The music filled the room and he sensed her walking up behind him. She wasn't coming close but remembering the other knives in the kitchen he glanced over his shoulder.

Mesmerized by the sounds she stood staring at the speaker.

Walking back to the kitchen, he checked the pancakes, flipping them over and then returned to the living room. She was now sitting on the floor with her ear to the speaker, eyes closed, and body swaying with a look of complete rapture on her face. His wolf stood at attention. Shaking his head to get his mind to focus, he walked back into the kitchen to finish preparing their meal alone.

Her demon calmed and her body relaxed. The sound was gentle, beautiful, and eerie. She instinctively swayed to the low beat. No anger, no pain, it soothed her beast. All the fury which grew over the previous weeks relaxed. Good memories flooded her mind; Carolynn rubbing her hair through the bars when she was small, Christmas with a new dress and enough food to fill her belly, her mother's voice reading about the baby Jesus. They were her only good memories and they trailed like smoke through her mind. Tears ran down her cheeks.

Everything was new; her rage, his touch, her fear, his voice. The music beckoned and her demon quieted. A soft touch on her shoulder had her opening her eyes and wiping away the tears before she turned. She could fall into his dark eyes. They mesmerized her and she yearned to reach her hand out and touch him.

"It's time to eat. I'll turn the music up so we can hear it in the other room."

Sitting silently at the table they used their fingers while listening to music play in the background. After seeing him add syrup, she poured some on her plate and then added more. His she-wolf had a sweet tooth. They finished off the bacon and pancakes. There would be no table scraps with her around. When finished, he handed her his plate and turned to pick up the other items. She followed and he led her to the kitchen showing her how to rinse the dishes and place them in the dishwasher.

Concentrating, Emily connected his words with what he showed her. So many questions fired through her mind but she didn't want him angry.

Multiple sudden loud knocks coming from the front door sounded through the house.

Instant crushing fear sent her running for the back bedroom. Escape, it was all she could think of.

Brandt missed grabbing her by a hair. Using the key from his pocket, he walked over and unbolted the front door. Samson stood patiently, stern faced and holding a large wooden framed Cheval mirror.

"How are the lovebirds this morning?" Unable to hold his facial muscles still any longer, he burst out laughing. "I'm glad to see you survived the night. Why do you want the mirror?"

Grinning, Brandt grabbed the monstrosity from his friend's hands. "Wouldn't you just love to know?" He kicked the door closed with a satisfying thump and Samson's laughter slowly faded. Carrying his gift to the bedroom, he passed the closet where he knew she was hiding. He sat the mirror in the corner of the room and opened the window's curtains wide. He then left the room to turn up the music even more. When he came back, she wasn't in the closet or standing in front of the mirror, she was looking with heartfelt longing at what lay beyond the window.

"I'd love to take you out but I think we should hold off a day or two. The mirror is so you can look at your wolf form without falling down." His voice teased gently and it surprised him when she answered.

"My demon will kill you."

"No, you might try but I won't die easily. You can control your wolf; it's not a demon that does the killing." He had no idea how to get through to her so he let instinct be his guide. "We need to talk but it's hard because I don't know your name. Sit in the chair for me."

Turning away from the window, she immediately sat in the chair by the mirror.

Finally, it dawned on him; she did what he said if he didn't ask and only commanded. Swallowing his ire, he closed his eyes for a split second to gain control. No alpha should be this broken. It killed him but he needed information. "What is your name?"

Dropping her head in submission she whispered, "Emily."

"Do you know how old you are?"

"Nineteen."

"Do you know what you are?"

No hesitation, "The devil's child."

His voice thickened but he spoke slowly and evenly, "No Emily, you are a werewolf, a species of beastkind. Your wolf is beautiful, you are beautiful. Kinsee, the child we saw yesterday, is also beastkind. She is sweet and funny and would love to be your friend, but you scared her." His voice grew firm, "We don't believe in demons. There are over a hundred werewolves here and thousands around the world. We don't harm humans unless they try to harm us. Many stay separate but some of us live among humans if we choose. The wolves here belong to my pack; I am their leader, their alpha. This is where you are safe and where you can let your wolf free." He waited but she would not meet his gaze. He began removing his clothing. "Look at me Emily."

Ocean blue eyes cautiously traveled upwards, his body; muscled strength, alluring, so different, so perfect. His deep penetrating gaze caught and held hers. In a blink, a large black wolf replaced the man. She scrambled out of the chair but the beast stepped between her and the door. Gasping for air, trying to control her terror, she remembered the black demon's first attack; chasing her down, sinking his teeth into her leg, the pain and the terror. But mostly she thought of it as God's retribution for killing her mother.

He took one step in her direction and then another.

Frozen, she could not move.

Linking with her mind, he ordered, "Sit down." Her backside suddenly met the chair.

Another step closer, her shaking hands fisted in her lap.

Using his snout he nudged her fingers and softened his tone "Release your hands Emily." Her fingers untangled and his wet nose sniffed her palm. "Touch me." He didn't think she would.

Finally, trembling fingers ran over his long nose. They glided over the short and bristled facial fur and up to his eyes.

Changing back into his human form he knelt naked at her feet, his head tilted up, brown eyes never left hers. He brought his hand up taking her fingers and drawing them to his lips. He slowly, sensually kissed each one.

Sad, chaotic thoughts consumed her mind but one overruled them all. He was like her. Fur, bristly but soft, his smell strong but compelling, she wanted to rub every inch of her body along his. She wanted to touch his demon body with hers. Oh how she wanted.

He stood. Taking her hand, he pulled her up to her feet. He turned with her toward the mirror and gathered her silken hair in one hand. He used his other to caress her neck. Releasing her hair, he reached down to the bottom of her t-shirt and swiftly pulled it up and over her head, giving her no time to object. His hand went to the waistband of her flannel pants and pulled them down her long legs. "Step out."

Her feet kicked free. She focused on his every move in the mirror.

"You are beautiful just like this." He flowed back to wolf form and mentally spoke, "Emily, change now."

Her demon looked back from the mirror, white fur in striking contrast to his larger black wolf, both of them different and so very much the same.

Backing up, he instructed her to do the same.

The other two wolves born from Malcolm's assaults did not have her coloring. His mate was unique. Prodding her gently to move slightly, he put his head next to hers so they stood together in the mirror. "You are exquisitely beautiful. I need you to stand still and not move." This one thing was driving him crazy. He needed to inhale her female scent, the fragrance of his mate. His nose began trailing slowly over her body, imprinting her essence into his brain, into his cells, and into his heart.

Her alpha was incredibly strong and she had no idea the damage she could do. He took his time. Spice; sweet and savory met his nose as he tasted the aroma on his tongue.

Arousal hit him hard.

It was torture, it was bliss, and it was not the time. His nose traveled back to her snout.

Her pink tongue tentatively came out and licked the side of his mouth.

It was exactly what he wanted to do and returning the favor, he tasted deeply of her scent, his rough tongue skimming over her face.

Emily stood so still, her world collapsing. Her demon was never touched, never accepted, never loved but his monster caressed her.

His long snout became the angular jaw of the man. His hands settled on her beast's jaws, holding her head in place. Looking directly into her eyes, he spoke, "There is no evil here. There is no demon. You are a beautiful wolf. My heart aches for what you have endured. You must trust me to keep you safe. You will soon be free to let your wolf run, I give you my word."

Emily shifted to her human form, her knees lowering until she was beside him. Turning from the mirror, watery eyes met his. Longing to trust him, she felt a small spark of love fill her heart. Her physical body felt something different though she had no idea what it was. The need felt like hunger but this hunger consumed her entire body.

The expressions shifting across her face told their own story and gave him hope. Her thoughts easily coursed through his mind but his thoughts froze on her last. Desire. Feeling himself stiffen and grow, his frustration came through in his voice. "Get dressed while I take a quick shower. I'll only be five minutes." With a groan and unable to handle his own simmering need, he turned and walked away.

Cold water did little to relieve his body. Stupid, he was stupid and needed to go gently, slowly. He quickly washed up. Who knew what she could find in the cabin to hurt herself with. When finished, he wrapped a towel around his waist and went to check on his mate. Now clothed, she gazed out the window with longing. It broke his heart. Making a quick decision, he dressed and sent a mental message to his pack telling them to clear the area. This time he told them to make sure Kinsee was away too. The pack had three children of various ages but Kinsee was the only one able to get more than a few feet from her parents. He didn't want any accidents. If Emily killed a cub, her life would be forfeit and he would carry out the sentence. He would die with her if it came to that.

Taking the comb off the dresser, he walked toward the bathroom to fix his hair.

"Can I do it?" Her shy voice held hope and longing.

Smiling, he changed direction and went toward the couch. They reversed the sitting arrangement from the evening before. He felt the comb run through his short brown hair. He usually only swiped a comb through it once or twice but he let her familiarize herself with his body and scent. He felt the comb pass across his head several times and then her small hands traveled along his shoulders, gently rubbing like his hands did the night before. Reaching up he took her fingers within his, stopping her movements. Tilting his head, he gazed into her eyes. "That feels wonderful but if you let me braid your hair, I'll take you outside to feel the sunshine."

He stood and went to the bathroom and then the bedroom. He couldn't find any hair ties so he broke off a piece of thread from a spindle. He went back to the couch where Emily waited. Combing through her hair quickly, he then plaited it into a single braid down her back. Her fingers went to the woven hair feeling its texture. He wasn't very accomplished with female grooming but she looked adorable.

Standing, he clasped her hand, giving it a gentle squeeze. His authoritative voice compelled, "You will not change form. You must learn to control it and going outside will temp your wolf to run. We are staying near the cabin. Do you understand?"

Irritation changed her scent slightly. Her jaw went rigid. Glowing blue eyes challenged him for a split second and then looked down. Not understanding the shifts in her mood, anxiety flooded her. One minute she wanted him touching her and the next she wanted his blood to flow. She spent years lowering her eyes to her mother but that was becoming harder to do with him. She wanted his eyes to lower and felt a strong need to make him do it. Remembering what happened in the bathroom, she knew she wasn't strong enough but that only increased her apprehension.

He fought not to grin. His she-wolf had sharp claws and he knew in the coming years they would have many fights for dominance. She wasn't even near the peak of her strength. Pulling her close, he gave her stiff body a brief hug then released her. Taking the key from his pocket, he unlocked the door. He intertwined their fingers and used his stronger grip to subdue any urge she had to flee. They stepped outside.

Her heartbeat accelerated rapidly. She tentatively followed. He knew it was partially instinct that she tried not to show fear to a stronger wolf. He also admired her bravery. Inhaling deeply, the clean air leeched into his wolf and he knew it was doing similar things to hers. His fingers tightened to remind her of his words about controlling her wolf and not changing. He noticed too that her alpha scent was growing stronger. Challenging was in her blood. It would take her months to fully control her beast. His sexy grin turned in her direction. Thoughts of dominating his alpha she-wolf spiked his desire again.

He squelched his thoughts and sat down on the edge of the porch drawing her down to his side. One of his hands remained entwined with hers and the other went to her thigh and gently rubbed in a soothing motion. Her unease dissipated. When her wolf completely calmed, he released her hand and jumped to the ground not bothering to make use of the steps. "Come and get your feet dirty," Raising his arms he beckoned.

With no hesitation, she jumped.

Unhurriedly, he lowered her to the ground. His eyes, etched with desire, held hers and his hand lifted to her chin. With a gentle squeeze her mouth opened slightly and he rubbed his finger over her bottom lip. He blinked and then pulled himself together. Looking down with a bemused grin, he wriggled his toes in the pine needles.

    Bending her knees, she placed her hand in the dirt then lifted it to her nose. Her lungs expanded. Wild, like her demon, the earth called her. No cage, no longer hidden from the world. Fur fought with human skin. Shaking her head she controlled the need to become demon. Fighting the change was something she had done for years but the outdoor smells made it harder. When she won the battle, she tempted herself again and bringing her hand back to her nose, took another deep breath and smiled.

Chapter 10

Bemused, Brandt cherished every change in her facial muscles and relished her wild, musky scent. He craved a time when they would finally run free side by side.

Snapping his head up, a scent grazed his nostrils interrupting his thoughts. Against his direct orders there was another werewolf coming toward them. It was Clem's brother Zeb and without breaking stride, he walked within twenty-five feet of Brandt and Emily. Showing no submission, he glared into Brandt's eyes.

Brandt's rage flared. Emily's look of fear and uncertainty increased his fury. Channeling his anger he focused on the other werewolf. "What the fuck are you doing?" He said and followed his words with a low deadly growl.

"I'm here to challenge." Zeb could feel the hot violent pressure swirling around his alpha but he wasn't backing down and he wasn't lowering his eyes.

"You're a dead wolf."

"It won't be easy to kill me. I'm not my brother." Spitting on the ground, Zeb's loathing and resentment exuded from his voice, "You've brought a feral into our pack. She needs to be put down."

Two hundred pounds of angry alpha used every ounce of will to hold his ground and not tear the other werewolf to shreds. "It might not be easy but I think I'll enjoy killing you more than killing Clem." The waves of Brandt's fury flooded the air.

"The challenge has been made and when I win I might try out your sweet little piece of ass before I slit her throat." Zeb deliberately turned his back on his pack's alpha.

Control shattered, Brandt's bare feet ate up the ground. Neither he nor Zeb could shift easily and risk being caught up in their clothing.

Knowing his words and actions would cause this type of response; Zeb turned and launched himself at Brandt. The ground absorbed the impact of their bodies. Bone crunched. Brandt's fist connected with Zeb's nose. Blood sprayed through the air. Alpha fists pummeled his enemy's face. Lust, his need to mate, his anger over Emily's anguish, and fear took hold and his need to kill Zeb intensified.

Zeb, realizing his mistake, scrambled to get away. His fist connected a solid blow which allowed him to put a few feet between himself and his alpha. His deliberate bating of Brandt was not his original plan. Seeing the beautiful she-wolf egged him on and he reacted with little control.

Neither noticed the white wolf until she launched herself into the middle of their battle. Her body took Zeb to the ground and razor sharp fangs descended into his throat.

"Stop!" Brandt's voice conveyed complete command.

She hesitated, her eyes traveling from her prey to the man looking at her with authority. Her teeth bit further into Zeb's bare throat. Shaking her head, his blood flowed into her mouth. She finally released her hold, backing away with a low rumbling growl from deep in her throat.

His rage tapered down and he watched his mate control her need for the same blood he was after. His voice betrayed no concern that she had not followed his order immediately. His mind linked with hers. "Zeb challenged me and I will kill him soon enough." He thought about telling her to go inside but then decided he'd pushed his luck by ordering her not to kill Zeb.

Derision and fury laced his words, "In the almost impossible event that I lose, she will challenge you for alpha." He let that sink in. Emily's dominant scent mingled with his and
finally overpowered even Zeb's rage, forcing him to lower his head and eyes.

With growls coming from his human throat, Zeb backed slowly away and faded into the heavy forest growth.

Deadly dark eyes turned to Emily, softening immediately. She was underweight, abused, and deadly. Perfect.

"We need to talk." Brandt grabbed her clothes and walked inside.

Emily followed cautiously dreading her punishment but refusing to show fear.

"Change." An order. Waiting with patience, he realized she did not obey immediately. The same happened when he told her to stop tearing Zeb's throat out. He wasn't used to having his authority challenged unless death was the consequence. He knew an alpha command was difficult for another wolf to disobey. She packed a shit load of alpha power. He wondered if she was feeling the same tingling beneath her skin that he experienced after his first challenge to the death. Her body was adjusting and she would be on unsteady ground until it settled.

She shifted and he placed his hand out but did not vocalize his desire that she take it. Leaving it there, he allowed her to make the decision. Her fingers tentatively sought his. He pulled her toward him and held her for a moment, torturing himself before helping her put on a shirt and pants. Sitting on the couch, he pulled her onto his lap feeling the adrenaline pumping through her body. He wrapped his arms securely around her and nuzzled her neck with his nose. Inhaling her scent he felt her body tense.

"Please I need to hold you while I explain a few things." He waited and finally she relaxed. "Your body, your scent, and the power of your wolf are changing. The same thing happened to me after I killed my pack's alpha. It was like dynamite exploding in my bloodstream, but over the next few months, it settled in and became a part of me. I know you don't understand but your wolf is dominant and your subconscious is fighting with your fear of the unknown. Your wolf does not like to be told what to do." He gave a low gentle growl. "My wolf does not like to be disobeyed. I'm stronger and alpha of the pack you now belong to. We have a lot to learn about each other and our wolves must adjust."

She was listening intently and not objecting. It was a good sign. Due to her change, the braid no longer held her hair and he ran his fingers through the soft strands. "Zeb challenged me. Pack law dictates that there can be no interference. You will stay here and I will have another wolf stay with you." His hand continued to travel through the silky texture of her hair but her body stiffened at his words.

Sudden fear emanated from her. When Brandt charged Zeb, she had immediately shifted to her wolf form but her clothing tangled her arms and legs. The rage she felt had no control and she only wanted to administer death. Brandt's voice in her head, soothed her anger, and allowed her to release the man and not kill him. The attack gave her a sense of power. Now, she listed to Brandt's explanation and fear consumed her. The thought of him leaving caused panic. For the first time her voice was shaky but commanding. "I will not stay without you."

The pain in her voice gave him pause. She was such a contradiction of bravery, terror, sadness, anger, and uncontrolled alpha but he had no choice but to control her. "I will not be disobeyed in this and I will return within a few hours. You will have food, freedom to move around the cabin, and company. I will not leave you alone. Dominique, the she-wolf I'll call, will help calm you. She is not dominant like us. Just the scent of anger will scare her but her need for protection gentles us too. She's defenseless and could die very easily. I will need your word that you will not harm her."

"No."

"Explain no?"

"Do not leave."

"You cannot come to the challenge. There can be no interference. Being alpha means I fight my own battles within the pack." His tone left no room for argument and he felt her body shudder in defeat. Her anger left on a long outward breath but desolation replaced it.

Tipping her chin up, he looked into eyes brimming with tears. His patience was at an end and his lips slowly descended. Her texture and taste caused his control to slip even more and his breathing to accelerate. His whispered words, into her mind urged, "Open your mouth." She didn't hesitate. Twisting his body, he lay back on the couch, and brought her fully on top of him. The kiss deepened and a painful erection formed between his thighs. Stop. Take her. His mind and body were at war. Growling with frustration, he pulled his mouth away and sat up while keeping her on his lap against his pain filled heat.

Blue eyes gazed into his eyes with uncertainty.

He tried to keep the sexual frustration from his voice but didn't succeed. "I don't even know where to start. I'm not sure if you understand the birds and the bees." At her puzzled look he searched for another way to explain through his own embarrassment. "Do you know how babies are made?" Her body stiffened and she looked for a way to escape. He tightened his hold remaining still and calm.

Anguish tinted her words, "The devil gave Carolynn a baby. His seed created me and I am one of his demons." She looked down and then twisted slightly, trying to extricate herself from arms made of iron.

His muscles flexed minutely and gave her no opportunity to push off. His words contained anger even though he tried for control. "The man who attacked your mother was not the devil. He was a werewolf. He wanted to get her pregnant, but what he did to her body should only happen with the mutual consent of the two people involved. I'm sure he frightened and hurt her deeply but she didn't understand what we are. There are no demons. You are beastkind, a werewolf."

She didn't allow his words time to sink in, "I killed her." She revealed her biggest secret, the one which would make him hate her.

Her mind traveled back to the blood and unrecognized body on the floor of her cell. The body of her mother and the only person she knew during her life. She killed her mother and she had no doubt God sent this demon to punish her for her sin.

Loosening his hold, he ran slow meticulous fingers over her trembling back. Pulling her hair slightly at the base of her neck, he drew her mouth to his. Soft at first, then demanding, his teeth nipped gently on her lower lip, kissing the side of her mouth and then stroking inside again.

Control; he fought his need to take her on the couch and sink his body into hers, the body of his mate.

Control damn it.

He disengaged his mouth from her soft lips and looked at her with violent intensity. He used his words to satisfy her wolf, "I killed your father. I tore him to pieces and relished his blood. Your mother was not the only woman he took by force. Two of the females he attacked gave birth. Those children grew up with the pack. You have a sister and a brother. If we had discovered you when young, I would have taken you from that woman. I wish my fangs were the ones that sank into her flesh and killed her. It's a memory I would enjoy having."

Her eyes changed and the stunning blue became a deeper pool of darkening sky. Their depth pulled him in. Bringing her hands up to his neck she drew him to her seeking mouth. With tentative lips, she mimicked what he had done to hers moments before.

His groan rumbled against her lips.

Time stopped, but the madness had to stop too. His growl was longer this time and she gave one of her own. He forcefully separated their mouths and then their bodies. He sat her to the side and stood. "Our alphas call to each other but not yet. Not now." He managed to calm his breathing and continued. "I want you to meet Dominique. She will be with you during the challenge. I can speak to my pack together or one at a time. I don't want to frighten you by opening the link so you need to know what I'm doing."

He waited and saw the question on her face. Only thirty minutes passed since Zeb left but the entire pack would have heard of the challenge by now. He opened his link with Dominique but kept his connection with Emily. "I need a favor. Can you sit with Emily during the challenge?"

It wasn't Dominique who answered, it was Cheri. "Do you think this wise? I will not have Dominique harmed. Your mate is too strong, uncontrolled, and dangerous."

Emily looked confused by the censure in Cheri's voice.

He tried to keep the frustration from his thoughts. "You can both come to dinner tonight and we will talk. I think it best that my father not be here, but only because I don't want her overwhelmed and was hoping for Dom to come alone. I understand your worry and think she can handle the two of you."

"Seven o'clock." The connection ended.

He looked at the uncertainty on Emily's face. "We will make dinner together. Dom will eat what we do but Cheri usually just drinks wine. I know you will like Dominique and you need to be around other females before having contact with our males. We are rougher and can be aggressive. They are not accustomed to a dominant female and you need to gain additional control of your alpha's temper so you don't accidentally hurt someone. Dominique is completely submissive and you will notice shortly after meeting her that your instincts to protect will be stronger than your instinct to attack." He stopped not knowing if she followed everything he said.

"Can I eat now?"

He laughed, grabbed her hands, and drew her to her feet. "I'll make sandwiches to hold us over."

"Can you make the brown food like last night?"

He realized she was talking about the brownies. "I have a better idea, let's bake a cake. We can do it together."

A barrier was crossed. Thoughts of killing him were no longer forefront in her mind. She continued to battle her wolf for control but it would come. So would the sexual release their bodies craved.

Patience. When that didn't work he would take cold showers. His wolf needed to wait.

They ate lunch first. Brandt put enough steaks out for three people and then added an extra for Emily. He would stuff her at each meal to fatten her up. He showed her the back of the cake box so she could read the directions.

The scent of anxiety began to roll off her body in waves. "I don't read. Carolynn read to me but said I didn't deserve to touch the book."

Placing the box on the counter, he took her hand. "What did she read to you?"

"God's book."

He could barely hear her voice but the scent of her distress didn't diminish. "Reading lessons will be added to your daily activities. I know my dad keeps some of my favorite childhood books here at the cabin and I'll gladly read them to you. Come with me." His voice had changed from that of a commanding alpha to the tone of a playful boy.

He led her to his father's office. He knew the book he wanted was there along with his father's books on philosophy. First though, he reached for the large leather volume, turned to her, and put the book into her hands. "This is my father's copy of the bible. It's a book that needs to be touched, but after today if you never want to see another, I'll make sure there are none in our home."

Her fingers gently ran across the leather in reverence. She thought of the many times Carolynn sat outside the bars and read from the book of God. Most of her words held anger but Emily never wanted the words to end. When her mother spoke Emily was not alone. She gazed up with longing. "Please, I want the book. One day I will understand."

Brandt smiled and replied with humor, "If you ever make sense of it, let me know. You can then argue with my father on the merits of Christianity. He believes in the Goddess and loves nothing better than a good philosophical debate." He turned and picked up another book. It had a picture of a wolf with a snowy mountain background. "This is Jack London's Call of the Wild and it's the one we'll read first. Let's finish the cake and then get ready for our evening company."

Chapter 11

Brandt tried to keep Emily busy. They took fifteen minutes and straightened up the cabin for guests. Clothing was another problem, knowing she had nothing appropriate for company he stayed in sweats so she would feel comfortable. He brushed her hair and because of the earlier braid, it flowed down her back in gentle ripples. It was pure silk and the color of white gold.

His voice was gruff when he spoke. "Dominique will keep her eyes down. She gets nervous easily and your scent will worry her. The power that makes you alpha is growing; I can feel it and smell it. If you stay calm she will too but any agitation will cause upset. This will happen with most wolves you encounter. Learning to control your internal emotions is what keeps those around you settled. They look to me for security and soon, they will look to you for the same."

Emily's eyes conveyed a slight understanding and he felt she would be okay. The power that made her alpha, oozed from her pores and made it instinct to protect those weaker.

He unlocked and opened the door when Cheri let him know they were approaching. The vampire entered first.

Striking green eyes looked to Brandt and then his mate. Lifting her hand to Emily's, Cheri spoke mildly, "I know we met yesterday but it wasn't official. Welcome to my clan." Taking a long steady breath in, she smiled. "Your blood has chosen the strongest among my wolves."

Brandt also inhaled. The mingled mate scent was there and would only grow stronger. When their physical bodies claimed each other, every beastkind and vampire they encountered would know they were life mates.

Amazingly, Emily's voice broke into his thoughts, "You honor us my queen." She didn't lower her eyes and stared straight into the smiling eyes of violence and death that forever remained just below the surface of Cheri's gaze.

Earlier Brandt explained the proper greetings to her but found it surprising that she managed so well. It was against an alpha's instinct to break eye contact and the vampire understood.

Cheri turned slightly, "This is Dominique. She's my friend and has been my companion for many years. She will not fight you. She will roll over and bare her throat. I will kill anyone who harms her."

Emily looked toward the she-wolf giving off a strong odor of uncertainty. Instantly Emily's demeanor changed. She took the other woman's hand gently in her own. "It's okay, we can be friends. I have much to learn."

Dom looked up with a quick glance and brief smile but then cast her eyes down again. It was a start.

They ate dinner and Brandt looked forward to inviting his father when Emily could handle the strain a little better. She needed time, friends, and love. He had no difficulty in providing all three.

Cheri glanced at Emily, "When Dom comes tomorrow night, she will bring you more clothing. Sweats are fine for males but females require a few fancy items. We also need to get you some shoes. When you think you're ready, we'll go shopping and see where your tastes lie and get everything you need."

Emily smiled, her eyes going to the necklace Cheri wore.

Brandt followed her gaze and knew the first thing he would buy her. He looked forward to draping her bare skin in diamonds.

"Eh hum...Brandt, I think you need to reign in your mating aroma. The scent is filling the room and you have three ladies present." Cheri looked at him with a wicked grin.

Brandt blushed, which only made Cheri laugh. It was wonderful to see him happy. She loved the stupid wolf and at one time felt great passion for his amazing body. He deserved his half-wild she-wolf. When Emily came into her own, she would be a mate to be proud of. The clan needed a strong pair to lead the pack. She abhorred the recent violence and knew it had to stop.

Changing her focus, she asked, "Clem has three brothers. Do you think you will be challenged by the other two after you kill Zeb?"

The air in the room changed with Brandt's irritation, "I am no longer playing the alpha game. The fight will be over in minutes. Zeb's brothers court certain death if they challenge but I'll oblige if needed."

"It's about time my alpha was back. I've missed you." Her voice softened and she remembered a night long ago after he won a bloody battle.

Electricity charged through the room and a low growl came from Emily's throat. Clenching her hands into fists, Emily stood and was a split second from launching herself across the table.

Propelling out of his chair, Brandt placed his body between Cheri's and his mate's. Steel arms locked onto Emily's but he gave a rebuking glance over his shoulder at the vampire. She had a chagrinned look on her face and if things were not so serious he would have laughed. They'd shared wonderful nights of passion but he realized it was only sex mixed with his yearning for more.

Turning back to his mate, he spoke with stern amusement, "Emily look at me." Her eyes rose to meet his. "Our queen grants you privilege because you are new to the pack. She does not want to harm you nor does she want to mate with me. She loves my father."

Frost blue eyes glared back, her voice challenging. "I scented what she was feeling. It smelled like you did a moment ago."

Brandt wasn't sure what to do because Cheri's scent smelled of lust and want. Pulling Emily close, his mouth took hers possessively not caring about the other two women in the room.

Cheri spoke up, "Come on Dom. Let's get you a slice of that cake. I've smelled it since we arrived."

Brandt was aware the two women left the room but he knew they could still see Emily in his arms. He pulled back and looked into her eyes. "It doesn't matter how many women throw off that scent, only you and I will share it with each other." He placed his forehead against hers and waited while she calmed.

"Kiss me again." It was a direct alpha command though she didn't know it.

He groaned loudly meeting her lips halfway, quickly tasting what she offered. Finally pulling away, he laughed and the two women in the other room laughed too.

"I'm sorry Emily," this from Cheri. "Our ways are difficult to understand. You will feel better once you meet Brandt's father. I think Dom has a boyfriend too and maybe sometime the six of us will get together at the main house."

Cheri cast her eyes in Dom's direction. Her face was bright red and she turned her head down into her shoulder. "You didn't think I knew did you? Mitch is not good enough for you but if you like him,

I'll keep my opinions to myself. Now eat your cake and let's get home. I have a need for Thomas and I don't want you walking by yourself."

Their guests left after enjoying dessert.

Taking Emily's hand, Brandt directed her to the couch and grabbed his book off the side table. The next hour he spent reading, trying to keep his mind off her delicious lips and body. Her head was nodding to the side and he asked gently, "Would you like a bath?"

Sleepy eyes looked back but she nodded her head up and down.

Dom had left a small bag with a few items he requested. He grabbed it on the way to the bathroom. Sitting her on the toilet seat, he began running the bath water and pulled a bottle from the bag, he removed the cap. The scent of roses was stronger than his sensitive nose liked. He poured a small amount under the faucet.

The bubbles rose with the water and Emily looked on with inquisitive fascination.

Scooping suds into his hand, he turned to her and touched the bubbles to her nose. Her nose wrinkled when the strong odor hit.

His husky voice filled the small room, "Werewolves' sense of smell is more sensitive than humans. Humans make their soaps for their own noses. You'll get used to the strong fragrance quickly but when we have a chance to shop, we'll find something a little less overwhelming. Get undressed and I'll leave you to your bubble bath."

Her soft but strong hand caught his, shadowed eyes imploring. "Stay."

He looked at the tub and then at her hand. This was going to kill him slowly. His voice held sexual longing, "I'll stay if you say my name."

Her smile was shy but her scent rose to match his. "Brandt." Hesitant, but she said it.

Smiling riley, he realized tonight would be death by sexual frustration.

He watched each piece of clothing leave her body. She blushed and looked away, her legs stepping into the steamy bath and quickly sliding down into the water. If their pheromones were strong before, they were raging now and he could no longer smell roses. Kneeling beside the tub, his eyes glowed with appreciative desire, following the silky path of skin exposed above the bubbles.

Lifting a sudsy hand, she brought it to his nose, leaving the bubbles behind mimicking what he had done to her. "You're eyes are black but they were brown before."

Brandt's laugh was low and husky. "I've been told that happens when I'm angry or thinking of a beautiful woman." His hand caught hers and brought it slowly to his lips. His tongue licked the additional suds from her fingers and an electric charge went straight to his groin. Placing her hand on his cheek, he closed his eyes trying to gain control of his racing heart. It didn't work and a low growl vibrated up from his throat. He lifted the upper part of her body out of the water. His kiss was possessive and untamed. He wanted this woman, his mate. The feel of her breasts and water absorbing into his t-shirt, caused him to momentarily release her mouth and back away. His hands grabbed his shirt and the sound of ripping cloth echoed. His lips descended again, his tongue taking possession and learning every detail of her mouth, its taste, and scent. He would never get enough.

She groaned.

He broke away.

Cerulean eyes slowly opened. Filled with desire, they begged for more.

"Your eyes change too. Now finish your bath and we'll talk when you get out." His voice was almost harsh and he didn't wait for a reply. Standing, he practically ran from the room. On the other side of the door, he took deep breaths trying to control his need. Not yet, he told his wolf, soon.

Emily dressed in a long nightshirt that was in the bag brought over by Dominique. The feelings running through her body were strange. Every nerve ending focused on Brandt and just being a room apart made her nervous. His hands and mouth swept her senses with longing. Her lower body ached with need.

Memories of Carolynn's voice sounded inside her brain, her mother describing the rape with every detail. Explaining what the monster did to beget Emily. Confusion stirred within her but she needed his touch. She needed him.

He waited on the couch and smiled deeply when she left the bathroom and walked toward him with a towel and comb. Moving his legs apart he made room for her to sit on the floor. He began their ritual and dried her hair before running the comb through it.

"Will you make the music noise?"

Her voice had its own melody and it took him a moment to realize she meant humming. With a laugh, he gave her what she asked for.

"I remember her touching me when I was very small. I only wanted to feel her fingers stroke my hair. I never wanted to be evil."

His hand stilled, resting on her shoulders and he stopped humming. "Tell me."

Chapter 12

Years of loneliness and abuse poured out. Her voice remained monotone though she could not control the change in her scent and it weighed heavily throughout the room. Anguish, despair, and hopelessness continued year after year. Her words described a small tortured child becoming a lonely and sad woman.

Brandt felt every emotion and he released his own scent to calm and soothe his troubled mate. Listening brought forth the miracle that was the woman in his arms. Every word imprinted on his brain, all the pain during every day of her life. He listened.

"Carolynn gave me crayons and white paper. I drew pictures with bright colors. I loved them. She brought me tape so I could put them on the walls. I knew she didn't care for me, but at those times, I thought some day she would. I loved green and blue but yellow was my favorite. I drew drawings from my memories of the bible storybook pictures. I drew the sheep that walked in my mind. Carolynn told me that demon's kill sheep. She told me I was born evil and I would be the devil's hand if she let me out of the cellar."

Brandt's arms traveled around her midriff giving her a gentle squeeze.

"My mother had favorite passages in the bible and she read those to me over and over, 'Beware of false prophets, who come to you in sheep's clothing, but inwardly they are ravening wolves.' She told me I looked sweet and innocent but inside I was evil and no one could know I existed. I was the sheep that turned into the wolf and I needed to die. She kept me hidden because she couldn't kill me. Her heart was pure because she couldn't drown the demon's seed."

He closed his eyes and took short shallow breaths in an attempt to hold his anger in check. He could feel his wolf's rage and he drew it in, using his internal strength he channeled the power. Inhaling her spicy scent, he was able to stabilize his emotions.

"She would talk about housework, mopping the floors, washing the laundry. She told me I gave her more work to do and how much she resented it…me. I didn't care about her words; I just wanted to hear the sound of her voice. Sometimes, if I was careful, she would answer questions. I wanted to know about everything and she would describe things I never saw. I would paint pictures in my mind. Those were the best days."

Silence descended and Emily took deep calming breaths.

"She left me in the dark when I was bad but my eyes always adjusted and I could see. She never knew. She would leave me for days and my stomach hurt all the time. When I changed to…" Emily stopped and didn't say demon. "When I changed to wolf my stomach hurt worse. I was always hungry."

Taking another slow breath, she went on, "I tried not to change but it happened in my sleep and Carolynn always knew. She said I stunk like my father. She used the hose to clean the smell away. It was ice cold and it burned my skin."

Emily remained quiet for a few moments before continuing. "She made me wear shoes that hurt my feet. She only wanted me to take them off when I went to bed but I never knew why.

Turning she looked up at Brandt and smiles slightly. "I hate oatmeal. I never want to eat it again."

"I assure you, it will never be in our home." His grin answered hers though it was painful to hear about her lack of food.

"We always celebrated Christmas and Easter. That was how I knew there were other foods besides white paste. She would cook all day and the smell would seep into my room. Then, she would bring the meal and sit with me while we ate. I fell asleep those nights without pains in my belly. Those special days never came often enough."

Brandt lifted her off the floor and sat her in his lap. He leaned back against the couch. His wolf needed her close while she spoke.

Her voice became softer, "Punishments with no food were lasting longer. Sometimes I didn't know what I did because her yelling made no sense. Once, she locked me in the dark for a week without anything to eat. I thought I would finally die and the devil would take me, but he didn't want me. I was barely able to crawl to the food and don't remember eating it. I think the demo---wolf got it. Carolynn began telling me I was going to die. She spoke of the Lord sending her messages and said my time was coming. She brought a candle with her one day and struck a match to it. She told me to touch the beautiful yellow flame and I did. It burned my skin but not like the water from the hose. She explained that she would light the house on fire with me in it. I was terrified but I was growing older and stronger and I dreamed almost every night of killing her. The devil spoke to me and I kept dreaming of her blood. If I couldn't kill her, I hoped she would kill me."

Emily began rocking in his arms. His strong supple fingers massaged the tense muscles of her back. Taking a deep breath, her next words were rushed and one flowed into another, "The day it happened, I had been left in the dark without food for two days because I changed. I was hungry and angry when the light came on. My skin felt itchy, not like when I didn't change but something different. I can't describe it but I yearned for the feel of the water even though I knew it would hurt. The sound of Carolynn's shoes on the steps made me look up. I smelled no food. She sprayed me until I got into my small cage. I thought about what I would do many times but I was so afraid. She started tearing down my pictures and yelling her strange words. She took a needle from her pocket and I knew it was time. I wouldn't put my arm out so she sprayed me again. My hands went to the bars and the demon took over. I remember her screaming for a few minutes but then she was silent. When I woke up there was blood everywhere just like my dreams. I wasn't sad."

Her body stiffened and drew slightly away from his. Troubled eyes met Brandt's. "I should have been sad."

He used his greater strength and pulled her back against his chest holding her tightly. "Your mother was not in her right mind. No one does what she did to a child. Our cubs are loved and cherished. They are rare and we do nothing to harm them. They are God's gift."

"Do you have a child?"

"No I don't. Beastkind cannot mate with each other. We must mate with humans to have children but we do not rape women."

"I can never have a baby?"

"No." His voice was almost violent and she jumped slightly. He slowed his breathing again, changing the conversation, and leaving so much unsaid. "I want you Emily, I want this," his hand stroked through her hair and traveled down, "I want this," his hand found her breast and squeezed gently, "and this." His fingers skimmed down her belly and over her hip. His palm came to rest on the ache between her thighs. "I so want this." He whispered in her ear and kissed her cheek gently. "We both feel it but not yet." His hand traveled back up and came to rest on her shoulder.

"Why?" Her voice was pleading, breathy and filled with the longing she didn't understand.

When we mate and my wolf claims your body and yours claims mine, separation becomes difficult until we adjust. I need a clear head in the challenge tomorrow night and I'm trying to give you time to understand our ways. So much is out there for you and I want to show you and experience it all with you. We can't stop our wolves from bonding once they've found each other but we can delay part of it."

Ducking her head slightly Emily contemplated what he told her.

Resting his chin on top of her head he changed the subject again, "Tell me more about your drawings."

"I noticed pictures hanging on your walls and they are beautiful. I don't draw like that but now I've seen more and I want to put pictures on paper while my memory is good."

"You will never need to draw by memory again. I'll show you beautiful things you can sit and paint."

"I want to put you on paper."

His laughter brought a smile to her face and lightened the mood. "If you must, I'll have art supplies delivered but please be gentle my ego needs a boost."

"What is ego?"

"Hmm. That's a little hard to explain. It is the sense of importance I feel for myself. It has been low lately, and I need to start doing my job and repairing the damage I've done to the pack. I also think myself quite handsome and I'm not sure I want to see me through your artist's eyes."

Tentatively her hands came up to his face and slowly traveled the contours. "You are the most beautiful person I have ever seen."

"You see, that's the kind of boost my ego needs. I won't mention that you have only met a few people to make the comparison." Bringing his hands up to hers, he trailed soft kisses on her cheek and neck. His control was at its limit and he avoided her mouth. Talking was best.

"I need to explain feral wolves to you. If beastkind grow up with no close interaction with others and or with no touching, they can go crazy. Your mother gave you just enough to keep you sane. For another wolf, one like Dom for instance, the little contact you received would not have been enough. She would have gone feral and killed anything in sight. You are strong, mentally and physically.

Only the strongest of our kind could stay sane in the world in which you lived." He hugged her tighter. "We don't kill humans without careful thought. Their laws are different from ours and we make adjustments for their weaknesses. You were never the evil one. Your mother was insane. Maybe it happened because of what your father did to her or because her mind could not accept that someone special like you existed in this world. We have been around longer than humans and far outlive them. My feelings of God are often confused so it's something I spend little time thinking about. We are magic and I do not believe we come from evil. I don't believe in demons or the devil. We follow our own path. We are similar in that both species have members who are bad and those that are good. You are part of me. Our souls intertwined. Your wolf killed your mother before she could kill you. It will always be your stronger side. Most of us don't mix well with people but some make it work. Whatever our feelings, we live in the same world and tolerate them. Few humans know of our existence and we prefer to keep it that way."

Emily was still and her breathing calm. Her body did not shake and he smelled her mating scent emitting from her pores. It was rolling off them both, mingling, becoming one essence. He would take it to the challenge the next night. When the fight was over, he would declare her his mate before the entire pack.

Taking her hand, they walked to the bedroom. He quickly removed her clothing and then his own. He had no intention of making love to her but their bodies needed to be close. Turning off the light he thought about what she revealed tonight. "Would you rather have the light on when you sleep?"

"No, I know I'm safe when I can hear your heartbeat."

He crawled onto the bed and brought her close. Her body wrapped around his. His erection swelled and he wondered if she understood its meaning. Finally, her breathing slowed and became even. His eyes remained open. He thought of ways he could have tortured Carolynn. His anger turned to cold fury. He held tight to his rage, it would go with him into the challenge.

Chapter 13

The sunlight peeked through the curtains while they ate breakfast. Then Brandt grabbed the comforter off the bed. Taking Emily's hand, he led her outside and down the steps of the porch. A direct patch of sunlight fell through the trees where he shook out the blanket. Pulling her down beside him, he lay back.

It was early in the day but the summer heat made it warmer than most wolves liked. He didn't think it would bother her. Rolling over he drew her close and then without warning rolled them off the blanket onto the pine needles.

Giggles spilled from her lips. His hand came up and with gentle fingers he picked the long pokey needles from her now ruffled hair. "I want you to smell the soil and feel it in your pores. This smell is freedom and magic. The earth feeds the magic and we need to spend time outdoors being wolves. After you are good and dirty, I want us to change. You need to explore the differences in our wolf forms. It's miraculous and the only way to explain is to show you." He then proceeded to roll them over the dirt and fallen pine needles again.

Her giggles became full laughter until he stood and removed his clothing. Her heart stopped for a moment. Hard sculptured lines of muscle moved; flexing, and then relaxing. His shirt then pants dropped to the ground. His knowing smile picked up her scent change, she wanted him. His hand came down and with no hesitation she took it.

Shedding her clothes quickly, her change followed his by seconds. Inhaling, her wolf gloried in the wild scent. Sudden impact tilted her world momentarily. Brandt nipped at her hind leg after his tackle. Running a short distance away, he charged in for another gentle bite. She sidestepped and then took off.

They ran.

She caught her stride and her legs became stable beneath her. Wild with her freedom, four legs carried her across the terrain in her demon form. She felt no guilt or shame for what she was.

Following behind, he gently nudged her side giving her silent direction.

He smelled the child before Emily realized she was there. Kinsee was in wolf form but immediately switched to human when she noticed the two wolves. Plopping down hard on her bottom, she began crying. Loudly. Emily approached cautiously and a few feet from the child she dropped to the ground. Rolling over, displaying her soft white underbelly, she waited. Childish giggles replaced tears and a small hand tentatively reached forward landing in soft white fur and rubbing back and forth.

"You're silly. You shouldn't call people bad names. I'm not a demon, I'm Kinsee."

Shifting her wolf form to human, Emily rolled to her side facing the child. "I'm sorry. I didn't know. I'm Emily. I would like to be friends?" Emily's voice was hopeful with a singsong childish quality to match the little girls.

"I will ask my mom. She says you are wild and I shouldn't be around you. She says Brandt knows what he's doing and if you stay wild he will eat you. I hope he doesn't. That would hurt."

Brandt spoke into their minds because he had no intention of changing form. "You young lady, need to stay closer to your parents. This is the second time I've found you away from adults. I don't think you would taste very sweet but if I catch you again, I will find out." He leapt forward and licked her arm. "Nope, not sweet but I'll suffer through a few bites if I must."

The little girl squealed with delight and changed back into her wolf form scampering off through the trees. Brandt turned and headed in the opposite direction, back toward the cabin. He didn't go fast allowing Emily to catch up. Two hundred yards from the cabin, he saw a rabbit run through the trees. Giving chase, he relayed orders to his mate without thinking, "Circle around and then don't move. I'll bring her to you."

Emily complied but when the rabbit came close and Brandt yelled, "Get it." She grinned delightfully and turned her head to watch the gray fluff scurry by.

He approached her side, not quite knowing what happened, "You were supposed to catch her."

"She was beautiful. Why would I catch her?"

He growled into her mind. It was more chiding than angry. "Hmm, we have things to work on. Your killer instinct came out with Zeb yesterday but when a meal is at hand you let it get away because it was cute?"

"You wanted to eat her?" Her she-wolf nose soured up and there was disgust in the words.

He couldn't help himself. Tackling her, his rich laughter flowed into her mind. Tumbling on the ground, his wolf form changed to human. His hands held both sides of the scruff of her neck. "Change Emily." His voice was a husky order.

Cerulean blue eyes met liquid brown, her body naked and aching with desire.

His lips claimed hers, thrusting his tongue deep while bringing her on top of his firm chest. Strong fingers gently skimmed her luscious curves. The kiss seemed to continue forever. But finally, he stood and picking her up, carried her to the comforter.

Both dirty, with a light sheen of sweat coating their bodies, they lay side by side facing each other.

Taking her hand, he placed it on his chest. His words came out choked with sexual need, "My body was made for you, but I don't think you're ready for all that entails. Not making love is killing me." He instantly saw the concern on her face, "No, not that kind of killing." He grinned, "It's the kind that aches from deep inside and won't go away. The union of our bodies is the only thing that will give relief. First though, you need to know and understand how my body works. I'm different from you." This time he saw a slow smile touch her lips. He rolled to his back and placing his hands to his sides, he encouraged her with dark eyes.

Small sparks hummed across her nerve endings. She brought her hand back to her side but her eyes traveled downward. His face; beautiful with sharp angles, eyes now black, his clenched jaw accenting broad lips, she wanted to touch but her eyes continued their path. The corded muscles in his neck strained, becoming broad shoulders with defined lines melding one solid muscle to the next. The skin on his chest, at least a shade darker than her own with two small pointed nipples and shadowed by a thin line of dark hair captured her gaze. She stared in fascination at the trail, the light dust of curls running down the center of his chest. Her hand came up, her fingers unable to resist. She touched the hair centered in the middle, splaying her hand, feeling a slight tickle across her fingers, pressing downward, her smooth palm met the heat of his skin.

He sucked air sharply into his lungs. His chest muscles expanded and unable to breath for a moment, he closed his eyes feeling her caress; light, inquisitive, and killing him. He finally breathed raggedly, in and out.

Her hand followed the path of her eyes past his belly button. His large erection extended up from the patch of hair between his thighs. She touched hard silky flesh, this amazing part of him, completely different from her. He expelled a low growl and her eyes snapped to his.

"I don't have one of these," she said with soft wonder.

"Oh God," he groaned.

"God?"

"God has nothing to do with this," was his tight response. "It's a figure of speech. When you touch me this way, it feels like the most incredible thing on this planet but it leads to other amazing things and now is not the time."

"What if I want it to be the time?"

"I am most definitely not going to survive this." Gently, he unlocked her fingers and moved her hands to his chest. "Your body was made to receive mine." His hand trailed down past her breasts and traveled to the soft down between her legs. This is where my body wants to be. It's a special place and only for me." His finger gently entered the soft moist opening waiting for his touch. Her eyes grew large and he could feel, more than hear, the growl coming from within her. It reverberated throughout her body. He looked into her eyes. "Kiss me."

Smiling, she brought her lips to his. His finger delved farther. The rumble in her body turned into a full groan. He released her mouth and soft wet kisses trailed to her breasts. Silky and slightly rough at the same time, his tongue twirled around her nipple then drew it into his mouth, sucking gently.

Dark knowing eyes slid up to hers. Head tilted back and eyelids closed, she was exquisite. "Watch me." He whispered and then continued the sweet suction of first one nipple and then the other. Her eyes opened partially and followed his every move. Kissing his way lower, he stopped at her belly. She inhaled sharply. "It's all right Emily, trust me." His words were low and sexy, filled with want.

Her sweet intimate musk spiked his sexual desire. Removing his finger, his tongue tasted wild honey. Emily's cry jolted his senses and tightened his groin painfully. Placing his hands under her bottom, he pulled her tighter against the invasion of his mouth.

Her desire centered on the entry of his tongue and the gentle pinch of his teeth. He consumed her, drawing out a need she didn't understand, a craving she couldn't control. Her knees came up and her breathing became harsh. His finger entered her again sliding smoothly inside. He then took the soft nub, waiting for him, between his lips and sucked.

Closing her eyes tightly, she felt the hum across her nerve endings turn to delicious shivers, growing from the center of her sex, up and over. Her scream echoed through the trees.

When the last pulse of her internal muscles vibrated around his finger he slowly backed away from the taste of honeyed spice traveling through his senses. He kissed his way up her body, his lips touching each breast, avoiding her tight pink nipples, he couldn't take any more.

Finally his eyes, shards of black crystal, gazed into deep ocean blue.

"God." Her smile was wicked.

She had a dark smudge of dirt on her cheek, pine needles threaded through tangled blond hair and more stuck to her skin. He had never seen anything or anyone so exquisitely beautiful. He took a deep breath, his desire raging, he had to stop. Grabbing her hand, he helped her to her feet and then released her. Touching even her hand and not giving into his need was beyond him.

Deep slow breaths helped his control. They entered the cabin and he walked straight to the bathroom, her gentle steps behind him. He turned and picked her up placing her bottom on the edge of the counter. His hand encompassed her smudged cheek. "We need a shower. I know it frightens you but the water will be warm. There is no evil to wash away but there are evil memories and I want to replace those with good ones. I'll hold you if you will do this but I'll also understand if you cannot. Trust me Emily."

Indecision, fear, pain…they all traveled across her face, paralyzing memories of the harsh force of the pressure hose made her heart race. She closed her eyes, "Yes."

He adjusted the temperature but stopped looking in her direction. Her tears were close to the surface and he was close to changing his mind. When the water was perfect, he scooped her from the counter, stepped under the spray, and held her stiff body in his arms. Time slowed.

Finally, her hands came up and cupped together to let the spray fill them. Releasing the water, it slid through her fingers. Wet eyelashes lifted to his gaze and then her arms went around his neck and her head relaxed against his shoulder.

Gently, he kissed the side of her face and slowly lowered her legs to the shower floor. Picking up the soap, he began washing them both. Covering her in lather, he turned her body around in a full circle letting the water rinse away the soap and caress her skin.

"It feels so good."

Bringing his forehead to hers, he whispered, "You are beautiful, your body calls to mine and I want to hear your cries of pleasure." He nipped her shoulder gently.

Her blue eyes looked into his and pheromones exploded throughout the small room.

His erection throbbed. He should receive saint status for his stamina in not giving in to his needs. Not yet, soon. He backed away from her body and shook his head, his damn wolf wasn't taking no for an answer and the need to sink into her body was endless torture.

With deep steady breaths he closed his eyes and gained control but knew, if he looked at her, he would ignite.

Turning off the water, he grabbed two towels and heard her stomach rumble. "The change makes us use energy and I need to add weight to your skinny bones." He pinched the side of her hip.

"Ouch."

He ginned, "I'll kiss the bruise later, come on."

Chapter 14

The day continued and thoughts swirled through Emily's mind. Unrelenting fear for Brandt terrified her. She needed him, wanted his touch, and wanted him to teach her everything in this strange new world. With him she was no longer evil or unwanted. She knew he was going to die.

He read from Call of the Wild trying to soothe her, knowing she was afraid.

His voice wrapped around her and she remembered.

Running through the woods after killing her mother, she saw the large beast from the corner of her eye when it attacked. The pain from his bite was almost welcome because it brought the horrific killing of Carolynn into focus. When the huge wolf stood over her, pain from the injury kept her from moving. Black dots confused her mind, but there was something in his scent that broke through the dark shadows.

Even now, while he recited the wolf story, his intensity was overwhelming, troubling, but calming at the same time. His touch caused her heart to accelerate and desire to flood her senses. When he wiped his blood across her lips, every nerve ending in her body burned. He told her he felt the same way after tasting her blood.

She struggled to understand what was happening around her. Doubt made her anxious. To fast, too much and she momentarily yearned for a dark room away from her new world. Waves of sadness consumed her.

"Hey, are you okay?" He was looking at her and no longer reading.

"I'm okay."

"You, my not so smart she-wolf, are lying."

Indignation shown in her eyes but he didn't let her speak. "I can smell your sorrow; talk to me---trust me."

She inhaled his scent deeply. It calmed her thoughts. "You speak of your pack, wolves, and beastkind with love but I'm afraid of this world. Don't leave me." Her beseeching eyes begged. "You will never come back."

Competent arms gathered her close. "There is nothing and no one in this world that will keep me from you. I will walk beside you always. Two days Emily, it's only been two days."

He knew what would help. "Close your eyes for me." He waited.

Her eyes closed.

"Now, don't change to your wolf but picture her in your mind. Breathe in through your nose and feel the texture of the air. Feel the wild magic and the fur just beneath your skin. Now bring it in, *feel* your wolf."

He gave her a moment before he continued, "Alphas are born, but it usually takes the blood of an alpha to release the magic. Their scent only changes after blood spills and the old alpha breathes his last. You are different. No battle warranted the energy inside you. It just happened. You are a miracle. When you are frightened, or unsure, use it. Your wolf will always guide you and if you trust her she will teach you what you need to learn."

Her eyes opened, the sadness dissipating, joy causing her lips to widen and smile.

"I know something that will brighten your day even more." His voice held mischief.

He lay the book down on the side table and grabbed her hand pulling her to her feet. "Follow me."

He showed her how to use the washer and dryer, and he was right and she brightened, her fascination with her new world endless. She then questioned everything around the cabin. She took his hand and pulled him into his father's office. He explained the computer and told her he would teach her how to use it, soon. Then he taught her the controls for the Ipod and they listened to music.

They ate and her questions continued. It reminded him of Kinsee. The world was a puzzle and every piece had to fall into place. She managed to awkwardly cut a small piece of meat because she wanted to use a knife and fork.

She touched it to her lips but pulled the fork back. "Is this rabbit?" Her voice was horror stricken.

He laughed, "No, it's a cow, they're huge and don't have nearly the cuteness. I can show you a picture on the computer although it's probably not a great idea because you will find something appealing about them. You need meat." His voice gentled. "Would you like a pet rabbit? It will need to be caged so none of the wolves have a snack but you would probably enjoy its softness."

Anxiety tore through her. She could never put anything in a cage.

Realizing what he said, Brandt was out of his chair and lifting her into his arms immediately. His hands ran gently over her back. "Sorry baby, no cages." His lips came down on hers. A minute later, he lifted his head and placed her feet back on the floor. "Eat. No rabbits for pets, I promise."

In the early afternoon she stood looking out of the window through the outside bars.

A kiss landed on the side of her neck. "Let's run."

The bristles from the underbrush rubbed against her fur. The smells fascinated her wolf. Everything was different. Her legs gained a sense of balance and she didn't feel clumsy like the first time she changed outdoors. She let her wolf take over and guide her.

They ate a large dinner and then Brandt continued reading from his wild book. His voice reverberated gently around her. She watched his fingers turn the pages and the muscles change in his face. The inflection of each sentence flowed with the story. She closed her eyes and imagined her wolf.

Her wolf had no problem taking over, she knew what she wanted. Silky fingers traveled up his jawline; bristly, hard and strong.

Turning, he kissed her hand but continued reading

Cautiously, her fingers traveled, and smoothed across his neck and further down his shirt. She needed to touch skin and her hand traveled to the end of the material and up underneath. Not warm but surprisingly hot. Gently, her fingers trailed the light dusting of hair. Her wolf also found it fascinating. Traveling to the center of his chest and then down, skimming below the waist of his pants. She smelled the change in his scent; tangy spice, raw.

Steel fingers gripped hers. Laying the book down, he pulled her onto his lap, and lifted her hands from their travels, placing them on his shoulders. His whisper sounded low in her ear, "You are being a naughty wolf."

"My wolf wants to touch you."

Laughing huskily, he kissed her.

His taste and the texture of his mouth made her want more.

With a frustrated groan, he lifted her and placed her back on the couch beside him. "Dominique will be here in a few minutes." He took a moment to control his breathing and then continued. "I'm sorry you cannot go with me to the challenge. I will declare you my mate after I kill Zeb. The bond won't completely seal until we join our bodies but that is for us and not the pack." He looked intently into her eyes. "I am leaving a key to the door with Dom. I will not trap you inside but I'm asking you to stay here. The challenge cannot be broken. If it is, the challenger has a right to fight the wolf responsible. You're not ready for a fight and I want you safe."

There was a soft knock on the door and Brandt rose to let Dominique into the room. She was carrying a large bag with handles. Casting Emily a shy smile, she took the sack into the kitchen.

Brandt took Emily's hand and guided her into the bedroom. Once there, his movements showed a single minded purpose. He removed his t-shirt and sweatpants then put on a pair of faded jeans that hung low on his hips. The muscles on his arms bulged and his chest undulated with his movements.

His eyes were almost black when he turned her way. Suddenly, his mouth came down hard on hers and his tongue invaded savagely.

His scent, which filled the room, was strange. She could feel electrical energy blanketing his skin. It almost hurt. She opened the link to her wolf and immediately the sparks arced between them. It wasn't pain---it was power.

Finally, he broke the kiss. Holding her away but gripping her firmly, shadows rolled over his eyes. For just an instant they softened. "I love you."

He walked away without looking back. The front door closed solidly behind him.

Dominique's hand slid the key into the lock, securing the door. Her fingers trembled. She dropped the key in her pocket.

Emily heard her inhale before Dominique turned in her direction.

"I know this is difficult but I brought a few things for you. The first is hot chocolate and I think you will like it." She smiled shyly though her eyes were downcast. "I brought you a dress and some other things so you can be ready for your mate's return."

Putting her hand out, Emily took Dominique's fingers into hers and instantly felt her own panic recede. Walking to the kitchen, Dominique showed her how to make the hot drink.

It tasted like liquid cake.

When finished, the two made their way to the bathroom, Dominique carrying the bag from the kitchen.

"Take off your clothes." Dominique wouldn't look at Emily but her voice held a small bit of command.

Emily thought this funny, and followed orders. She knew the timid she-wolf was helping to keep her mind off Brandt.

Shimmery red silky material fell over Emily's body, hugging her curves. The low cut V-neck accented her cleavage and the hem stopped just below the crease where her bottom and thighs met. Feeling odd, she tried to walk past the other wolf to look in the larger mirror in the bedroom but Dom stopped her.

"No, you can't look until we're done. Please?" Dominique's voice was excited. She plugged in a cord with a long thing at the end. "I'm going to curl your hair and then put makeup on your face. Your mate needs a reward for winning his challenge tonight."

Emily stood still under the onslaught of attention. She could see herself in the bathroom mirror and saw the changes take effect. She wondered if Brandt would like it. When Dom completed her tasks, they both walked into the bedroom. Emily slowly turned in front of the looking glass.

Completing a second slow circle, the electrical spark she felt on Brandt's skin earlier multiplied and painfully charged through her body.

Dominique dropped to her knees, her hands coming up to her head making her distress evident. She struggled to get her words out so Emily would know what was happening. "It's the call of the alpha. Brandt is telling the wolves that he is our leader. The battle will start soon." Dominique was breathing heavily.

Emily's entire body focused on Brandt's call; his fury, his need. It was need for her. She could feel it coursing through every nerve in her body.

Rage grew thick in the room and Dominique tried to run. A steel grip landed on the terrified wolf's arm and deadly blue eyes flashed. They drilled into the woman holding the key to the front door.

The red haze Emily knew so well was closing over her eyes. Control; she could not hurt Dominique. Breathe deeply in, out. She steadied herself enough to speak, "Get into the closet, and stay there. I don't want to hurt you." She released Dominique and walked out of the room placing distance between them. With each step her rage grew. A dining room chair flew across the room; the splintering noise only feeding her frenzy. The table landed with a louder crack. Pieces of wood splintered and shot through the room while the larger pieces fell to the floor. Nothing appeased her overwhelming need for blood and methodically one by one, each piece of furniture flew from her hands.

"Brandt." Her scream was lethal. She charged into the living room and picked up the table in front of the couch, she threw it into the door that was keeping her from her mate. The door didn't budge. Her hands lifted the side of the couch.

"Having a temper tantrum are we?" Cheri appeared a few feet away.

Emily's breath was leaving her lungs in hard bursts. "I didn't hurt her."

"I know that or you would be dead."

Rage shot from Emily's eyes locking on the deadly vampire.

Cheri's calm voice broke into her wolf's hot fury, "I think it would be best if you attended the challenge. You cannot interfere which means you will control yourself."

Emily slowly lowered the heavy piece of furniture and watched Cheri hold up the key. The two women walked out the front door and Cheri led her to the ring. Emily's feet were bare but she hardly noticed. She had to see her mate.

She could smell the wolves' diverse odors and walking closer she could see the clearing.

Taking her hand in a forceful grip, Cheri squeezed so Emily would control her emotions.

She found Brandt through the red haze.

He was lighting during a storm. His body naked, power rolled in thick waves calling to her wolf.

She didn't at first notice the man standing opposite her mate.

Brandt suddenly launched himself into the air and attacked.

The hand on Emily's became a vise.

Brandt's wolf exploded out of human skin. Sharp claws tore skin and muscle from his enemy's side. Blood flew. Brandt's teeth savaged the other wolf. Zeb tried to scramble away. Black fur flowed to human skin and his shoulder muscles strained. He wrapped his arms around the other man lifting him from the ground. Then, threw Zeb flew across the ring. Brandt seamlessly became wolf and he followed. This time Brandt's large jaws went around Zeb's throat. A vicious jerk and blood sprayed the surrounding wolves until the death gargles faded. Large jaws unfurled and fangs glistened with the blood of his enemy. His head tilted back. The cry was savage and again the waves of power resonated through the clearing.

"Shit, he's calling the pack to change. Emily, don't remove your clothes. Fight it. You are his equal."

The words sounded in her ear from a distance. The alpha's call was brutal for the pack wolves but Emily only felt an irritating sensation. After years of isolation and hiding her beast, this was nothing. Wolves writhed in pain and dropped to the ground around her. She stood tall, unruffled.

The howl tapered off. Breathing hard Brandt shifted to human. He stood naked, his power rippling, hot molten lava smothering everything in its path, destroying but promising rebirth. He was alpha.

Emily walked blindly, her wolf needing to play with fire.

Every fiber of his being felt her presence, from the moment she entered the clearing she was his beacon.

Her gentle arms went around his midsection and her supple body leaned into his.

Energy merged.

His hands came up, peeling her arms away and brought her forward, reversing their positions. He whispered in her ear, his voice filled with aggressive intent, "You are mine."

His gaze; hard and lethal, looked out at his wolves. Death punctuated each word, "If you choose to challenge, your blood will flow into the ground, your body will burn on a funeral pyre, your family will mourn, and I will relish the taste of your death." He let his words sink in and continued, "Emily is my mate. She was strong enough to withstand my call and she is strong enough to fight and kill beside me. Go home. If you wish to die, challenge tomorrow. Tonight is mine."

Chapter 15

Zeb's brothers carried his body away and the wolves dispersed into the surrounding trees.

She turned in his arms and his palms trailed down her sides and then to her backside cupping her bottom. Sinking to his knees, with Zeb's blood streaked on his face, he tilted his head forward resting against her stomach and the cool silk of her dress. His body trembled beneath her fingers. She feathered them softly through his sweat dampened hair.

"I couldn't think straight without you here. My focus was on the mate bond. I needed you and here you are." He slowly drew air in through his nose, breathing in her scent.

Tipping his head back, his black irises matched the now dark outer color and met hers. Strong arms pulled her closer. He inhaled deeply, again.

"You no longer have a table and chairs," her words were hesitant.

Rough, choked laughter spilled past his lips. She was his. He'd waited lifetimes. A thick growl came from deep in his throat. "I have an idea. Let's destroy the bed."

Standing suddenly and scooping her into his arms, his long muscular legs carried them swiftly to the cabin. He leapt onto the porch, bypassing the stairs.

He pushed open the door letting it slammed against the inner cabin wall. He left it standing wide and carried her to the bedroom but then stopped. Back-tracking he entered the bathroom.

"Zeb's blood scent is coming off."

Slowly, releasing her legs, her body drifted downward. The silk of her dress glazed over the taught muscles of his abdomen and then his jutting arousal. A deep growl vibrated through his chest.

His hand found the cold water nozzle and turned then found the hot. Hitting the knob to activate the spray, he stepped into the tub before the water adjusted and let cold ice hammer his body before it turned warm.

Leaving the shower door open, Brandt watched the soft mist spray outward soaking the front of Emily's dress, molding it to her curves.

Lathering soap over his flesh, her eyes changed from ice blue to deep cerulean and followed his hands. Her tongue came out and traveled the contours of her lips.

Impossibly his erection swelled larger. He rinsed and then shut off the water, his expression dark, his wolf barely contained.

Unease suddenly flared in Emily's eyes and her feet carried her backwards.

Brandt didn't grab a towel. He stalked forward with infinite slowness.

The cool hallway wall stopped her movement.

Corded muscle, a breath from her head, flexed with tension. His large hands landed on either side of her head. So close. Hot breath swept her face causing shivers to course through her body.

"I need you Emily, don't run from me." His words whispered out on hot breath. His nose ran along her neck to her shoulder inhaling deeply.

Her fear receded and scalding desire replaced it.

His hands traveled to the front V-neck of her dress. The tear started at her breasts. Agile fingers parted the material like tissue paper.

Feasting on her body, his eyes lowered and devoured every inch of uncovered flesh. The sides of his lips tipped up. She wore nothing beneath the material which now pooled at her feet.

His palms smoothed over her hips, across her back ending at the soft globes of her bottom. His fingers splayed and lifted her to his waist.

Her legs secured at the small of his back, her eyes drowning in his.

Turning, and with determined strides, he took them to the bedroom. He stopped when his knees touched the side of the bed. Bending, he gently sat her down on the soft mattress. His hands went to her ankles, releasing them and placing her feet flat, her knees bent, arms remaining around his neck.

His palms cupped her face, fingers splayed into her hair and his thumbs rubbed her jaw line. Going to his knees, his face now even with hers, he grasped her hair in a steel grip, bringing her mouth to his.

Texture, taste, scent, it burned through their bodies.

His hands slowly traveled. He released her mouth and gently pushed her upper body back into the bedding. He nudged her legs farther apart, his shoulders sliding between soft thighs. His hands cupped her bottom. Sinking back farther on his calves, he slid her forward to his mouth. His lips, moist from her kiss went to the center of her desire.

She moaned; deep, low, sweet. It reached his soul.

He licked between the delicate folds. A low growl began rising from deep in his throat and vibrated through every part of his body.

Seconds, minutes, time stopped. Her body bucked, his hold tightened. Withholding bliss, he kept her from going over the abyss, licking, nibbling gently, but the hard nub waiting for him remained untouched.

"Brandt." She screamed his name.

"Shhhh baby." Stopping his sweet torture, he looked up past her glistening sex, meeting her eyes. "I want you."

Gliding up her body he flowed onto the bed covering her. His lips came forward claiming hers. He settled between her thighs, the tip of his heat finding her soft welcoming entrance. Brandt leaned his upper body away and gazed into the blue depths of her eyes.

"Please." Breathless anticipation escaped her lips.

His hips surged forward and in one stroke he sank fully into welcoming burning softness created for him. Her back arched, a scream tore from her throat. Sharp fingernails drew blood digging into his sides and back.

He discovered heaven deep inside his mate.

Withdrawing and then slowly sinking back into paradise, he began a sensual steady rhythm.

Her legs tightened around him, her fingers sank into the muscles of his butt urging him to move faster.

The little control he had finally snapped. His teeth sharp and deadly sank into the curve of her neck, drawing blood. It streamed through his cells, traveling, expelling sparks of white hot energy that careened straight to his groin. Their release exploded and her cries mingled with his.

His claim final, she was his mate.

Breathing hard, hands holding tight, the scent of sex filled the air. He rolled, bringing her on top, and running his fingers through the curls Dominique arranged in her hair. Its texture soothed. He drew a section to his nose and inhaled. Her stomach made a small rumbling noise. He grinned.

"I'm hungry."

With a short playful growl he rolled again trapping her beneath his weight. "I'm going to have a cooler of food placed by the bed so you can't leave for a week."

Her smile was playfully shy, "You make me hungry."

His eyes, starved with further need gazed back. "We need you well fed to keep up with me." She gave a playful squeal when he picked her up and carried her over his shoulder. Her hair tickled his rear and he gave her a playful slap because he could.

Depositing her on the kitchen counter, he fixed a quick meal, stopping to kiss, nibble, and touch her ever few seconds. She laughed when he wouldn't let her help.

Finally, when he came back within reach, she wrapped her legs around him and he obliged with a quick searing kiss.

"You ARE going to be my death." He groaned, swinging her down from the counter, twirling her around the small kitchen area until they were both laughing again.

"I'm still hungry." She said when her giggles faded.

He kissed her nose, "Then let's eat so I can take you back to bed.

His eyes followed every movement of the fork making its way to her lips. She licked the side of her mouth where a small crumb lodged. His growl rumbled up from deep in his throat but he let her finish.

She took a last delicious bite and looked up. Her voice low and throaty but conveying curiosity, "I feel odd, tingly everywhere."

"Hmm." He said standing and then walking behind her. His hands landed gently on her shoulders, whispering low in her ear. "I'm alpha. You are my mate you get some of the magic that makes me stronger." A light kiss pressed to her neck. "You are also alpha and you're magic has combined with mine. I feel the same way but I also feel complete, it's the mate bond." His teeth ran over the side of her jaw and then nuzzled her hair.

Her words came out on a sigh, "Will it keep feeling this way?"

"For a few weeks, maybe even months. Our wolves are more aware of one another and they need to settle. We will be jealous." He bit the lobe of her ear, "And possessive." He gave a small jerk to her hair tilting her face sideways so he could reach her mouth. "Cheri and the pack know and understand this."

His lips met hers, hot, intense, seeking.

They didn't make it to the bed until much later.

At four A.M. he carried her outside. She was tired but he insisted she change. They ran through the still dark forest. Small mice scurried out of their way. When Brandt caught one he snapped its fragile bones and then dropped it using his nose to push it her way.

"No. Did you need to kill it?" her distressed words entered his head.

"Yes, I did. They taste good." With that he picked it up and with one swallow it was gone.

"I can't believe you did that. No more kissing tonight."

He grabbed her haunch with his teeth and she let out a sudden yip. She turned and attacked trying to nip him back. He managed to stay a hair's breadth away from her jaws.

His voice, filled with mirth sounded I her mind. "We'll hunt with the pack and find a large buck for you."

"And a buck is?" her breathing became labored. He turned them back toward the house. "A buck is an extra-large rabbit."

He wasn't paying attention and she finally managed to bite his flank. There was fur in her mouth and she heard a loud, "Ouch," in her head.

The sun was rising through the trees when they made it back to the cabin. She ran in front of him and beat him onto the porch. She entered the door first and changed to human never slowing on her way to their bed. He was right behind her and launched himself through the bedroom door landing on top of her body. He tickled her ribs until she was screaming for him to stop. Their play eventually turned to sighs of pleasure.

Chapter 16

They didn't leave the cabin for five days except to let their wolves run and then only at night. A small refrigerator, complete with prepared meals appeared on their doorstep. Brandt placed it in the bedroom and refused to let Emily out of his site except for short bathroom excursions. No one bothered them and no one challenged. Gifts quietly appeared on the porch.

They talked. Emily asked unending questions about the pack, life outside the pack, and vampires. He introduced her to the Internet and explained television though there wasn't one at the cabin. Emily absorbed everything in her amazing new world, her brain a sponge.

She craved touch and closeness and her hand or body was always rubbing his in some way. Wolves needed a pack and she never had one. Her wolf was making up for lost time.

On the afternoon of the third day, a group of men arrived and dismantled the bars on the windows. When they left, Brandt took her to the loft and out onto the balcony. It didn't matter that the wood deck was rough; she tempted him playfully and didn't stop her teasing until they made love. They both had a few splinters but neither cared.

Two days later, Cheri mentally interrupted their love play and asked them to attend dinner at the main house. "I need to see if your she-wolf is alive and well. Your father also wants to meet her. Tonight. Dinner. Seven. And she was gone.

"She doesn't say much, does she?" Emily asked.

"She's female. Once you know her, she'll become like all the rest and never shut up."

He got a pinch for his answer, which he rubbed before pulling her back into his arms. Later, he taught her to play backgammon and they almost made it through an entire game before she was on his lap and another game took over.

Later, she pouted prettily, "You ruined my only dress."

"Hmm, nude would work for me but I have a surprise. A dress arrived earlier while you were taking a shower. I put it in my dad's office closet. It also has shoes if you want to wear them."

She ran into the office and opened the closet door. There was a long gown hanging in clear plastic. It was yellow silk. She knelt on the floor, running her fingers over the uncovered fabric at the bottom. "It feels wonderful and it's my favorite color." She had tears in her eyes, her voice choked.

He walked over and took an oblong black box off the desk. "This goes with the dress." He said.

It held a necklace with delicate links, each surrounded by diamonds. At the base was a large sapphire complimented with the same diamond design. She couldn't take her eyes from the sparkling jewelry.

"If you get naked, I'll fasten it around your neck." Carnal darkness shown in his eyes but his lips curved with a playful quirk.

Without taking her eyes from the glittering stones, her shirt, sweatpants and underwear dropped to the floor. He turned her around and lifted the jewels to her throat; sweeping her hair aside he attached the clasp. Turning her gently, he stepped back. His eyes blazed, taking in the curve of her neck and the color of her skin. A blush washed over her breasts and then upward.

Shy, adoring eyes followed his. Her heartbeat accelerated. His scent changed, desire swathed the room.

His voice was gruff, "When we get home, I want you just like this but lying on the bed. You're gorgeous." He leaned in, giving the tip of her nose a soft kiss, controlling his desire, he anticipated the hours until they returned. A smoky velvet promise belied his next words, "I'll help you dress."

Removing one item after another from the bag he inspected them and then placed each piece into her hands. The pushup bra made him laugh. "I don't think you need to be pushed up but I'm sure Dom knows what she's doing. She's the one that choose the dress. I just told her the color."

When the gown draped silkily over her body his eyes darkened even more. Taking her hand he tugged gently leading her to their bedroom and the large mirror. His hands came up from behind and covered her breasts, cupping and splaying over uncovered skin just above where the material barely covered her nipples.

He breathed a hungry whisper into her ear. "Maybe the first time, the dress can stay on."

She laughed quietly her own desire burning softly but also feeling nervous. Multiple questions ran through her mind and she voiced them aloud. "What is your father like? What are you wearing? Oh, I need to try on the shoes. I never wanted to wear any but I think the dress needs shoes." She scooped up the hem and quickly ran back into the office and opened the box. The shoes were skin tone and beautiful. "Oh." She sighed and took them from the box.

They looked like four inch torture devices to him.

"Will I be able to walk?" She slipped them on with a smile.

"Probably not, so I'll carry you to Cheri's door." Another bag in the closet held his clothes. He quickly pulled the pants on and zipped them up.

"Do men wear panties?"

He turned her way laughing. "Yes, we wear panties but we give them the more masculine name of briefs or boxers. I prefer briefs but I also like to dress so I can disrobe quickly. It's an alpha thing but having you, it's now a get out of my clothes quickly for sex thing."

She smiled considering his words.

He finished getting dressed and finally put on his black loafers.

"My shoes will be more fun than yours."

He reached down and swung her into his arms. "You wouldn't catch me in a pair of high heels but at least I can walk through dirt and pine needles without breaking my neck. Are you ready?" He placed a gentle kiss on her forehead.

Her heartbeat accelerated, her scent giving off a small whiff of distress but she gazed at him. "Yes."

"You'll like my father. I can't believe he's managed to stay away from his office this past week. Cheri must be keeping him busy. He's a workaholic and a genius when it comes to numbers. He's going to love you. If he doesn't, I'll just kill him."

Her shock was instant and then she realized he was joking.

He smiled but he knew it wasn't a joke; he would do anything to keep her safe and happy. He carried her out the door and to the house that was once his home.

The main house was three stories of windows, balconies, and grandeur. Cheri called it a chalet but to Brandt it was just a big log cabin. He didn't see himself moving back in and decided he would have a home built for Emily. Not huge like this one, but definitely bigger than the one they were now sharing. He wanted a place they could play hide-n-seek and have more than five rooms to lose themselves in.

Brandt carried Emily up the front steps and one of her shoes slipped off. He bent over and picked it up while holding her, causing her to laugh. He took off her other shoe and hung them by the straps from his finger.

Emily brought her hands to his face. "You're giving off the sex smell again. Can we go home?"

"No, and you better be ready because I'll be giving off the "sex smell," all night until we're back in our bed making love."

"I'd rather go home now and do it."

"Imp; not going to happen."

Dominique opened the door seeing Brandt lower Emily to the porch. He knelt, lifted first one foot and then the other, putting her heels on while running his fingers up the back of each leg. Cheri looked over Dom's shoulder and laughed at the sight.

"Only you could turn shoes into sex." Cheri's humor was infectious and Brandt laughed too.

"I won't be laughing later when these shoes are over my shoulders." He stood and looked up into Emily's red face. She was mortified so he leaned forward and kissed her tenderly.

"If kisses get you out of the trouble caused by your big mouth, I'll rethink her for your mate."

"You can think or rethink; it won't change anything," he said with a growling edge to his voice.

Cheri laughed, "Pulling your chain is going to give me some entertainment this evening."

They entered the massive foyer and went into a larger room. Emily was captivated with everything around her. The room, decorated in *wolf,* had incredible artwork on the walls and wolf sculptures displayed on each surface. The beauty held her spellbound.

Finally, she drew in a steady breath and walked to the far wall raising her hand to touch a painting. "The demons are beautiful and this one looks like Kinsee." The picture was that of a wolf cub lying in tall grass while her mother groomed her.

Stunned silence descended.

Thomas entered the room overhearing the comment. He passed Brandt, walked behind Emily and said quietly, "Our littlest demons are our most beautiful and precious possessions."

Emily turned instantly at the new voice.

Thomas slowly took her hand so she wasn't startled, drew her fingers to his lips, and kissed the back of her knuckles. "I'm Thomas, father to the young man keeping you separated from your family." He cast a sideways, discretionary look at his barely contained son who did not want another man touching his mate. He ignored the low growl. "Welcome to the pack Emily, we are honored to have you. The Goddess has given us a surprisingly wonderful gift."

Emily inhaled his scent and scrunched her nose. "I smelled you at the cabin and your odor is similar to Brandt's but not the same."

"My scent has been found wanting by a beautiful woman." He smiled and looked at his son who was clenching his hands.

Brandt moved to Emily's side pulling her firmly against his chest. The sensitive ears in the room heard the low rumble, from deep in his throat. He rested his chin on her head and gathered her within his arms. "My old man is teasing me but playing with fire." He glared into his father's eyes.

Thomas' lowered.

Brandt didn't care that his father was with Cheri but he did care that his father was a wolf and male wolves needed to stay away from his mate.

Emily's hands went to Brandt's powerful biceps and squeezed gently. She felt the tension in Brandt's hold and wanted him to know she was his.

His muscles tightened fractionally and then he released her. His hand stroked down to her backside and gently cupped one cheek through the yellow silk. He whispered in her ear, "You're mine," before releasing her entirely.

Thomas walked to a sideboard and took out glasses without acknowledging his son's implied threat. "I propose a toast." He splashed dark liquid into each glass and passed them around. "Brandt, may your mate calm you and bring you endless love. Emily, may you find peace and happiness in his arms."

They brought their snifters to their lips.

Brandt could not take his eyes from Emily and grinned when she took a drink without taking time to scent. Her mouth and nose scrunched sharply at the taste of the strong liquor.

Seeing Brandt's grin, she brought the glass back to her lips and downed the rest. Her eyes blazed but she didn't choke. Though struggling, she managed to keep the repulsed expression from returning to her face.

Thomas and Cheri looked on and then they all began laughing.

Cheri said, "We'll try some wine and start you slow. Brandy isn't my favorite but Thomas loves the stuff. Brandt, stop challenging your mate and everyone else in the room. She will most definitely give you a run for your money."

Brandt turned to Emily and drew her closer, his lips descending on hers. After a quick taste he raised his mouth, "Umm, the brandy tastes better this way."

Thomas pulled Cheri close looking into her eyes his showing content and happiness for his son.

The mood was broken when Dominique announced dinner. The four separated but the couples remained hand in hand walking through the house toward the dining room.

Before they entered, heavy pounding came from the front door. No wolves had telepathically announced their presence and it took a moment for Brandt to determine who was knocking. "Emily, I have kept your brother and sister from you. I wanted to give you time. They have decided they are not waiting. I will gladly make them leave, but if you are ready they are eager to meet you."

It was impossible for him to decipher the look on her face and all she said was, "Yes."

"Yes you want them removed or yes you want to meet them."

Emily did not look at her mate but walked straight to the door like invisible rope pulled her. Her hand reached the handle and pulled the door open. Mandy and Caleb were standing outside. Emily stared.

Mandy took Emily's hand first and brought it to her nose. She inhaled the scent, closing her eyes letting the essence wash over her. Her eyes opened and filled with tears. She released Emily so Caleb could take her hand.

His eyes shown bright, "We couldn't stay away." He ignored the growl coming from Brandt but Emily didn't.

Reaching her other hand to his, she brought him to her side. "I am Emily. This is my mate."

"Two extra places have been set for dinner so everyone come in," said Cheri from behind them.

Emily, Mandy, and Caleb continued to stare at one another and another low rumble escaped Brandt's throat. Emily's hand gently touched the side of his face. Going onto her tiptoes, she placed a fleeting kiss on his lips. "Stop that, you are scaring them and I would like my family to join me for dinner."

Brandt's gaze turned to hers. "Disobedience in the pack is not acceptable." His disgruntled look was just a hair's breadth from full anger.

"Please." Her eyes begged but also sparked with just a touch of power.

His eyes blazed quickly but then softened.

Standing back, he let the two wolves enter. Both their scents held fear. He needed to remember how young they were.

Brandt took Emily's hand and walked beside her to the dining room.

Reaching back Emily took Mandy's hand drawing her along.

Mandy was beautiful; her medium brown hair thick, falling in gentle waves down her back. She had a beguiling smile and green eyes. Caleb, at least six inches taller than the women shared his sister's green eyes but where her body was small and compact his was large and muscular.

Brandt's many lessons on pack dynamics reminded Emily about the younger male wolves and the trouble they had controlling their aggression. It was obvious Caleb was suffering the consequences of his age.

Caleb's scent was turning from fear to anger.

Brandt looked over his shoulder and let the other wolf know he was putting off the wrong odor to his mate. He stopped at the entryway to the large room, his eyes piercing into those of the young wolf.

"Do you have something you wish to say Caleb?" Brandt's voice was tight and he let a touch of alpha temper release from his pores.

Caleb immediately looked down.

Brandt finally let up on his scent because he was afraid the other wolf was going to drop to his knees. He also sensed exasperating sparks from his mate.

Caleb's voice was shaky, "I shouldn't have disobeyed my alpha, but we could not stay away." He glanced up briefly but quickly lowered his eyes. "If Emily lived among us and you claimed her for mate, she would have been sent to another clan until she was twenty-one. I had to be sure she was okay." His nervousness increased and his words ran together.

Inhaling a deep calming breath, Brandt placed a kiss to the inside of Emily's hand then nipped the soft pad of her thumb. She needed to trust him. Turning back to the other wolf he reined in his irritation, "Emily is mine. I will kill anyone who tries to take her from me, but I understand your need and later I will let the three of you visit alone." He looked to Emily to see if she agreed. Her smile was all he needed.

"Let us eat. If my she-wolf is not fed, she becomes grouchy."

The tension dispelled and everyone took a seat. They shared more wine and enjoyed the food and conversation. Thomas and Brandt discussed finances and Thomas said he would need to retrieve some records from his cabin.

"You and Emily are welcome back here at the main house but if you wish you may have the cabin."

"I've decided to have a home built, but we will probably stay at the cabin until it's finished. Thank you."

"You're building a home?" said Emily.

"Yes, if you don't mind. I need roaming room and I would love to build a house for you. I want us to design it together and make something we both want."

Emily's burning smile caused the mate scent to roll off Brandt and fill the room. Her face reddened.

"You are embarrassing her in front of her brother and sister. Somehow you need to find a way to control yourself while in polite company." Cheri said but then the unmistakable scent came from her own mate and she folded her napkin and placed it on the table. We either eat dessert or end our party sooner rather than later."

"Brandt promised me time with my family and I'm not leaving without speaking with them." Emily's gaze traveled to her mate.

He swallowed his threatening growl and his lips quirked. Having Emily out of sight even for a short time was going to be hard. However, he knew that her wishes came first in this instance and he would survive.

"I'll have dessert served to the three of you in the den and Thomas, Brandt, and I will discuss a few things needing our attention."

Emily stood but Brandt pulled her close and gave her a quick kiss before releasing her to go with her siblings.

Thomas began speaking but opaque alpha eyes followed his mate from the room. He tried to pay attention to the conversation but knew he wouldn't feel calm until Emily was where he could see her.

Caleb entered the den first holding the door for the women and then shutting it behind them. Mandy dropped to her knees in front of Emily and buried her head against Emily's legs.

Emily gazed at Caleb helplessly but Caleb was fighting tears. The longing in his eyes saying he wanted to be on his knees with his sister.

In a choked voice he explained, "Family is everything to wolves. The two of us were united when we were young and have been with each other ever since. Now we have you and it's hard to keep from rubbing our bodies with yours and sharing our combined scents." He looked down at his sister with adoring sibling love. "Mandy and I slept in the same room until we were young teens and she still sneaks in and lies at the bottom of my bed when she's upset. Forgive us for pushing our way into your evening but we could no longer wait."

Tears formed in Emily's eyes and slowly they made their way down her cheeks. She sank to her knees beside Mandy and placed her arms around her sister's shoulders.

Caleb was suddenly there, kneeling on the floor, his larger arms around both women.

Mandy sobbed while Emily held tight, and Caleb gave comfort.

Lifting a tear stained face and looking at Emily, Mandy spoke pleadingly, "Can we change?"

"Please Emily. Our wolves need to scent you." Her brother's longing was evident.

"Yes." With all the years of her life spent hiding what she was, she would never stand between anyone and their beast. Brandt taught her to love and find glory in her wolf.

Caleb shed his clothes and Mandy followed. They shifted before the falling material settled. Both wolves were all over her, licking her face and arms, and sniffing her body. Emily couldn't help but laugh.

At a sudden sound from across the room, she looked up to see Brandt standing in the doorway. Her look was unsure and worried about his reaction.

"I forget how young the three of you are. Do you want to change? We can skip dessert and run."

The look on her face gave him her answer. He walked over and helped her slip off her shoes. He knelt down, lifted her gown, and brought it over her head. Wasting no time, she removed her bra and panties. Brandt shed his outerwear his shift following hers. He turned and headed for the front door, which Dom opened for them.

"Will Thomas join us?" Emily spoke into his mind.

"No, they have other pursuits. This is for you and your siblings. I'm sorry, but I'm not yet able to let you run alone. I need to be near you."

Brandt stopped and his snout rose into the air. He let go with a loud howl. Caleb's followed and then Mandy's. It was more than Emily could stand and hers rang through the night. In the distance fellow pack members answered their call.

"Who can keep up?" Came Brandt's challenge.

They ran into the night.

Chapter 17

When they tired of running, Brandt and Emily left her siblings at their own home and then continued to the cabin. On the porch, they changed back to human and went inside. He noticed that Dom had neatly folded the discarded clothing they removed before their run and left them on the new coffee table she had brought over after Emily's display of temper. On top of the clothing rested the necklace.

Picking it up, his desire ignited. "You promised me this, you naked and the bed," his husky voice intoned.

He followed her to the bedroom.

She turned away, allowing him to secure the clasp. Her need permeating the air, she crawled onto the bed. Before she could turn over he pulled her legs toward him. She landed gently on her stomach. Peering over her shoulder, she watched him. With infinite slowness he trailed soft moist kisses from the arch of her foot slowly up the length of her body. His other hand massaged her calves and then the backs of her thighs. His lips traveled higher. Finally, his warm breath blew out lifting loose hair from her partially covered face so he could bring his lips to hers. Lifting his body, he shifted her to the side and then rolled, bringing her body over his.

She pushed up slightly. The heat of her eyes burning into his.

"This is a perfect memory to cherish," he said with a deep throaty groan.

Her breasts hung down, the sapphire necklace swaying between them.

Passion ignited.

She lifted the lower half of her body and brought the warmth of her sex to meet and then surround his. Setting the pace, she slowly lifted herself up and then back down.

His hands moved to her hips but she fought the gentle coaxing of his grip to make her move faster. He accommodated her need and relaxed his hands though need burned through his blood. His face showed tightly leashed desire. His eyes drilled into hers.

Her body found its own rhythm and the musky spice of her mating scent filled the room.

When her inner muscles began pulsing in release, he rolled them over. Trapping her beneath him, his passion unleashed, and his erection thrust hard.

Her fingernails raked down his back. He shouted her name and their cries filled the night.

***

One day flowed into the next. The weeks passed in happiness and contentment. Emily spent hours learning to read. Brandt downloaded several programs on his father's computer to help her progress more easily. When alpha business took Brandt's time, she went to the main house and watched television. She absorbed large pieces of the world she never knew existed.

Food was another thing she couldn't get enough of. Her reading improved and she began cooking and experimenting with simple recipes but her favorite remained barely seared steak.

Every day, she explored a little more of the green forests surrounding the cabin. Brandt had art supplies delivered but she had yet to use them. She didn't know what was holding her back but her mate seemed to understand the things she couldn't put into words.

Late one night, while running through the forest, Brandt tackled her and after shifting to human they made love beneath the stars. When their breathing slowed, his fingers threaded through her hair. His other hand made slow circles over her sweat dampened skin. He didn't still his touch when he said, "Friends of mine are getting married, and they invited us to the wedding. They live quite a distance from here and we will fly to attend the ceremony."

"They know of me?"

"No, but they soon will. They invited me through Cheri, which is the proper protocol. Our queen won't attend but it is expected of me."

"We will fly?"

"Yes, the clan has a private plane. I will take several of the pack's wolves too. The proper number is ten. We're mates and count as a single entity so nine other pack members will go with us. Before we leave I will take you shopping to buy you clothes. Humans have a thing called a birth certificate that you need too. We have the means to get one and to establish a past for you but it must be handled in the city. Will you come with me?"

"We can fly in the air in a metal bird?"

He could tell she hadn't heard anything else he said. "Yes, and you will love it."

"Can Mandy and Caleb go with us?"

He smiled, "Gregor, their father won't be happy about them going to the city during your first trip but he shouldn't have a problem with the wedding. I will make up the rest of our party with strong pack members." Twirling his finger through her hair, he continued speaking, "When we attended the naming ceremony of the Central Clan, one of my younger wolves got out of line. The fault was mine and wouldn't have happened if my head was out of my ass. We need to make up for my last visit."

He kissed her gently, soft nips falling to the side of her mouth until he bit down gently on her lower lip. He inhaled deeply, loving the smell of her wolf, her human skin, and sex. Just on the edge he could smell slight apprehension.

"You'll like Marcus and Amy. Marcus recently turned her to vampire and she is Marcus' mate. The mate bond of Vampires is different than ours but just as powerful. Wolves don't have weddings, we have always been part animal. Vampires were once human and remember that time. I think you will enjoy our visit."

She smiled gently into his eyes, her scent calming. "I will enjoy anything with you. Right now though, I'm hungry."

His rich laughter filled the night. "My mate, you are always hungry. A midnight snack is waiting in the kitchen but I get my snack when we return to our room." He laughed more when she changed form and raced for the cabin on four fast legs.

***

The following morning, Brandt informed her she would begin training in self-defense with his father.

"Your wolf-self will learn the more it runs free, but your human side must learn control too. We are stronger than humans and if confrontations occur, we must remember to contain our strength and protect our secrets. Pack/human interaction training usually starts at an early age and you must learn too. I know you will catch on fast and my father is the best person to prepare you. He is not the most dominant wolf but he's a killer in a fight. I also don't want another male scent on you. It will drive me crazy. You have already absorbed my father's scent by living in this cabin. I think I can control myself after he touches you. I have other concerns I must take care of and I'll stay busy while you train."

"When will I start?"

"I was thinking we would take a warm-up run and then I'll leave you at the gym. We'll run as wolves but clothing will be waiting for you when we arrive."

They left the cabin and Brandt took her through a rougher course than usual. Other werewolves and pack mates in human form were interspersed throughout the area and going about their normal day, but none did more than glance up when the two streaked past. They were cautiously accepting Emily. Brandt took her to a small canyon and scaled an incline of rocks. On four legs, Emily was becoming more stable and tackled the loose rocks and steep incline with little difficulty.

After the canyon, Brandt led her to a large metal barn. It smelled of sweat, blood, and wolf. The double doors were open and they went directly inside. There were other wolves within but Brandt ignored them and led her to the showers and some shelves that held clothing. They shifted and both dressed in sweats.

"I'll leave you with Thomas and come back in two hours. Will you be okay?"

She saw the concern on his face. She knew it would be a long two hours without him but she would survive. "Yes, but don't forget me."

He pulled her close and kissed her passionately then breathed deeply of her scent. "It would be no different than forgetting to breathe." He took her hand and led her to his father. He said nothing just walked away.

"He'll be okay. He's alpha and life should be hard." Thomas smiled at her. "Come on and I'll introduce you before I kick your ass."

She appreciated his teasing knowing he would never seriously hurt her. One by one the wolves welcomed her. They did not meet her eyes for more than a heartbeat but she detected no animosity, only the same curiosity she felt.

Her training began.

"You can kill a human with one blow, rip off their head with your hands, and not break a sweat. Not good. To the public eye, we are nothing more than human. And, we need to stay that way. I'll start you on the heavy bag and show you what I mean. We will spend the last half-hour of every workout going full out. With Brandt by your side another wolf should never challenge you, but a situation may arise where you must fight and you need to know how to use everything you have. Ready?"

Lines of silver tape wrapped around the black heavy bag. It hung from a thick chain. Thomas showed her how to make a proper fist and he began striking the bag to show her what he wanted her to do. He moved over and let Emily stand in front of the bag. "Bend your knees and find your center of balance."

Her first strike sent the bag ten feet back on the chain track. Thomas laughed and told her he wanted her to feel her own power. "Now you must hold back. It's almost harder than fighting your own kind full-out."

Emily was finally able to pull her punches and move the chain mere inches rather than feet. Even with what Thomas considered the light part of the workout, sweat dampened her brow and shirt.

Next was the speed bag, which caused the sweat to run down her face. Her hair was no longer damp, it was wet. Twenty minutes later they went into the ring for some sparring.

"It's not hard when you're calm. We will work on control when you're angered tomorrow. That is another reason we don't want Brandt here. He will have trouble controlling his reactions if you are feeling stressed. These lessons are important. We need to know humans are safe from you when you go out into their world." He spoke while blocking her strikes and ringing her teeth a few times. They weren't hard blows but he wanted her to remember to protect her face and knew the fastest way to impart the lesson was to cause a little discomfort.

Emily's arm muscles were beginning to shake with the strain but Thomas wouldn't let up. He barely broke a sweat.

Thirty minutes later, with a nod from Thomas, the other wolves left the gym. Emily looked around and then gazed questionably at him. "I thought you might feel more comfortable with our next lesson if we are alone." He pulled his shirt over his head and then dropped his pants.

Emily watched until he stood naked. Brandt was a tougher version of his father. They had the same olive skin and dark brown eyes but a different kind of intelligence sparked from Thomas'. Brandt's were more alive with his animal and the domineering force of being alpha.

Thomas spoke in her head, "What are you waiting for? It's time to fight using your wolf." He shifted and then used his powerful wolf body to send her flying.

Emily's clothes were off in seconds and she too changed forms. Thomas came at her again and she twisted and nipped him on the shoulder. The fight was on.

He changed to human and clocked her K9 ear and head.

It hurt and she quickly spun away and shifted. She was breathing hard but before she could catch her breath, Thomas came in close and landed another punch to her jaw. He caught her nose too and blood streamed down her face, "Had enough?" His voice taunted in her mind.

She shifted at the same time she launched herself. Thomas was not where she expected him to be when she landed, and she spun feeling his teeth bite into her flank. Her painful howl reverberated throughout the gym

Two-hundred pounds of angry male alpha sent Thomas flying. He stayed down, which was smart. Emily defused the situation landing on her mate's back and taking him to the ground. She stood with her front two paws on his side and spoke gently, "If you wanted to play, you only had to ask."

Thomas laughed and rose to his feet to leave the gym. "I think you need to stay away until the two-hours are up. I have no intention of inflicting lasting damage to your mate, and if she grew up with us, she would have a few scars. You know she needs this."

The large doors closed behind his father. Outside sunlight shown sparingly through small windows high up, casting shadows on the dark interior.

"You didn't need to do that," Her teeth circled her mate's throat and she growled with a low rumble flexing her jaws slightly.

The body beneath her became human and his strong arms came up to grab chunks of fur and muscle on either side of her body.

Startled, she released her jaw muscles and in a blink she was airborne. Emily rolled, landed, and came up with her sharp teeth displayed.

"I thought you wanted to play?" Brandt's voice was low. His hand came up and gave her the come hither signal.

Emily shifted, "No, you come here."

He placed one foot in front of the other and stalked toward her. Her nose was bleeding and she had a large bruise on her cheek. He didn't care, he knew she wasn't seriously hurt and she was beautiful in fight mode.

Emily noticed the scent change and shifted back to wolf. "No, you don't. You need to finish my lesson since you interrupted it." She sent the message to his mind and danced away on four legs.

His shift was seamless. He turned and sprang in one move. His body hit hers and they came to a stop with her neck between his jaws.

"The only way this battle will end is with you on your back." He shifted. Her body also melded to human. She was pinned. The kiss was savage. He could taste her blood and sweat. Lust overcame his anger at seeing his father hurt her. Breathing deeply through his nose, he gentled the kiss and his teeth took her lower lip, applying pressure. "I'm sorry. I'll stay away until your training is complete tomorrow." He gave her a soft kiss on her bloody nose. "Let's go home and get you cleaned up."

Emily was no longer in the mood to argue.

Chapter 18

That night Brandt spoke more about Cheri and the gift vampires give to beastkind. He wanted his queen to take care of the bruise on Emily's face. "By drinking our blood, vampires grant us immortality. They also speed our healing. Cheri has fed from you twice and monthly is more than adequate, but you are the mate of the alpha and need to appear at your best. It is expected but must be your decision."

"I barely remember the past two times when I was given no choice. You're telling me I don't have a choice again but I can refuse. That doesn't make sense."

"It's part of being my mate and I'm sorry if it's difficult for you to accept. You can refuse now since it isn't necessary except to improve your appearance for our trip but you will share blood with Cheri over many lifetimes. If you were raised here, it would begin when you turned twenty-one unless an accident befell you and required her bite."

"My brother and sister mentioned that I would be sent away until I was twenty-one, if it was discovered I was your mate?"

"They are right. I'm robbing the cradle with you but I can't help myself. A wolf usually stays at home or goes to another clan until age twenty-one and then they have options. A mated pair can be together then. It's very difficult when the mate bond is discovered early. The older wolf is in a constant state of need for the mate until he or she is at an age to allow them to bond sexually. Physical bonding without sex happens with supervision if the older wolf is having too much difficulty. But then, both wolves suffer once the younger wolf feels the pull. A wolf's sexuality begins at around sixteen. It is frowned upon in the human world and in ours for an old man to have sex with a young teenage girl."

"You are the old man in this picture, aren't you?" She smiled at him.

"Yes, I'm archaic compared to you."

"Are we talking more than five-hundred-years-old?"

"Yes, we are talking more than that."

"Cheri keeps you young?"

"Yes, she keeps me from using a walker to make my way around."

"You're teasing me."

"Yes, I don't like talking about your age compared to mine."

"But what you're really telling me is that in over five-hundred-years, you found no mate." She could tell her words bothered him. His scent changed but it was neither anger nor passion, just different.

He swept her into a deep kiss. Suddenly, she felt the vampire's presence. Brand's mouth released hers. "She has a need for you my queen."

"Thomas said he was rough on her today." Cheri could feel Emily's apprehension. "I've already tasted your blood but I'm sure Brandt has explained how it will help you heal."

"He did, but I'm not certain what you want me to do?"

"I can drink from your arm until you are more comfortable. Most wolves prefer the neck for closer relationships. When offering to another clan's vampire, always give your arm."

Emily took a step toward Cheri and moved the hair from her neck without saying a word.

Cheri moved faster than a blink and her fangs entered Emily's throat. Her eyes went amber and locked on Brandt while drinking deeply of Emily's sweet blood. This was part of the bond all her wolves shared. She sensed Emily's fear but the young woman was mentally and physically strong, making her perfect for Brandt. Cheri's fangs receded and she pulled away. Emily's eyes had drifted closed. The enzymes in vampire blood now flowed in the bloodstream of the wolf. Cheri took a step back, waiting to see what Emily's body needed. The exchange always gave the greatest gift.

Emily walked straight into Brandt's arms, "Take me to bed." Her voice oozed sex.

Cheri left with a laugh. Brandt picked up his mate and gave her what she wished.

***

The following day brought more of the same punishment at the gym, with one difference. It was time to get Emily angry.

Thomas knew this would be tough on her. He didn't clear out the other wolves because it would be more difficult for her to handle with them looking on. This was a test and needed to be hard. Killing a human was out of the question and she would leave wolf territory and go to the city in two days. He kept his plans for today's workout from Brandt. His son would go ballistic. Thomas knew Brandt would sense her feelings but hoped he would keep his promise and stay away. This was a test for them both. Emily needed to be able to fight her own battles and not kill a human while doing it.

She concentrated and worked hard to pull her strikes. Thomas taught her to use her legs to trip her opponent and put them down. He checked her speed several times. She listened and understood what he wanted from her. It felt good.

For their human session in the boxing ring, he had her put on gloves, "If your claws don't come through the material, you're doing well. The gloves will help you focus." He did not glove up. The wolves circled the ring and he began with a few jabs toward her. "Slow your evasion of my punches. You can take a punch from a human and it will feel like a bee's sting. Use your legs and take your opponent to the floor."

She tried, Thomas did not go down. He pulled his punches so the few that landed were mere tickles. He had no trouble skirting away from hers and she became frustrated.

"Has Brandt told you about his mate bond with Cheri?"

Stunned, Emily put her arms down. Her penalty was a punishing blow to the jaw.

"Get your guard up. He hasn't fucked her in twenty years but I know he wanted to."

That was all it took. Her claws exploded through the gloves and she attacked. Her canines enlarged and Thomas didn't have a chance. His shoulder took the first punishing bite and her nails ripped deep furrows in his side and leg. Emily momentarily saw red and she wanted that red to be his blood. Her clothing ripped and a white wolf burst completely from human skin. Thomas was down but breathing. The angry she-wolf deliberately circled his throat with her jaws.

She spoke to the mind of every wolf present. "Brandt is mine; never forget that. It doesn't matter who came before, it only matters who tries to take him from me now. That person dies." Emily released her sharp teeth and gave a long lick to Thomas' face. "I think you're finished for today but I still need my beast workout."

An unclothed Brandt stepped between the ropes surrounding the ring. "My old man will never learn. There is only one wolf in this pack who can give you a run for your money sweetheart."

"I don't think sweet is the word you will use in a few minutes." With that Emily launched herself at her mate and the fight was on.

The wolves stayed to watch. Brandt had no illusions about who they were there to see. She was his mate and his pack wanted to judge if she was truly worthy. A sharp bite to his thigh and damn close to his manhood brought his thoughts back to the fight.

Thomas got out of the way, blood trailing from deep gouges on his shoulder and leg. He was proud of her. She lost control for a few damaging minutes but managed to contain herself and think rationally. With a few werewolf babysitters she would be safe around humans. He wasn't so sure about his son. "Emily, it's time to let your wolf out and teach your mate a lesson for dreaming far too long about my woman."

"Thanks old man. I hope your woman gives you a few hours of suffering before healing your injuries." Brandt rolled to the side. Her teeth came within an inch of his nose. His wolf replaced the man and spun, catching her with his teeth and sinking them deep in her flank. She growled with pain and scrambled away. She turned human and grabbing his back leg, pulling it hard and propelling herself backward. Everyone heard the pop when the limb dislocated. Brandt turned human and using his greater strength brought her in close, rolled on top, and pinned her to the mat.

Emily stopped fighting and looked at into Brandt's pain filled eyes. Her breathing was heavy, "You're my mate, and I don't care to hear about past females in your life. Do I need to kick your ass a little more to remind you?"

He couldn't help but laugh and Cheri joined in. "It's the middle of the night for me but I think the winner gets first choice."

Emily rolled Brandt beneath her without resistance. She disengaged from him and stood to walk toward Cheri. She met the vampire's stare straight on. "He is mine and I don't care what happened before me, but if you change your mind about his father and want him back I will fight."

"You will die." The words held no humor or softness.

"So be it, he is my mate, and I will die defending my rights if I must."

"Thomas is mine. You never need to worry about a challenge from me." Cheri looked around. "I don't think you need to worry about a challenge from anyone here."

Emily looked around too. Pack werewolves lowered their eyes while her gaze made its way around the gym. The internal power, which made her alpha, flowed from her skin. Electrically charged, every wolf present felt its weight.

She let additional energy flare before speaking, "The only reason my mate didn't win," she glanced over her shoulder at the man in question, "was because he would not seriously hurt me. I may need to teach him a lesson a time or two before he gives me a real fight." Emily looked back at Cheri pulling her hair to the side of her neck. "I have need of you my queen and the defeated can wait."

After Cheri released her, Emily walked to the changing room and got in the shower to rinse the blood from her body. No one entered the room. She left the gym on four legs, not seeing Thomas or her mate. This time, vampire enzymes didn't cause her body to desire sex. Her wolf just needed to run.

In front of a medium sized cabin, Kinsee played with dolls. A grown woman sat on the porch steps watching Emily approach.

"I won't harm her." Emily stayed in her wolf form connecting with the woman's mind.

"I know that, she speaks about you often. You are the wolf who called her demon, Brandt's mate, and an alpha in your own right."

"I am sorry for what I called her." Emily's eyes went to the child. "I am very sorry Kinsee."

The small child lifted her dress over her head. "You're silly; can I run with her Mama?"

The woman laughed, "I'm Patricia and mother to this little demon. Will you let her take a jaunt with you while I get some work done?"

Emily was stunned but replied with a look of devotion at the child. "I will care for her and have her back shortly"

"Take your time, if you tire her out she will go to bed early."

Emily looked toward the small wolf who gave a little yip. The two of them took off. Emily slowed her pace for the child and couldn't believe she had the opportunity to be alone with her. The two of them ran for an hour. Kinsee talked nonstop and asked every question conceivable.

"You never went outside when you were a child?"

"No."

"No one loved you?" It was obvious Kinsee's mother had devoted considerable conversation to the new pack wolf.

"No, no one loved me until Brandt."

"I will love you and now you have two, like I have my mom and dad."

"You have a dad?"

"Of course silly. His name is Wolfred. He says I am the most beautiful wolf ever born."

"I think you are too. Thank you for loving me." Emily wanted to cry. She also remembered that Brandt told her wolves were unable to produce children together and required a fully human mother or father. She wondered how Kinsee's parents managed. She couldn't help but feel a pull in her heart for her own child but knew no other man would ever touch her. She would also kill any she-wolf that placed a hand on her mate.

"Look, a rabbit. Can we get it, can we?"

The chase was on and even though Emily mourned the outcome she could deny the child nothing. Kinsee made a quick kill and for that Emily was grateful. The child brought the rabbit to her and dropped it at her feet, nudging it closer with her nose. "It's for you."

"I've eaten too much today, why don't you take it home."

"I can eat it now; I'm hungry and can eat the whole thing."

Emily sat by and guarded Kinsee while she consumed her kill. She refused to think about one beautiful creature being devoured by another.

Shortly after, the two of them trotted back to Kinsee's home. Brandt was waiting out front when they came into sight.

Kinsee changed back to human and pulled her dress over her head. She hugged Emily around her shaggy neck and then ran into the house. Emily took off, giving Brandt a run for his money until they reached their own cabin and shifted to human. Brandt took her hand and brought her fingers to his lips.

"I'm so proud of you." His gaze met hers.

"Well, I'm not happy with you and think you have a few things to explain."

Chapter 19

Emily sat on the couch watching Brandt paced back and forth. It was obvious he felt uneasy, but she was not going to help him.

His agitation was more apparent when he finally spoke, "I thought I loved Cheri and was quite stubborn about it. We were together for a short time and then she no longer returned my affections. I was eaten with jealousy and thought her my mate. I told you before that vampires do not share the mate bond like we do. I put her rejection down to that. I was unable to accept that she loved my father. I knew for many years that they were seeing each other."

He stopped for a moment and gave her a beseeching look. He needed Emily to understand. His hurt and betrayal came out with his next words. "I wanted to kill him. He raised me alone, nurtured me, and supported me but I wanted him dead. I craved his blood on my hands. It made me crazy."

Deep, slow, steady breaths strengthened his voice. "Cheri and I slowly regained our friendship but for me it always felt like more. I couldn't stop my jealousy and my anger began having an effect on the pack. My rage simmered slowly and my wolves became unsteady. The night I found you, my father challenged me and I was mere seconds from ending his life." His eyes closed briefly, remembering his father's blood.

He didn't look at her. A soft touch brought him back. Warmth flowed from her fingers sending small sparks along his skin.

"Do you still love Cheri?" Her voice was soft, worried.

He turned. No hesitation, "No."

Her eyes changed and she exhaled, "Do you think you would have killed your father?"

With a look of complete anguish he took both of her hands. "Yes." He hesitated before continuing, thinking back. "When we were tracking you, I decided to leave the pack. I knew I was destroying my wolves and I feared my friend Samson would challenge me. I didn't want to kill him and I knew killing my father was not the answer. Finding you cemented my place again. One taste of your blood and Cheri was a distant memory. There is no comparison in my feelings. If I thought you were with anyone but me, I would not stand by in anger. He would be dead." He grasped her hair at the base of her neck, pulling her head back and his mouth came down on hers.

He was her world, the reason her heart beat, the reason she was alive. She matched the kiss, no softness only hunger.

Mating pheromones rolled off their skin. Her stomach growled loudly and he pulled away, his grin chiding. Breathing in her scent he tried to get his passion under control. His voice husky, "I won't take a hungry she-wolf to bed." He took her hand and pulled her into the kitchen with a laugh. I smelled the rabbit on Kinsee. I take it you didn't have a bite or two?"

"No, but I did help her catch it and then let her do the killing. Set me down so I can get my clothes on."

"Oh, but I prefer you naked."

She laughed but her eyes grew steamy, changing color.

The low growl started deep in his throat, rising. His eyes darkened.

Her stomach rumbled again and they both laughed.

"Let's eat light and I'll call a pack hunt tonight. It will be dark soon and in a few hours I'll teach your wolf to stalk prey. Before that, I'll stalk you."

"Call the wolves."

***

They met at the clearing. Fifteen wolves divided themselves into three separate hunting teams. Samson, Thomas and a she-wolf named Josie were in the alphas' group. The teams split up. They would branch out, seeking a fresh scent trail, and then hone in and move the prey toward each other.

Samson found the scent first and the rest of the team followed. Brandt relayed information to Emily while running, "Samson is my best tracker. When we get closer to the deer, we will work together. For now he has the lead."

Emily's excitement took over, squeamishness forgotten, her wolf took over. The forest floor gave beneath her paws. Gangly in the past, her legs were now steady and strong. Her ears pricked at the sound of snapping branches and then she saw a large buck charging through the undergrowth.

The wolves surrounded the large animal and attacked. There were three does on the run too. Only one escaped.

Emily launched herself forward, instinct taking over. Her fangs sank deeply into the buck's throat, tearing through hide and muscle. With help from her pack mates, she took the magnificent animal to the ground.

The tangy scent of blood filled the air. Brandt's snout rose to the moon in the age old call of the wolves and his song rang through the night. The others joined in and when the last cry echoed through the trees, they feasted.

Brandt's team tore into the buck while the other teams went for the does. He growled a few times at his pack. The best morsels belonged to his mate.

When they finished, the wolves lay around in smaller groups and groomed themselves and one another. The alphas stayed apart while Brandt cleaned Emily's muzzle with his rough tongue and then moved to the top of her paws and ruff of her neck.

"I think it's time to go home," her sultry voice sounded in his mind.

"I think you're right, loser must scrub the winner's back." And he was off.

Emily had no chance to catch up, but she enjoyed washing his back. She might have lost the race but the night was hers.

***

The next day, she kept her appointment at the gym.

Thomas looked away when she approached, so she gave him a brief hug. He glanced over her shoulder looking for Brandt and she laughed.

"I value my hide and your mate will have it if he sees you hugging me."

"Then my mate and I will have a serious talk. You are his father and my family too. He can learn to live with it."

"Hmmm, if you say so." Thomas spent the morning teaching her of human habits versus those of wolves while she dodged his fists. "No growling if a human male tries to come on to you. A polite and firm 'no' will work. If a human female does the same to Brand…"

"I rip her throat out?" Her voice was eager.

He gave her a crooked grin, "No, you place your hand firmly on her arm, soften your voice, and look her in the eye. Besides the gesture, you won't need to say a word."

"What if the arm thing doesn't work?"

It wasn't Thomas that answered it was another she-wolf named Maggie. She was one of the pack's fighters and gave Emily a lot of space. Emily wondered why, but hadn't asked anyone. "Just move Brandt behind you, look her in the eye, and ask if she wants to lose her right nipple."

"You're not helping here Maggie," said Thomas.

Emily grinned, "I disagree, and I think she did. I'll be sure to use that line if it's needed."

Maggie walked away and began working on a speed bag.

"I'll pass your little talk on to Brandt so he knows he better stay away from other women."

"I think that would be smart. He's too beautiful. Now, let's see if I can spill your butt on the mat."

"I'm at your mercy, my alpha." Thomas dipped his head and then twisted away. Emily attacked.

***

Departure day arrived. Samson and Maggie were to be Emily's babysitters. Maggie would even enter bathrooms with the recently tamed werewolf.

Brandt explained things would eventually be easier but they were taking no chances with her first time in the city. "If you're good, I have a special treat planned." He teased to get her mind off her first airplane flight. He could hear her accelerated heartbeat and smell her apprehension. He wanted excitement to overcome any worry she had.

"More than the couple of hours in the whirling hot bath you promised me?"

"The Jacuzzi, and yes a bigger surprise."

"What is it?"

"If I tell you, it won't be a surprise."

Emily leaned over and nibbled the side of his jaw. "Could I kiss the secret from you?"

"No, but go ahead and try."

She didn't notice the plane take off until they broke apart and she looked out the window. "It's beautiful."

"Not more beautiful than you." His eyes met hers.

Emily could see over his shoulder. Maggie made a gagging gesture to Samson. Emily's voice carried to the two wolves, her eyes drilling into Maggie's. "Which nipple would you like to lose?" Her tone held a challenge.

Maggie looked down, "I'm sorry my alpha."

Brandt chuckled, "It's your own fault Maggie. My father told me you were trying to teach Emily a thing or two."

Samson snorted. "Oh Mags, you've more than met your match with Brandt's mate and I like you with both nipples."

The tension eased. Brandt took Emily's hand and held it during the two-hour flight. Denver's population was just over five million and had museums, art walks, shopping, and just about anything a city dweller could wish for. Brandt wanted Emily to see some of the wonders she missed in her childhood. The three days would be jam packed but he would bring her back to the city soon and let her explore.

Emily's nervousness increased after they landed and the smell of humans became overpowering. Her slightly shaking hand sought Brandt's and she was grateful when he sent a soothing vibration through his touch. People stared and watched their every move. They traveled by limousine and the buzz began again when they entered the luxurious hotel. It put Emily even more on edge and her tension escalated. Two bellhops took them to their suite. Once the door closed, strong comforting arms came around her shoulders and a gentle kiss landed on her nose. She took a deep breath and her body relaxed. Another breath and she was back in control. Pulling away she looked around the suite.

A large living room with several couches and chairs took up the front area. A dining table for eight separated the room from a luxurious kitchen. Emily made her way through each room and finally walked into the master bedroom. An extra-large bed was the centerpiece with a grouping of plush chairs next to bay windows in the shape of a wide "U" setting off the beauty of downtown Denver. Emily looked out over the skyline completely amazed with the city. Eventually her eyes traveled back into the room and she spotted the walk in Jacuzzi in the corner. It was easily eight feet wide and five feet across. White marble with gold streaks and gold fixtures made it a work of art.

She grinned at her mate and received a wicked smirk in return.

Samson and Maggie would be in a suite across the hall and two other males, Jordan and Morris, stayed further down the hall. Their job was to run interference, make sure everything ran smoothly, and alert Brandt to any trouble coming their way. Samson and Maggie were exclusively on close wolf sitting duty.

Emily looked longingly at the large tub.

"No, we'll have time for that tonight. For now, I want to take you shopping. You will enjoy my surprise more if you have the proper clothes."

"You promise that we can share the bath tonight?"

His kiss was gentle, "I promise."

Samson and Maggie met them in the hallway. Jordan and Morris followed a short distance behind. The limo was waiting and Larimer Square was their destination.

Brandt kept a tight hold on Emily's hand. He knew the crowds would be difficult. He released some of his own scent to help soothe her nerves.

She gave him a grateful smile understanding what he was doing.

"I'm here. My arms are waiting and if you cuddle close to my chest, it will ease some of the strain."

He stopped on the sidewalk and she gave him a quizzical look. Bringing her into his embrace, he hugged her tight and whispered in her ear, "See, we can do this any time you need." His gaze burned hotly into hers.

Samson and Maggie understood and gave Emily some space keeping humans from getting too close when possible. They found a small non-crowded boutique where Emily could shop without being overwhelmed.

Maggie asked Brandt to go with Samson and get a beer while the women did their thing. Emily's anxious eyes turned to Brandt but she gave him a slight smile. "Go on, I can do it but don't go far."

Brandt was unsure but knew she needed to try. Placing a brief kiss on her lips, he left with Samson.

Maggie waited until the two men were gone before whispering to Emily, "You need some girly items and the men don't need to be around. I won't hug you but I'll help if you begin to panic."

Surprised, Emily looked at the other woman. "How?"

"I have some great raunchy jokes about men and they're good for releasing tension."

Emily laughed and had to ask, "Okay, tell me one, please."

"What did the elephant say to the naked man?"

The look Emily gave her was not what Maggie expected. "Do you know what an elephant is?"

"Brandt showed me one on the internet, gray, long nose right?"

"Yes, now let's start over."

"Okay."

"What did the elephant say to the naked man?"

"I don't know."

"It's cute but can you pick up peanuts with it?"

It took Emily a moment and then she started laughing.

"See, I can help you relax and I have a million men jokes."

"You don't like men?"

"Hmm, there are a few things men are really good for. But, most of the time I only tolerate them. Now let's shop or your man will come back and we won't be finished."

Emily needed everything; lingerie, evening wear, jeans, t-shirts, and shoes. Maggie had a good eye and helped choose colors to accent Emily's hair and skin tone. After a childhood hating shoes Emily purchased hiking boots, stilettos and everything in between.

Maggie talked Emily into some fun lingerie with the promise that Brandt would enjoy them more than Emily. Maggie pointed out a classy pair of jeans and told her she needed them for her surprise. Emily chose three inch heels and a lace, partially transparent cream shirt to wear over a rose colored corset.

Emily wanted comfort clothes too. She chose sweats and flannel pants along with shorts and sun tops. She had the most fun picking out five pairs of colorful flip-flops. The two women received royal treatment and shopped unhampered by bags since delivery to the hotel was part of the service. The men joined them in the early afternoon and they went to a café and ordered a large lunch.

The women spent the rest of the afternoon getting their hair, nails, and toenails beautified. Still excited by their day but with energy on the wane they arrived back at the hotel at five. Emily wanted to take a short nap but was unable to rest due to the excitement of the day and concern that she might squish her updo. Brandt sat on a large luxurious couch and pulled her over. "Lie here and I will make sure your hair isn't mussed. Take a nap so you can enjoy a night on the town and not fall asleep for your first real date."

If I lay on the couch with you and nap, won't that be what I'm doing?"

"Imp." He said and gently pulled her down.

A little over an hour later she woke to soft kisses and whispered longing in her ear. "It's hard having you lay here when I can't run my fingers through your hair. You had better get up before I break my promise and undo your stylist's hard work."

Emily kissed him and then jumped up, instantly communicating to Maggie that she needed help with her makeup. The she-wolf had promised to assist Emily in getting ready. The two of them laughed and kicked Brandt into the suite across the hall to get his own clothes on. The men were to meet them down at the bar in an hour.

The corset pushed Emily's breasts up. They spilled lusciously over the silk edges. The heels gave her added height and the entire effect was that of classy seductress. Her sapphire necklace was a little much for jeans, so the long curve of her neck was bare. Their sensitive noses did not allow the use of human perfume but any beastkind within a hundred yards would smell the essence of the mated pair.

The women took the elevator down to the ground floor. Maggie wore jeans with a silver studded black sleeveless t-shirt displaying her toned arms and outlining her figure. The top ended two inches from the hip hugging jeans and accented her defined abs. The effect was lethal sensuality.

They crossed the expansive lobby drawing the attention from every man they passed. Emily didn't take a deep breath until she finally saw her mate.

Brandt's eyes darkened when her scent invaded his thoughts and then went black when he saw her. She would be beautiful in a burlap bag but tonight she was seduction on a stick and he wanted to lick every inch of her body. Standing, he pulled her into his arms. She leaned away from his mouth and batted her eyes teasingly. "Maggie said not to allow you to mess up my lipstick."

He nuzzled her jaw and a low growl rumbled from his throat. "This is going to be a very long night." He reluctantly pulled back but looked at her lush cleavage on display. "Are you ready for your surprise?" The husky words rippled through her body.

"Are you going to tell me what it is?"

"No, I'm just going to take you there and let you enjoy."

She pursed her cherry red lips in a pretend pout and he was unable to resist a quick peck. She used her finger to wipe the red lipstick from his lower lip.

"Okay you guys, the mating scent is becoming a little much for us single wolves." Samson said with a laugh.

The limo was waiting and the night began.

Chapter 20

The venue was outdoors at a large park on acres of land. Brandt wanted tonight to be special but knew Emily might have a problem with large close crowds. They removed two blankets from the limo and made their way to a secluded spot on the grass. More people arrived. Jordan and Morris sat on the blanket's edge and added an additional buffer zone.

Excitement and unease battled within Emily's mind. More people arrived and her nervousness increased.

Brandt pulled her back between his legs holding her tightly within his arms. Giving a gentle kiss to the top of her head he whispered, "I wanted you to enjoy some music. If this becomes too much we can leave."

Tipping her face to look at him, she smiled. "I'll be okay, they just smell funny."

"It's the perfumes. They don't get it." His nose nuzzled behind her ear. "Umm, you smell wonderful."

The music began; a mix of country, jazz, and blues. Jordan left for a short time and returned with two clear plastic cups of beer handing one to Emily and one to Brandt. No one else would be drinking but Brandt wanted Emily to experience the concert to the fullest. He laughed when she made a face with her first sip of the malty liquid. "It's an acquired taste and I'll drink the rest if you don't want yours."

"You challenge me and know I'll drink it but it's definitely not my favorite beverage."

"Cheers." He tipped his cup to hers.

An hour later the music softened and a lovely melody ran through the night. Finally, she was able to unwind until Brandt stiffened and whispered into her ear, "Cats."

He began giving rapid orders wordlessly. "Leave the blankets, stay together." Taking Emily's hand, he kept her to his left with Maggie on her other side. Samson walked in front of them, Jordan and Morris at the rear.

The wolves were large and people mostly cleared out of their way.

Emily concentrated on containing her panic. She remembered Brandt's lesson on letting her wolf deal with difficult situations. Breathing deeply she looked around with her wolf senses. In Brandt's pack history lessons, he covered a lot of the animosity between the wolf and cat clans. The hair on the back of her neck bristled. *Cats; deadly, enemies, protect.* Her wolf helped focus and the humans around them faded from her danger list.

"Good girl." Brandt realized what she was doing, his own wolf bristling just below his skin.

They escaped the large crowd and walked quickly through thick trees. They could see the parking lot in the distance.

Three large shapes stepped from the shadows.

Brandt mentally gave his instructions, "No blood unless necessary. Let's see what they want first." He snapped shut his link to the other wolves and sent another message privately to his mate. "Emily, tap down on the alpha scent and try for a little nervousness, we may need you for a surprise." He knew the cats outnumbered them. He had faith in his team and Emily; two alphas could do a lot of damage.

"Alpha of the northern clan, we are honored at your presence." The cat's voice held derision."

"We are visiting neutral territory. There is no *honor* in delaying our departure." Waves of alpha power magnified.

"Mating does not become you. We've offered proper greeting. No blood has spilled." Menace rolled through the air from the cat.

It was a new odor for Emily; off, different, not so nice.

Brandt walked forward using his hand and placing Emily behind him.

Holding back a growl was difficult, she wanted to be by her mate's side.

Brandt's next words threatened any peace they might have. "I believe you're courting death before I even know your name."

"My name is not important; there are twenty pride cats here. Your death is imminent." The scent thickened.

Brandt's growl was low, building. "Is this a challenge?"

For several minutes there was no response. "No, we only wanted to say hello." The last came on a whisper and the cats melted into the night.

Blazing fire shot from Brandt's eyes. This time, it was Emily who used her soothing abilities to calm her mate.

"Come on, we're going back to the hotel." His fingers grasped hers tightly.

"What was all that about?" Samson's thoughts carried into Brandt and Emily's minds.

"We'll have that discussion later." Brandt's voice was tight, his control barely leashed.

***

Their conference was short. Cats were difficult to understand. Their clans worked differently than the wolves. Brandt also notified Cheri with an update on what happened. She was no happier than him.

Emily spoke little. She continued to send out soothing waves to calm Brandt.

He finally looked directly into her eyes. "You can let up now. I'm in full control." His mouth tipped up at the corners, letting her know he wasn't angry. This was what mates were for.

The other wolves left the suite and Brandt and Emily were finally alone. Brandt turned, placing his hands to either side of her jaw, his eyes gazing softly into hers. "This is not what I planned for your first night out." His thumbs rubbed her cheeks and then his hands moved back, his fingers going to the nape of her neck, rubbing the tense muscles. Moving in closer, his breath traveled over her face, feathery light, and then his lips gently touched hers.

She raised her arms and rested her hands on the backs of his, her fingers holding him still. Drawing back slightly she looked up, her eyes deep blue changing to cerulean passion, her voice husky, "You promised me a bubble bath."

"Yes I did. Shall we?"

Scentless bubble bath sat next to the large tub. He adjusted the nozzles and began filling the bath. Emily shimmied out of her jeans and shirt. When Brandt turned she was standing in her corset, garters, thigh high stockings, and four inch heels. His breath caught at the erotic sight.

"You like?" Need filled her sexy voice.

With a growl, he began unbuttoning his linen shirt, but his fingers were not working at their best. "Fuck it." The buttons went flying and the shirt ripped at the seams. His shoes and pants quickly followed.

Emily gave a gentle laugh while watching his clothes fall to the floor. He always called her beautiful, but he was breathtaking. Her eyes followed the light trace of hair trailing down to the juncture of his thighs. Her gaze stayed there for a moment, taking in his large erection, and then traveling back up to his strong shoulders and powerful muscled arms. She hadn't realized that she moved closer.

His hands covered the swell of her breasts. "I like," he said in answer to her forgotten question. He dropped to his knees and moved his mouth to the juncture of her thighs. Inhaling her scent and nudging her legs slightly apart, his tongue came out. He slowly licked across the material covering her sex.

Her legs weakened and she inhaled sharply.

"You like?" His eyes sparked.

"Please don't tease, not now." Her voice begged.

He stood and lifted her, her legs wrapped around his waist. He bent and shut off the water, but instead of stepping in he carried her to the bed.

"If I don't taste more of you, I'll go crazy." His hard husky voice left no room for argument.

She didn't even try.

He laid her on the bed and removed the small scrap of material in his way but left the corset, garters, and heels. Pulling her legs forward, he lifted them to his shoulders. He remembered the night on the porch of Cheri's home. "I think I like these heels over my shoulders even more."

Her eyes were alight with sexual wanting, her voice soft and needy, "Maggie calls them fuck-me pumps. That's one of the reasons I bought them."

"Then I'm obliged." Words stopped. His lips traveled down her leg until his tongue found her heat and then delved inside. One finger entered her moist sex and her legs tightened as she groaned. He sucked, nipped, feasted, and then added another finger. Her cries carried through the suite and the sweet torment caused her body to finally explode. Rising up, he buried himself deeply, a loud groan sounded from his throat. With a few deep strokes his body shattered, joining hers in release.

He stayed locked deeply inside her body while their breathing slowly returned to normal. Their hands continued to journey over the other's body, his drifting down her sides and hers traveling the contours of his arms. When he tried to withdraw she tightened her hold. "I'm too heavy and you need to breathe."

"This feels so good."

"I will die this way if that is your wish."

"No, I just want you inside me."

"I'm there sweetheart and I'm not going anywhere."

Finally kissing his chest, she allowed him to pull away and shift positions. Laying her head on his chest she breathed deeply scenting the odor of their love making. Her lips replaced where her head rested and traveled downward. Each kiss had a goal, each kissed caused him to inhale deeper. "It's my turn and I want to taste you." A low groan was her answer. Cupping one of his testicles, her other hand went around the base of his erection. It tightened in her grasp and a loud growl tore from his throat. Slowly, taking him into her mouth she used her tongue to swirl and drive him crazy. Slowly, learning every inch of his silky hot length, she took him over the edge. His release was wild spice, reminding her of the taste and smell of the untamed forest of their home.

She looked up. Pure onyx burned into her eyes making her voice wobbly "I, I asked Maggie what I could do for you, so she picked out the corset and explained you would like this."

"Ah." He took a few breaths and then continued. "Remind me to send you shopping with her more often."

She smiled in relief and then wiggled from his hold and stood on the floor at the bottom of the bed. Kicking off her shoes, her wicked smile found his. "We aren't done but I need your help getting out of this contraption," her smile deepened, "Please."

Making short work of the corset, he unclasped the garters, and rolled the stockings down her legs. Lifting her into his arms and walking to the Jacuzzi, he slowly lowered them into the tepid water. He turned on warmer water to finish filling the tub and then pressed the control for the jets. Grabbing the bubble bath, he poured some in.

The jets massaged her muscles and relieved the ache brought on by her shoes. "This is heaven."

"I've just decided I'm having one put in our new house."

"Perfect. We'll get a lot of use from it if your father keeps pummeling me."

His eyelids were barely open. He leaned back and pulled her with him. "You won't have a chance to sneak in without me."

"Never." He began to massage her arms and back. She finally turned over to face him. "I love you. I never mentioned that after you told me. Thank you for taking me to the concert."

"You did well in the crowd. I'm sorry for the way it ended."

"I liked the extra excitement and I wanted to practice what I've learned in the ring."

"You are amazing." Brandt kissed her. His palms trailed over her slippery body and passion filled the room.

Much later, he said gently, "We have a full day tomorrow and should start early. We need to get your birth certificate and some other documents. Our attorney is handling everything but we have an appointment to meet him in his office first thing in the morning."

"I never want to get out of here." Her sigh was dreamy.

"You can sleep on my chest and I'll keep your head above water. I won't be responsible for your wrinkled skin tomorrow though."

"No, I'll get out, just give me a minute."

A moment later she was asleep. Picking her up, he carried her to the bed. He crawled in and fell asleep with his nose in her hair.

***

They arrived at the high-rise office building at eight the following morning. Maggie and Samson stayed outside the door while Jordan and Morris stood at the elevator.

Entering the luxurious office, Emily and Brandt sat down in large plush chairs. Once introductions were completed, the attorney, Tyler, began handing documents to Brandt. Placing her new driver's license in his wallet, he then put the other documents in a manila envelope.

They didn't stick around for chit chat. Tyler was approximately fifty years old and one of the few humans that knew their secrets. Brandt didn't know if he worked with other beastkind and didn't want to know. Their unorthodox partnership had begun many years before.

Next, Brandt took Emily on a sightseeing tour. The Botanical Gardens was their first stop and they enjoyed a walk through an oasis of flowers and greenery. Emily found it hard to hold her wolf back. She wanted to explore the sights and scents with her canine nose. Brandt told her he would bring her another time and they would sneak in at night and let their wolves run free. After lunch, he took her to Confluence Park where they visited the downtown aquarium.

It was a day filled with wonder and discovery for Emily. She grew more accustomed to human scent along with the crush of the crowds. Availing herself of Brandt's chest became more for cuddling than settling her nerves. His quirky grin proved he knew her secret.

When they returned to their suite they took a nap and woke with the rising moon.

"We can have a quiet night in the room or I can take you out on the town. I have a friend who owns a nightclub and we won't be bothered by cats but it's your choice."

Emily stretched overused muscles. "What if we compromise? We enjoy each other now and then go out."

His hands moved to her breasts.

Much later they showered and dressed. She let him choose a black skirt and off the shoulder white top for her to wear. Handing her a small box, he looked like a young boy as she peered inside. A two carat diamond solitaire pendent necklace rested on the soft velvet. It was beautiful and less ostentatious than her other piece of jewelry. Kissing the side of her neck, he connected the clasp.

Shivers trailed across her skin. "I have nothing for you and you keep giving me gifts."

"Not so, every piece of lingerie you possess is for me and I intend to unveil my next gift later this evening."

"You're sure you don't mind going out? We can stay here."

Turning her around, he placed a tender kiss to her lips. "Tonight is for you to have some fun."

Samson and Maggie stood holding up the walls when Brandt led Emily from the room.

Samson was the first to speak. "It's about time the two of you came out, we were about to leave for dinner without you. I would have had food sent up so my alpha could keep up his strength." He put his arm out for Emily but Brandt gave a low growl.

He not so gently moved Samson aside and possessively placed her hand on his forearm. "You have your own date and unless you wish to lose a limb your hands will remain off mine." Hard eyes glared.

Samson laughed loudly and winked at Emily.

They enjoyed perfectly grilled steaks. Emily ate but kept looking between Maggie and Samson. She sent a thought to Maggie practicing her newly acquired ability to single out a pack mate and send a message directly. "You would make a good couple."

"Not going to happen." Came Maggie's return thought.

Emily just grinned and replied, "But he's very sexy."

"Yes," the she-wolf said giving a covert glance to the man beside her. "But not my type."

"Not your type either baby," was Brandt's rejoinder but said out loud with a slight grin and a very direct look.

"That's not fair. You said I could communicate with other wolves privately." Emily looked at Brandt with a chagrined smile.

"You can and a lesser wolf like Sam here can't hear a word but you forget sweetheart, I'm alpha."

"What brought me into this and what's this 'lesser wolf' crap anyway?" Samson sounded mystified.

They all laughed.

"I believe you have been the butt of the ladies' jokes."

"Maggie thinks you're sexy but not her type," said Emily with a sugary sweet smile.

Samson coughed and grabbed for his water. Maggie's face went red. "Emily you will pay for this my no longer girlfriend."

At the hurt look on Emily's face, Maggie gave in. "Okay we're still friends, Sam here doesn't get choked up too often. It might have been worth my red face. Sam dear, you know I find you sexy but you're not even close to my type. I like my men gentle in the bedroom and I have no intention of fighting for dominance between your sheets."

Samson's eyes sparkled. "I'll take that as a personal challenge---dear." He drew out the one syllable word. His gaze burned into the startled eyes of his new conquest.

"I think we are finished here and it's time to head to the nightclub. Will the two of you go with us or do you need some privacy?" asked Brandt.

Two pointed glares directed themselves at their alpha and then quickly their gazes lowered. Emily couldn't help but laugh. Her mental message held promise, "Alpha indeed, when we're alone, I'll teach you to listen in on my conversations"

"I look forward to it."

Chapter 21

Curious eyes followed them when they exited the limo and walked passed humans waiting in line at the nightclub. The red cordoned off entrance opened immediately with two gigantic bouncers holding the doors. When Emily passed she noticed the men smelled odd; not cats and definitely not wolves.

She slowed but Brandt gave her a gentle nudge and whispered in her ear. "It's okay; they're bears."

They were much larger than her mate, *dangerous* her wolf warned. Their scent didn't blend with the surrounding odors of perfume and sweat given off by the humans. It wasn't bad, just different.

Emily looked around in awe trying to take in what was happening around her, feeling the excitement in the air. The music with its heavy bass vibrated across the floor. Lights flashed from the ceiling sending different color streaks over their party. They made their way to a reserved table.

A man, his dark complexion at odds with his blue eyes stood by and greeted Brandt formally. "Welcome Alpha of the Northwestern Clan. We are pleased to accommodate you." Energy rippled with his voice but his demeanor changed immediately after reciting the formal greeting and he boyishly grinned, allowing warmth to soften his features. He pulled Brandt into a tight hug before releasing him. His gaze traveled questioning to Emily. He inhaled deeply, hesitated momentarily, and then continued. "And to the alpha's mate." He brought Emily's fingers to his lips and he gazed at her appraisingly. A low grumble from Brandt made the vampire's eyes sparkle with humor. Turning, he then looked to Samson and Maggie. He shook the male wolf's hand and then swept Maggie in for a passionate kiss that lasted until a rigid hand landed on his shoulder.

"I think you've said, 'hello' long enough," Samson growled softly.

Brandt stepped between the two. Emily placed her hand on her mate's back knowing the man before them was vampire and quite deadly. "Emily," Brandt said reaching for her hand and bringing her around for a proper introduction, "This is Dmitri. He owns this establishment and is a longtime friend of mine. Obviously he is also a friend of my wolf, though I wasn't aware." His glance left Dmitri and landed on the she-wolf in question.

Maggie bristled slightly, she enjoyed the kiss and had known the vampire intimately, but that was long ago. They were now good friends. "I'm sorry Dmitri but Samson seems to think he has some say over who I have a relationship with. He has no right to be possessive."

Sam continued to stare at the vampire and muttered between gritted teeth, "Yet."

Dmitri laughed and looked between the two. "No worries from me. I can keep my hands off. It was a kiss for old times' sake; I wasn't aware she was claimed."

Incensed she-wolf eyes turned from the vampire to Samson. "I believe a union between us would end with our alpha having to find a new second in command. Wouldn't that be a shame?" Her tone dripped sarcasm while she imagined the sound of his bones breaking.

"Ah Brandt, you've always maintained a wild pack. I like my bears gentle and sweet, though they too can be a little crazed when it comes to mating."

"Come on Emily, I need the Ladies' room. I would hate to shed blood before I have a chance to dance."

Emily flashed a slight smile at the men then followed in Maggie's wake.

Brandt's eyes followed the women until they were out of sight and then turned to Samson. "I hope you know what you're doing?"

"I believe it was your mate who began this challenge. I will thank her later. That she-wolf has been in my sights for a while but getting more than a word out of her in private is impossible." His eyes turned to the vampire, "Any suggestions?"

"I wouldn't recommend talking."

"I was thinking the same thing but I kind of like my male anatomy and I'm not sure it would survive."

"Only one way to find out. Now, what would you both like to drink?"

Brandt gave an order of wine for the ladies and whisky for himself and Samson.

"Make it a bottle," said the disgruntled wolf.

Maggie pulled Emily into the bathroom, "I'm going to kill you."

Emily could only laugh. "I think he likes you."

"You don't understand. I've had a crush on him for years and he never gave me a second look. Now he has the mating scent all over him. And it's not the lasting we'll be together forever kind either. It was easier when he treated me like one of the guys."

Emily eyed Maggie's shimmery silver tank top and black leather skirt that hugged her ass, ending two inches above decent. Her arms and legs were muscled and defined. Her dark hair flowed around her face and down her back to end at the top of her hips.

"If he thinks you're one of the guys he has a problem."

"That's not the point. I'm third in command and got here by fighting my way up. I was planning to give challenge soon and now, I don't know if I can."

Emily's expression changed from cheerful to panicked, "You would kill him."

"No, only the alpha challenge is to the death. A non-alpha challenge is last wolf standing."

"Okay, so what's the problem?"

"He will break my heart. I've seen him do it to countless women. Oh, he's nice enough while he's with them but he doesn't stay around for long. I would rather not go there."

I should probably say I'm sorry, but seeing how quickly his jealousy came on, I think his attraction to you has been building for a while."

"Well aren't you suddenly the expert on men." She said with a snarky hiss but then slowly she grinned. "So maybe I should use that gorgeous body for sex and get him out of my system. If I did and then dumped him first it might work. I can kick his ass in challenge using my anger to help me through."

Emily wasn't sure what to think. They walked out of the Ladies' room and Maggie pulled her onto the dance floor. Brandt danced with her a few times at the cabin but it was to slow soothing music. This was strong, sexy, and wild all at once. Emily watched Maggie's body pulsate with the beat. She began swaying with a little less exuberance. No one seemed to be paying attention to her and she gradually let herself go. There were more women on the dance floor than men but she felt a quick tug on her hand and was whirled around to face a man she didn't know. Immediately, strong fingers grasped her hips and Brandt pulled her back against his body. The young man's eyes got huge. His hand released hers and he quickly backed away.

Using a firm grip, Brandt moved her hips provocatively against his growing erection and pressed into her bottom, all to the sexy rhythm of the music. "It won't be his nipple he loses." His words were possessive but whispered softly in her ear.

Emily tried to turn in his arms but he kept a secure hold and swayed a little more. She wiggled and moved until his low groan caused her to smile and melt further into him.

"Vixen." He said. The music changed and a slower song began. The lights dimmed and he turned her around bringing her close again. With a soft sigh, she rested her head on his shoulder.

The music continued and Emily leisurely opened her eyes, seeing Maggie and Sam dancing a short distance away. Maggie did not look happy but moved her body to the music. Sam slipped his hands lower than the she-wolf's waist and Maggie took them in hers and moved them back up. Emily caught the grin on Sam's face when the couple turned. She then closed her eyes and again drifted with the music.

Back at the table, they enjoyed their drinks and people watched for a while. A short time later Emily felt Brandt's thigh tighten against her hand.

"We're going to have some company but I don't think we need to be overly concerned, they're wolves."

Emily looked around and saw four men heading to the table. She felt a presence behind her and by scent realized it was Jordan. She kept her eyes on the advancing men and taking Brandt at his word, tried to tap down on her edginess.

Brandt removed Emily's hand from his thigh, and pulled her up next to him then dropped her hand while Maggie and Samson stood and spread out slightly. He might not perceive a threat but he was ready.

The largest of the men stopped and the other three followed suit. He was easily three inches taller than Brandt but managed to keep his eyes cast down, "My alpha, you seem to be a long way from home."

"This entire territory is my home or you wouldn't be calling me alpha." The words held lethal promise.

"We've been hearing the main clan has had a few…issues."

"I would be happy to settle any…issues quickly." There was no doubt that Brandt meant the words to be a threat.

An arm came from behind the taller man and rested a hand on his shoulder. Of the four this man was the smallest at around six feet tall. He spoke softly, "Max we don't want trouble."

Max exhaled slowly. "No---we don't but I felt it important to see which way the wind blows."

Brandt took Emily's hand in his. Without taking his eyes from the wolf in front of him, he drew her fingers to his lips and kissed them. "My mate, I would like to introduce you to Max and his brothers. They run some of our city business and have never given me reason to doubt their loyalty." His voice remained hard.

Emily's eyes went to Max's when he spoke. "And we never will my alpha, we are happy to see you mated."

"I'm not just mated. Emily is an alpha in her own right, and our clan will be much stronger with her by my side. That is the truth that needs to be passed along, not rumors."

"Yes alpha, may I greet your mate?"

Brandt stepped slightly away from Emily but relayed the protocol into her mind. "Give him your hand and react swiftly if anything feels uncomfortable to you. He wants to scent you but etiquette says it's only with your permission."

Max stepped forward and Emily put her hand out. He gently drew her fingers to his nose, breathing in deeply. His eyes closed and his nose traveled up her arm.

Emily pushed a small amount of alpha power from deep inside. It was not soothing or angry, just raw. At the same time she placed her hand on his shoulder and stopped him from going further. Using an extra burst of energy which caused a quick electrical charge to end his travels, she let the energy fill her eyes.

His opened wide. After he briefly met her gaze, his eyes lowered. With unadulterated worship in his voice he said, "Alpha, I am yours to command. I ask pardon for interrupting your evening?"

She had a slight smile on her lips when she answered, "I'm glad Brandt didn't need to kill you. I'm sure your brothers would be sad." Her voice was soft but her tone was deadly serious.

The brothers in question burst into laughter. One gave Max a robust slap on the back and pulled him away. "My man, our sadness over your death would last a few days and then we would forget you." Everyone laughed relieving the last bits of tension. The four said their goodbyes and departed.

Brandt leaned in close and whispered huskily, "You are learning my love."

Her grin was wicked. She was learning and her wolf loved nothing more than to show off.

Dmitri approached with a devilish grin of his own. "We haven't had a good brawl in here for a while. I'm surprised that went so well. Word is your pack is having difficulty."

"No longer true and just so you're aware," Brandt's eyes turned black. "There would not have been a brawl, only death."

"Then I'm glad you calmed the situation. A bar fight is easier to explain to the authorities than dead bodies. May I request a dance with your mate?"

Brandt grinned, "Ask her yourself, and if she says yes, keep your hands where I can see them."

"You've always driven a hard bargain." The vampire's gaze then landed on the she-wolf in question. He gave a slight bow. "Emily may I have this dance?"

Emily hesitated and looked to Brandt. The vampire made her nervous. Brandt's words in her mind enabled her to walk forward. "It's an honor for him to dance with you. He is my friend and you are safe."

Dmitri drew her onto the dance floor and after taking her firmly into his arms, began sweeping her across the floor. Emily had no idea what the dance was but the vampire made it effortless.

He finally whispered into her ear, "You are lovely my dear and Brandt needs you. He can be a thug sometimes but your power is growing and you will soothe his anger and balance his alpha with yours."

Emily squeezed his hand slightly. "You said your beastkind are bears? I've never seen a bear. Are they big?"

Dmitri laughed loudly. "Yes they are and someday I will let you see them in their beast forms. I think right now your mate has put up with my arms around you long enough."

Dmitri stopped suddenly and dipped her back. When he brought her up, his lips landed swiftly on her cheek and then turned her toward Brandt.

When Dmitri's lips move to his mate, Brandt stood.

Dmitri couldn't prevent his smile. "It was only on the cheek but worth the price of fire in your eyes." He thumped Brandt on the shoulder and guided Emily into her mate's embrace.

Feeling Emily back in his arms helped Brandt gain control. His heartbeat slowed and he quirked his lip at his friend. "You bastard, I owe you."

Everyone laughed and a short time later, they said farewell. During the ride to the hotel, Emily fell asleep against Brandt's shoulder. A soft kiss woke her and in their room he helped remove her clothes. They settled into sleep with their arms wrapped around each other.

Chapter 22

They left Denver the next morning to spend two days at home before leaving for Marcus and Amy's wedding. Brandt began preparations for building their new cabin and asked Emily to review the floor plans with him. Their home would sit on a piece of land half a mile behind the main house where Cheri and his father resided. After looking over the drawings for hours and making a few adjustments, they choose the layout they wanted and Brandt began making phone calls. Their new residence would be ready within six months.

They cleaned out the closet in Thomas' office so Emily's new clothes would fit. She would miss the small cramped cabin when they moved. This is where she truly grew up, fell in love, and learned about her wolf. It would always be special.

The afternoon of their return, Patricia stopped by with Kinsee and a plate of cookies. Refusing to hold back, Kinsee ran up to Emily and threw her arms around her neck. Holding her close, Emily inhaled the precious young were-child scent.

When they released each other, Kinsee began talking, "I helped bake the cookies, and my mom said you would love them. My mom told me you went away for a few days but you would come back. I stepped on a nail by my house and got an owie on my foot. My dad said I would be okay but I should be wearing shoes. You don't have any shoes on so I shouldn't need to wear shoes either. It didn't hurt that bad and shoes don't feel good on my feet. I killed a mouse this morning and ate it. It had crunchy little bones and I didn't like it much. Do you think the crunchy bones will get caught in my tummy?"

Patricia looked at Emily with a grin. "She's only just started. She's been saving all her stories and questions for your return."

Emily began commenting on Kinsee's summation of events since they last saw one another. The three of them sat on the porch and enjoyed the cookies with added milk that Emily brought outside. "These cookies are wonderful Kinsee."

"My mom said I had to be careful what I put in them and she showed me the right cup to use so they would be perfect. Do you think I'll know everything my mom knows when I grow up?"

"I think you'll be just as smart."

"My mom's having another baby, can you smell it?"

"Ahh." Emily looked at Patricia who was blushing slightly.

"Kinsee's father and I decided she needed a brother or sister."

"Is that why you smell different than before?"

"Yes and there is no keeping this secret from the pack. I guess you've never smelled it until now. My scent changed almost from the moment of conception."

"But I thought…" Emily stopped not wanting to ask about the human seed needed to create a child and her face reddened.

Brandt stepped out on the porch but she couldn't mistake the hurt she saw on his face though his voice was firm. "You thought right Emily and some wolves decide to have children despite knowing what it takes."

His hand feathered possessively through her hair.

Patricia took Kinsee's hand. "We need to go. I've been tired lately and soon I'll switch to wolf form so the baby comes faster. We will visit again after you return from your new journey."

Kinsee pulled her hand from her mother's and ran at Emily. "When you get back, will you take me to chase rabbits?"

"Yes sweetie, I promise."

Kinsee ran off trailing her mother and Emily smiled while listening to the fading chatter of the little girl.

Strong arms scooped her off her feet and carried her into the cabin, straight to the bed. Brandt made quick work of their clothes and followed Emily down on the soft mattress. Placing both her hands in one of his, he stretched them above her head using a steel grip to hold them in place. He kissed her with incredible need, running his tongue on the inside of her lips before sinking further into the kiss.

When at last he pulled away, his eyes were dark. "I would give you a child if I could but I will never let another man touch you. I'm sorry but I can't. Patricia's husband, Wolfred, has more strength than I do. I would kill the man that laid hands on you."

Again taking her mouth, his hand traveled her body until she squirmed and he released her so her hands were able to travel their own path.

When their breathing settled, Emily's soft voice reached his ear, "I love you, and no one else will ever touch me."

He held her close. Her breathing slowed and then took on the steady rhythm of sleep. His troubled eyes remained open.

***

The following day consisted of preparing for their trip. They packed the bridal couple's gift that Emily and Maggie purchased while in the city. That night they ate dinner with Thomas and Cheri. Brandt and Cheri discussed Marcus' clan. Ivan's disappearance was affecting everyone. Emily knew the cats and their vampire queen murdered Ivan's wife. Her own newly mated heart mourned for the devastated wolf.

"Can Columbus hold the clan without his father?" asked Cheri.

"I believe so. I didn't see him much when I was there but Ivan told me he was coming into his alpha and it was best to keep him away or in his young stupidity he might challenge. There's another son showing signs of alpha tendencies too. I can only hope his bond with his brother will keep him from doing something foolish."

"I've also heard they have a cat living with them and nursing the babies."

Thomas joined in at this point, "That should be interesting. Most of the cats scattered after losing their queen. I'm aware of the group you recently ran into but Cheri told me there was no sign of a vampire. They must find one or longevity will no longer be theirs though that would make life much easier for us."

"I'll drink to that." Cheri tipped her wine glass to her lips and took a sip. She then turned to Emily. "Are you ready to meet another clan?"

"I think so. I feel sadness over the loss of Ivan's mate." Emily looked to Brandt.

Brandt took her hand and kissed each of her fingers. "No more sadness at the table. How about a game of pool?"

"I don't know how to play."

"Oh, but it will be so much fun to teach you."

They carried their drinks into the large game room. Thomas grabbed another bottle of wine and they settled in to show Emily how to play.

She soon discovered why Brandt suggested it. His body bent over hers and he ground his hips into her soft bottom while adjusting her arms and hands to hold the pool cue. She could smell his mating scent and enjoyed wiggling her bottom against him.

"Stop that you two. We are going to start and finish this game if it kills us." Cheri insisted.

Brandt took a step away from Emily and put his hands up. "I know I'm strong enough to hold out."

"Humph," was Emily's short rebuke. She played the game horribly but took every opportunity to rub against Brandt's body when she walked past him. If his hands reached for her, she skipped away and gave him a stern look. They made it through three games before calling it a night.

"Can Brandt bring me here to practice so I can learn to play better?"

Cheri eyed Brandt, "Yes, but I'll be surprised if you get any practice in." They all laughed and the evening broke up.

Later, while lying in Brandt's arms Emily could feel his distress. "What's wrong?"

He kissed her hair, "I love you, and I won't let you go."

She turned to him, "I'm not going anywhere, and in Kinsee's words, you're being silly."

He brought her body closer and they made love one last time before falling asleep.

Chapter 23

Emily's apprehension with flying wasn't what it was the first trip and she was able to look out the window and enjoy the mountain scenery on the way to the wedding. Mandy chattered non-stop in the seat beside her with Caleb sitting by Mandy. Sampson and Maggie were also part of their entourage along with four pieces of muscled eye candy, which was the idiom Mandy passed on to Emily when seeing the men for the first time. Mandy's parents requested Emily keep a close eye on her sister due to her penchant for trouble. They were hoping she didn't find her mate for several years but after she was twenty-one, destiny could take its course.

Mandy and Caleb asked about her trip to Denver and they spent the journey talking about music and shopping.

Mandy educated Emily on pop artists and their music, "I love Adele, and I listen to her songs over and over."

Their brother's annoyed voice broke into the discussion, "Yes scamp, I can attest to that. I'm embarrassed that I know all the words and if I never hear another of her songs I'll be a happy man." Caleb ducked his head avoiding his sister's fist.

They obviously practiced this ritual often and Emily couldn't help but feel sad because she missed so many years of what the two of them shared.

Brandt, noticing her melancholy, leaned forward and kissed the back of her neck. Just his gentle touch changed her mood again and her and her siblings went back to speaking about every subject under the sun.

Comforting his mate was instinctual and Brandt didn't miss a beat as he continued his quiet conversation with Samson.

His second in command was fascinated with Emily's progress. "I had little hope this would work the night you found her."

"It was her blood, my wolf knew before I did."

"I can't believe how much she's learned these past weeks and how much control she's gained."

"Her mind is a sponge and she questions everything. She spends time at Cheri's watching television and she's captivated with human politics. My dad is thrilled and they've begun arguing about everything from financial breakdown to current government elections. A more boring topic I can't imagine but she eats up the knowledge. Her alpha is gaining power but I know she's been incredibly strong her entire life. She shouldn't have survived her mother and all the years of isolation with her sanity intact."

"Who would have thought Malcolm could beget an alpha female? He would have killed her once he knew."

"I agree, but that problem was eliminated many years ago. I only hope there are no more Emily's out there. I doubt they could retain their sanity and not go feral. The control it took in not killing her mother for nineteen years is more impressive than the deed itself."

"Does it bother her?"

"The woman was crazy and began speaking of Emily's death. I'm wondering if that's what brought her alpha to the forefront. Even though the woman deserved to die Emily mourns her. She hasn't touched her art supplies and I'm okay if she never uses them but I'd love to know what she would choose to draw."

Mandy giggled each time Brandt leaned forward and kissed Emily's neck or touched her hair. Caleb rolled his eyes, the entire mating thing being a complete mystery. He would leave soon for the military. He was a young male werewolf and his sometimes chaotic control and the urge to fight were intensifying.

The plane touched down and then they enjoyed the mountain scenery on a thirty minute drive to the ranch house in the northern Arizona hills. The surrounding mountains were a different green and the pine trees weren't as dense but the beauty was undeniable.

Columbus, the current alpha, and a few of his wolves met them upon their arrival at the main house. The sun was beginning to set and Marcus and Amy would awaken soon.

Brandt hugged Columbus in a tight embrace. "Have you heard from your father?"

"Yes, a few weeks ago. He's not coming for the wedding and he wasn't very forthcoming with information on his whereabouts or how he's spending his time, but he's alive."

Brandt released him and drew Emily to his side. "This is Columbus, Alpha of the Southwest Clan and son to my good friend Ivan. This is my mate Emily."

Before she could say hello his arms circled her and the world spun. Her feet left the ground and her head whirled for a moment after the big oaf finally released her.

Smirking, Columbus laughed at the ferocity in Brandt's eyes. "I heard the stories of your last visit and how you played with fire by tormenting Marcus. Payback is a beautiful bitch," he said moving his eyes to Emily. Slowly while leering intensely his gaze traveled suggestively over her body.

"Oomph." A solid fist to his stomach cured his laughter. The punch didn't come from Brandt, but from the female alpha he manhandled.

Emily's scent fanned through the air while her gaze never wavered from her less than gentlemanly target, "I believe the proper protocol is to maintain eye contact with another alpha."

When Columbus could finally breathe again, a devilish grin appeared on his face. "I believe you are correct in etiquette and I apologize, Emily, alpha and mate to the alpha of the Northwestern Clan." He made a short formal bow his eyes never leaving hers.

Brandt wasn't worried about Emily's sudden vehemence. Columbus deserved it and wouldn't hold a grudge. Fighting back laughter he introduced Mandy and Caleb. Columbus kissed them both on the cheek and welcomed them to his home.

They strolled into the house and made their way to the bedrooms assigned to them. Brandt pulled Emily into his arms once the door shut and Columbus' footsteps in the hallway faded. "Please feel free to punch any male that gets out of hand. If you don't, I will though I won't be quite so gentle." His mouth nibbled on hers.

Emily pulled away with a grin. "It wasn't gentle. I felt a crack and I'm surprised he was able to walk without showing pain."

"He would never show pain in front of another alpha. He'll visit Marcus and heal quickly but I'm proud of you. I was a naughty boy when I was here last and Columbus was just pushing my buttons."

"He can push your buttons all he wants but his eyes had better remain above my chest."

Brandt laughed and resumed their kiss but raised his head a few seconds later. "Marcus and Amy should be downstairs. Let's go."

He took her hand and guided her down two flights of stairs to the large gathering room. His gaze landed on Amy. She was more beautiful than he remembered. He had not seen her since she became vampire and now a menacing power surrounded her.

Not wanting his bones broke by his mate he gave Amy a brief hug and then shook Marcus' hand. He then gave Emily a reassuring smile and made introductions.

Marcus brought her hand to his lips for a kiss and then inhaled deeply; his eyes momentarily turning amber from the scent of Emily's power. He slowly released her and met Brandt's satisfied gaze, "Congratulations on finding your mate. She will strengthen Cheri's clan and add joy to your life."

Amy hugged Emily tightly. "Forgive Marcus; he believes formalities must be observed. I'm trying to get him over his boring habits." She winked at Emily and then gave a slight shriek when Marcus jerked her off balance pulling her in close for a heart stopping kiss.

Columbus stood by silently though he did roll his eyes at the display of affection his pack put up with continually.

A new voice challenged from the front door. "Aren't you past the kissy-kissy stage yet Marcus? It's been months and the rest of us shouldn't have to put up with your constant exhibition of sexual play."

Nicolas, the Eastern pack alpha, was standing in the entry hall.

Emily stared unable to take her eyes off the new wolf. Where Brandt and Columbus held their alpha power tightly in check unless needed, sizzling energy leached from Nicolas' pores consuming the room. He stood over six feet tall, lean, but muscular. Dimples appeared with his grin though his gray eyes took in the room with deadly intensity. Marcus told her of his friend but failed to mention he was drop dead gorgeous.

Brandt, knowing the effect Nicolas had on women, pulled Emily close keeping her out of the other alpha's arms. This was his gentle way of reminding her who she belonged to and taking her focus off the conceited scoundrel.

"A little possessive I see." Nicolas said with his devilish knowing grin.

Brandt loosened his hold slightly, "No, my mate will get over your pretty boy looks soon enough. She cracked a few of Columbus' ribs earlier and she has my blessing to break your nose."

Nicolas' sensual laugh filled the room. He knew not to push the newly mated pair too far but he would enjoy giving a nudge here and there at his friend's expense. His eyes went from Brandt to his she-wolf. "Warning heeded." Nicolas reached for Emily's hand and gently squeezed her fingers. "It's a pleasure to meet the woman who tamed Brandt. I'm sure Columbus was pleased too."

Columbus came forward and gave Nicolas a brotherly hug. "I was lucky; Amy took pity on me and was willing to help heal my injuries." His eyes met Emily's. "For shame though, that was our secret. I didn't think you realized what you had done."

"Thomas taught me how to stop inappropriate wolf behavior. You made a good practice session."

The entire room filled with laughter and conversation flowed allowing the pack alphas to solidify their friendships. Finally, Marcus announced that dinner was ready. More pack wolves entered through the front door. They all made their way toward the double doors of the dining room.

Emily didn't immediately understand why everyone stopped but then the beastkind odor hit her nostrils. It was familiar and a woman standing in the back of the room was slowly making her way to the opposite door.

"Cat," growled one of the wolves.

The female let out a terrified whimper.

A man suddenly pushed Emily forward trying to get past her. With no hesitation her hands grabbed material and muscle. Using little effort she tossed the offending wolf against the wall and sprang forward placing herself between werewolves and the frightened cat.

Amy was suddenly beside Emily and reached her hand back to reassure the cowering woman. "Thank you Emily for your help. Zenya is part of this household and nurse to the babies. If anyone has a problem with that I ask you to leave immediately. A car will return you to the airport. If anyone hurts what is mine, I," she looked at the protective she-wolf beside her, "or Emily will kill you."

Nicolas picked his unhappy wolf up from the floor. "Go to the car, you are returning to our home and don't let me see you for a while or we will finish this--- discussion alone."

Head down, but with angry strides, the man walked out.

Nicolas softened his voice, "I am sorry my dear. We are all surprised at the beauty before us and one of my wolves lost his head. I think one of Brandt's wolves had the dubious honor at our last gathering." His steady alpha power turned into a soothing stream. "Are you joining us for dinner?"

For maybe the first time in his life his effect on women missed its mark.

The she-cat gave him a quick discourteous glare and then lowered her eyes back to the floor. "Nn-no, I was helping to set the table. I must get back to the children." She rushed swiftly from the room."

"Well Marcus, you never cease to amaze me," said Brandt. He placed his arm around Emily's troubled shoulders and kissed her gently sending a calming message to her mind. "It's okay. We would not allow her to be hurt."

The anxiety in Emily's eyes slowly faded. He pulled out two chairs keeping their fingers laced while they sat down.

Everyone else was finding their own seat at the oversized clan table. The additional pack wolves made their way to the kitchen. They had been here before and knew there was a great meal waiting and an opportunity to catch up with their allied friends.

Emily whispered back into Brandt's mind, "I felt her terror and the anger coming from some of the wolves."

Brandt squeezed her hand gently his pulsing waves of soothing energy continuing.

Marcus stood and acknowledged the gathered clans. "I know that our having a cat here in the house is slightly unorthodox but she has nursed the cubs since Alba died. She now belongs to Amy and me and is under our full protection. She has a gentle soul and she's seen too much tragedy, her own child murdered before her eyes. She would die for Sierra and Roland. Please give her space. She has many adjustments to make, but is becoming accustomed to our clan. She shouldn't be upset or she might lose her nursing ability and the babies would suffer." He paused for a moment to let his message sink in, and then continued. "I want to thank each of you for coming to our wedding." He took Amy's hand and she rose from her chair and stood beside him. "I know we usually only meet for naming ceremonies but Amy's friends could not be here due to her recent transformation and I wanted our extended family to make her welcome. We will not let a young naïve wolf ruin our gathering. This is a time for celebration." He kissed Amy gently on the lips and they took their seats.

Dinner began and chatter soon filled the air. Caleb was talking to a young wolf from Nicolas' pack and the two seemed to hit it off. Mandy sat to the right of Emily and whispered into her ear, "I have never seen or smelled a cat before. It was different than I expected but not bad, the poor thing." Only taking a slight breath she continued, "I can't wait to see the twins. When Patricia's cub is born, I'm going to help her with Kinsee. A baby werewolf is a handful. They are always into mischief and must be constantly watched." Mandy took a breath and then a dreamy quality entered her voice, "Nicolas is a god. What I would give to kiss his feet and more."

Emily momentarily choked on her wine. Mandy and mischief went hand in hand. Her thoughts went to the cubs upstairs. It was hard for her to eat and she had to fight the urge to search them out. Again, she felt Brandt's sadness and for the first time fully realized its cause. Her arms ached for a child and he could never give her one. Her sadness blended with his.

He squeezed her hand and spoke into her mind again. "When we are finished with dinner, I will take you to see the twins."

Her fingers tightened on his. She had never known love and she loved him with all her heart. They finished dinner and the younger wolves decided to take a run together. Emily sent Caleb and Mandy off with a warning, "Watch your sister. Your mother and father will never forgive me if she finds trouble."

They were out the door before she could continue the lecture.

Marcus invited Brandt, Emily, and Nicolas to join him and Amy on the couches arranged in the side room away from the table. Amy gave Marcus a kiss on the cheek. "I'm going to take Emily up to the nursery to properly meet Zenya and the babies."

Brandt barely looked their way when the two women left the room. "I love you," whispered into her mind. She returned the sentiment but smiled sadly without looking back.

Chapter 24

Squeals sounded as they drew closer to the room. Amy opened the door and two beautiful naked babies rolled on the floor trying to avoid tickles from their nurse. Their bodies round and chubby with light unblemished skin and curly light brown hair were enchanting.

Both turned at the sound of the door and their eyes brightened at the sight of Amy. Then, noticing the stranger, they instantly shifted to their wolf forms and scampered under one of the two cribs. Two inquisitive black noses stuck out and watched Emily enter the room.

Going to her knees, Emily sat beside Zenya and spoke gently to the she-cat. "Hi Zenya, I am also new to this world and in need of friends. I know of no differences between the cats and wolves. I just want friends that will care for me and allow me to care about them."

Zenya smiled shyly and raised her eyes briefly to Emily's. Sierra chose that instance to fly out from under the crib and give Emily a small nip before running back to her brother's side.

"Sierra, you know better than that. Emily is our guest and you will spend time in the time-out room if you do it again. Come out here at once. You too Roland," said a stern sounding Amy.

Both pups made their way from their hiding place. Roland sniffed his nose against Emily's finger that rested on the floor. She slowly raised her hand to scratch behind his ear. His sister immediately pushed him away and squeezed in closer.

"You need to watch that one Emily. She's a bully and every member of this clan spoils her rotten. She's so bad we had to come up with a suitable punishment and we send her to the timeout room daily. Roland is wiser and learns from his mistakes." Now Amy's voice was chiding but her eyes twinkled.

Emily didn't want to know what the timeout room was. She was afraid it would be small, cold, and solitary like her own prison had been. Pushing away these thoughts, she gave Sierra the desired ear scratch and used her other hand to rub Roland. He rolled onto his back so his rounded belly was showing and Emily's hand sank into the baby soft fur scratching gently.

Sierra ran to the corner of the room, pushed a soccer ball out, and sent it in Emily's direction. Her intention to get attention away from her brother was clear.

"You are a new friend and these two have never known an enemy." Amy turned and smiled at Zenya with appreciation.

Zenya glanced up. Gold cat eyes filled with trust and love looked back at the vampire.

Emily was amazed.

Zenya turned back to the babies and joined in the impromptu ball game. The pups scampered and fought each other over the right to push the ball back to the two women. Laughter and small growls rang throughout the room and Amy joined in.

Emily pushed the ball away but was surprised when two balls of reddish-brown fur flew her way, pushing her to her back. Joyous giggles tumbled out while the pups began licking her face. She settled her hands on the wolf cubs and snuggled them in close.

Brandt entered the room and his heart froze in his chest. Emily needed a child and he couldn't give her one or allow another man to do it. He stood and watched as the pups exuberantly cleaned Emily's cheeks of tears caused by her laughter.

Before Brandt could close the door, she looked up and met his eyes. His pain was palpable and her heart clinched.

He quietly walked away.

Ten minutes later, it was time for the pups to go to bed and Emily had the honor of granting a kiss to each snout before they lay down in their cribs. Zenya had a room with a private door connected to the nursery. She smiled shyly and kissed Emily's hand before leaving.

After Amy closed the nursery door Emily asked, "How much time do they spend in wolf form and how much in human?"

"They are able to do more in wolf form and they are less defenseless. Their human legs carry them slowly and four is much easier. After their mother died it took them a week to change back to wolf. They were unsettled and preferred to be the infants they are. Have you discussed children with Brandt?"

"We aren't having children." Emily's voice was final.

"I'm not sure how Ivan handled it. He and Alba had a total of eight children though two sets were twins. The cat's queen killed their first twins. I don't know how Ivan was able to let Alba mate with other men. I would not allow it with Marcus even if it was our only chance at having children. I feel for you. I have the babies and they fill my life. Vampires cannot have children and I really never wanted any. Sierra and Roland changed that. If I could have a litter I would. Let's rejoin the men and see what trouble they've gotten themselves into."

Emily tried not to think of Amy's words but her heart broke over the thought of never having a baby. She wouldn't ask it of Brandt and she never wanted another man's hands on her regardless. There would be no babies for them.

The men were getting drunk. Amy and Emily joined them for a few glasses of wine before they went to their separate rooms.

Later, Brandt entered their private bathroom and took a quick shower. He didn't invite Emily to join him. Saddened, she removed her clothes and crawled into the strange bed alone. Brandt walked out of the bathroom and turned off the bedroom light before getting beneath the sheet. She could smell the soap he used to wash himself and the scent of his wet hair. His strong arms pulled her to his body and he guided her mouth to his. The kiss went from needy to fierce. He didn't say a word while he eagerly explored her body. The exquisite torture continued. His hands and mouth played her body long into the night eliciting moans of frustration followed by screams of pleasure.

Sated and exhausted her hands came up and she placed them gently on his cheeks. "I can live without a child but I can't live without you. I don't want you to feel pain for what cannot be. Patricia's child will be here soon and I will get all the hugs, kisses, and licks I can take. Be happy with me Brandt. You make me feel like I'm your entire world. Don't be sad. You rescued me from death and made all my dreams come true. You are my world." Tears spilled over her lashes and Brandt held her throughout the night.

***

The following day they took four wheelers out and toured the southern end of the property. Emily held on to Brandt's waist feeling the rush of adrenaline while he went crazy on the ATV. She screamed but urged him to go faster. He finally pulled over and quirked a devilish grin her way ruffling her windblown hair. "Would you care to drive my fearless lady?"

"Nope, I just want to hold on."

"As my lady desires." He took off again through the trees.

That night, they walked several miles to a large pit. It was similar in size to the ring Brandt's pack used though recessed approximately ten feet into the ground.

Wolves began issuing challenges and the first two jumped into the pit.

Emily's hand gripped Brandt's arm.

"This isn't to the death. It's only for fun though it does get a touch bloody."

"Will you fight?"

"No, the last thing we want is two alphas fighting one another. Our challenges are to the death. It's ingrained through the magic which courses within our bodies. When we get in the ring, only one wolf survives."

"Then I won't be challenged."

"Not unless someone has a death wish."

"You're so sure I could win."

"I know you would win but have no fear your challenger would die; win or lose."

A wolf from Marcus' clan challenged Samson. Fur, flesh, and blood flew as rippled muscle and razor sharp teeth caused painful damage. The match was a draw.

Emily asked about Samson's challenger.

"That's Ivan's youngest son Asia. He's also beginning to show alpha behavior. It will either make the southwestern clan stronger or tear it apart. It all depends how much the brothers love each other and how good they are at controlling their wolf. Marcus is going to have his hands full. Let's hope Columbus is half the leader his father was."

"Ivan could control the situation?"

"I have no doubt. Ivan is the only wolf who could possibly take me in a challenge though I don't count out Nicolas. I think I could take him though." Brandt knew Nicolas had come up behind them and heard his last words. He knew the thump on his back was coming and let it land. "So the truth bothers you?"

"My young man," said Nicolas, "if we could fight without it being a death match I would challenge though I would hate leaving this pretty lady without her mate. But then again, she could live with me while you become a distant memory."

Brandt's fist shot out and struck Nicolas' ribcage though it wasn't a hard blow. "How about we race to decide the outcome so we can both go home when it's over? Loser buys the beer for the next naming ceremony."

"You're on. Around the house and then back here should give me time to leave your ass in my dust."

Both men began disrobing and the other wolves started heckling the alphas. Brandt gave Emily a kiss before he shifted and then a big slurp after. She couldn't help but laugh and was happy to see Brandt's good mood return. She grabbed the ruff of his neck and said loudly, "If you lose, I might need to choose a better alpha."

He answered with a low growl and then the two were off. It was several miles to the ranch. Emily had no idea how long it would take to complete the race and her excitement grew. Bets began flying and Emily couldn't help herself, she put $100 on Brandt. She didn't have the money but knew Brandt would give it to her if he lost. It would serve him right.

The minutes ticked by but the laughter and jokes went on. Finally, they could hear crashing through the trees. Nicolas was in the lead by a head but Brandt put on a last burst of speed and crossed the finish line first. Both wolves were panting and trying to catch their breath.

Emily walked over and put her arms around her mate. "You had me worried there for a moment but you won me some money so I'm happy."

Brandt changed to his human shape and pulled Emily into his naked sweat-soaked body. The surrounding wolves whistled and shouted. Emily knew she was blushing but she leaned forward and gave Brandt a well-deserved kiss.

"Get a room," said a disgruntled Nicolas with a slight smile.

Standing, Brandt picked up his mate. He didn't say a word just began walking back to the house.

A loud voice called out, "Now they'll keep us up again tonight. I thought Marcus and Amy were bad."

Chapter 25

The day of the wedding arrived. The house and front yard were prepared for the reception but the wedding itself would take place in the gazebo by the pond. The sun finally went down and twinkling lights appeared throughout the yard.

Emily stopped to admire the work they had done throughout the long day. She hadn't slept much the night before and a blush covered her cheeks. A pair of strong arms came around her from behind. She sank backward into Brandt and then turned to give him a brief kiss. "I must get upstairs and help Amy dress."

"I know, I just wanted to say hi," he replied in a low sexy voice.

She quickly gave him another soft kiss and headed to the house. Approaching Amy's room, she could hear giggles and laughter coming from inside. She knocked on the door.

"Come in Emily." Amy said in a voice filled with happiness.

The twins were on the bed naked in their human forms. The day before, Amy explained it was impossible to keep clothing on beastkind children until their third year when the word "appropriate" sunk in. She said it usually took the entire year for them to understand the true meaning.

The soon to be bride looked up from her game of patty-cake, "Zenya will be here to get them in a moment. They will have a quiet dinner in their room and then it's off to bed."

Roland stood on wobbly legs and suddenly launched himself at Emily. In midflight he changed to his wolf form. She was surprised but managed to catch the little hellion.

Sierra tried to do the same but Amy held her back. "No you don't, she only has two arms, and you would land on the floor."

The angry baby she-wolf began to wail and with perfect timing, Zenya entered. Gathering the twins into her arms, she quickly removed them from the room.

Mandy arrived and the women helped one another with their hair. Emily followed Amy's directions closely. The first dress out of the closet was for Emily. It was a beautiful shimmery gown in royal blue.

"Brandt sent me your measurements and I had it made for you. I asked Zenya to be my maid of honor but she told me she couldn't handle it yet. I'm hoping you will stand with me for the ceremony."

Emily's huge smile was her answer. The next dress was a lighter shade of blue and fit Mandy perfectly.

It was then time to get Amy into her dress. Yards and yards of white silk, the back, cut low had thin strips of material to hold it together, it was exquisite. The front became sheer lace a micrometer above her nipples.

"I chose this for Marcus. It will drive him crazy tonight and I plan on partying for hours. I will only get married once."

A knock at the bedroom door interrupted the women. Emily opened it slightly and saw an unfamiliar man standing on the other side in a dark tuxedo similar to the one Brandt was wearing. From his scent she knew he was a wolf and the smell was somehow familiar. Before she could ask questions, a female hand wrenched the door completely open from behind her and Amy threw herself into the wolf's arms.

"Oh my god Ivan, you're here. I didn't think you would come."

Ivan held the vampire gently rubbing her back.

She finally eased away and looked up into haunted alpha eyes. "Have you seen the babies?"

"No, I'll do that tomorrow and then I'll be gone. I'm sorry but I am only here to give away the bride. My scallywag son may be alpha but it's my right."

Amy fought tears and then hugged him tighter.

His sad eyes looked over Amy's shoulder and gazed at Emily. He may have passed the reins to his son but this man would always be an alpha.

Brandt walked up behind the bride.

"It's time; I thought I would walk my mate and her sister down the stairs."

Emily and Mandy smiled with gratitude. Ivan and Amy stepped aside and Brandt took Emily's hand and brought it to his lips, "You are exquisite," came his whispered words.

A gentle shove against his shoulder from Amy made him laugh.

"You are supposed to compliment the bride."

He took her hand and gallantly pulled it to his lips. "You are the most beautiful bride I have ever seen."

A sigh from Mandy and he looked her way. "You are too beautiful for your own good, and I won't let you out of my sight."

Everyone laughed and they made their way downstairs for the wedding. It was a joyous night with love and laughter ringing throughout the house. Thankfully the fights the night before took the edge off the wolves and everyone was on their best behavior.

The only mishap was when Ivan requested to sleep in the babies' room. Zenya quietly disappeared. Her terrified scent left a trail behind her but Ivan showed no awareness. They all hoped he would change his mind about leaving but the next morning he was gone.

With the celebration over, the line of vehicles began to clear out one after the other. Columbus was there to see everyone off, while Marcus and Amy slept through the day. At the small airstrip, Brandt and Nicolas said their farewells and their packs separated into two jets.

Emily, Mandy, and Caleb slept the entire flight home. Emily hadn't seen much of Caleb after their arrival and she hoped he had stayed out of trouble. Her thoughts faded and sleep took over.

Strong arms lifted her drowsy body from the seat and carried her from the plane.

She and Brandt were the first to disembark. He took several steps down the stairs but suddenly turned his back, his arms loosening and then he tried to throw Emily back into the plane.

All hell broke loose and loud popping noises came from every direction.

Emily could feel the impact to Brandt's body as bullets pummeled his back.

Samson appeared at the plane's door and reached for her and Brandt.

Suddenly she felt herself falling when someone below the stairs pulled her feet out from under her. She landed hard on the tarmac and saw Samson grab Brandt and lift him into the plane.

Maggie managed to get past Samson and jump off the stairs. She landed a few yards from Emily but couldn't stop the first dart that entered Brandt's mate. A gun, with true bullets not darts, changed its site when the furious female alpha refused to go down.

Maggie didn't think. She launched herself high and landed on Emily, her stunned eyes, showed pain and then slowly faded to nothingness while bullets continued to strike her body.

Emily fought the effects but the drugs went to work on her nervous system. She was unable to do anything but watch when they heaved Maggie's body off her. The incredibly brave she-wolf was dead and Emily didn't know if her mate was alive. Her screams were deafening and she went wild trying to rise. Something hard landed against the back of her skull and her world went black.

***

The room was dark. She couldn't help the groan that escaped her lips and her eyes struggled to adjust. Thoughts of the attack at the airport filled her mind; Maggie's lifeless eyes and her last glimpse of Brandt when Sampson dragged his unresisting body into the plane.

Brandt couldn't be dead, she would feel it. Slowly she began taking inventory of her body and realized thick chains held her restrained. She panicked as the nightmare became real and the memories of her basement prison filled her mind. She wasn't aware she was screaming until the light flashed on.

The door flew open and two men entered. Emily didn't know who they were but by their scent knew they were cats.

One of the men walked immediately over to her.

The blow to her stomach caused intense pain and the air left her lungs.

"Shut the fuck up bitch," said the angry voice of the man who hit her.

The other man checked the chains holding her to a metal bedframe. Emily could feel some kind of straps beneath her and knew she wasn't on a mattress. After much needed air entered her lungs, her eyes met those of her attacker. Her fear was gone and only cold rage remained.

"My mate will kill you." She put every ounce of loathing she had into the words.

"No, your mate will see you die," said the man obviously in charge. He walked to the door and called into the next room, "Fredock, bring the camera."

Emily had no idea what was going on but if Brandt was able to see her die, he must be alive. Her joy was short lived.

The man named Fredock came into the room with a handheld video camera, "It's recording my alpha." He then pointed it at her.

Emily had no idea what they intended. The first blow hit her jaw and blood sprayed the wall. The second strike found her breast but no screams left her throat. She would not give them additional satisfaction and though she couldn't get away she did what Brandt commanded weeks before and let her wolf take over.

Time stood still and pain coursed through her body. Blood now slid down the walls. One eye, only able to see a small sliver of the room, watched the gun barrel lift and move toward her.

"I love you Brandt." She knew she hadn't said the words out loud but that was all that passed through her mind when the first bullet struck her chest. It didn't hurt until the second shot sounded. Slowly, her world went black and the pain faded at last.

***

Black agony, helplessness, and rage consumed her. Her blood; sticky, tangy, and dripping from her body onto the floor caused her mind to float. She knew she was dying, should already be dead. Tears squeezed out between her eyelids though they were swollen completely shut. Brandt would see the video. It would kill him slowly. Her world faded.

"Emily!"

It was Brandt's voice yelling in her mind. She knew she was dreaming and a smile formed on her swollen split lips but the darkness continued to close in.

"Emily damn you, don't stop fighting! God damn it don't." With those words, Emily revived enough to hear noises coming from outside the door. The solid wood disintegrated but Emily heard nothing more.

The next time she woke, a soft mattress pressed into her back, and when she tried to lift her head, arms instead of chains held her down. Red burning agony allowed her to take only shallow breaths. Pain traveled her body.

"Shhhh my love, breathe slowly."

She felt Brandt's lips kiss the inside of her hand. One of her eyes wouldn't open at all but with the other she made out a large shadow over Brandt's shoulder and terror made her draw in a sharp agonizing breath.

Brandt stepped back and Dmitri was there. His teeth sank into her arm before she had time to register that Brandt was safe. Darkness descended once more.

Chapter 26

Emily felt someone squeeze her hand and jumbled gibberish changed to voices that formed sentences in her brain. Struggling past the fuzz in her mind, she opened her eyes. Brandt, Mandy, and Caleb surrounded her bed. Her mate held her hand but Mandy's head gently came down to rest on Emily's shoulder and her tears quickly soaked the light sheet covering Emily's body.

"It's okay," she slurred past her dry and cracked lips. Her vision and comprehension slowly increased and she saw her brother take Mandy by the shoulders gently pulling her away. He gave Emily's hand a squeeze and walked his crying sister from the room.

The intense pain was now a memory and she could breathe normally with only a slight twinge.

Brandt lowered his head to her shoulder and inhaled deeply. She could feel a tremor run through his body. Her arm finally cooperated and she was able to rest her hand on his back.

His low and husky voice clogged with unshed tears murmured. "I love you so much. I was afraid you left me."

Emily couldn't hold back tears. She thought she had lost him too.

His kisses began on her neck and cheek then moved to her forehead and hair. He finally lifted his head, brought her fingers to his lips, and kissed each one slowly, never taking his gaze from hers.

Emily smiled through her tears.

Brandt divested himself of his clothing, climbed into bed, and gathered her body close to his.

She dreaded asking but needed to know. "Tell me what happened."

Brandt took a deep steadying breath. "We were attacked. Two vampires accompanied by more than fifty cats attacked the chateau and we believe approximately a dozen cats hit the plane simultaneously. It was well organized and meant to wipe us out."

"Maggie's dead." It wasn't a question though she had to know the worst. "Was anyone else killed?"

"We lost ten in all. My dad was severely injured, but will be okay. Two vampires tried unsuccessfully to stop Cheri and did keep her from getting to the plane when I sent a distress call."

"Why did they take me then attempt to kill me so quickly?"

"I think their original intention was to take you alive and kill me. When their attempt on me failed, they knew our mate link would lead us straight to them once you woke and they had to act fast. I lost consciousness when Samson pulled me into the plane. I could kill him for leaving you behind. I may kill him still."

"You know he saved you and Maggie did her job too." Tears slowly made their way down her cheeks. She looked around the room and recognized the décor and scent. It was the same hotel they stayed at when they came to the city to shop. "Why did Dmitri help?"

"Cheri is at the chateau with my father and other injured wolves but primarily she's there if we're attacked again. The cats transported you to the city. Dmitri is our friend. He and his bears took up residence on this floor for your protection. I think even Dmitri is a little spooked and it's safer if we keep our allies close. I'm sorry but I have more to tell you."

By his tone, Emily knew she didn't want to hear and closed her eyes to avoid his look of heart wrenching devastation.

Brandt's hand squeezed hers tightly and he took a deep breath. "Nicolas' pack is gone. They're all dead, even Franklin the clan leader."

Emily's tears fell harder and tremors laced her words, "Nicolas?"

"We haven't located his body but we have little hope that he's alive. We think they did to him what they did to you. We can't spare people to look for him right now but soon."

"What about Marcus and Amy," her heart stopped, "and the babies?"

"They weren't attacked. We think the cats didn't want to risk attacking a clan with two vampires although we know they were next. They thought they had a better chance of success by hitting Cheri and Franklin's clans first. They were right. They had two vamps on the team that hit Franklin and they managed to kill him quickly. Once he was gone, the vampires and cats killed everyone. They attacked Nicolas' airplane simultaneously like ours. The cat pride had four vampires total. Cheri killed one and more than twenty cats died."

"How could they do this?"

Brandt's teeth clenched and his jaw tightened. "We have no doubt there are traitors supplying them with information. We were all at the ranch for the wedding and we think Zenya gave them our flight schedule."

Instantly, Emily's voice became angry, "She wouldn't do that. She loves those babies and she loves Amy. I saw it with my own eyes. Is she okay?"

"Amy and Marcus feel the same way you do. I'm not convinced and there's a lot of disagreement right now about what to do. Zenya's safe at the moment."

"No, she is safe period. We will not let anything happen to her." Emily moved her upper body away from Brandt so she could look straight at him.

He gave a long sigh, "Nothing will happen to her." He pulled her back and held her close for another hour.

Emily's bladder finally protested and Brandt helped her to the bathroom and then ran a bath. He gently washed the blood remaining on her face and body. After the bath, he dried her off and against protests carried her back to bed.

Her sister and brother came in with food. Emily was ravenous and felt like she was on the brink of starvation, just as she had the first time Brandt made steak for her. He assured her that after her blood loss from the gunshot and Dmitri's feeding it was normal to feel so hungry.

After she took the last bite, Mandy curled up on the bed and began sobbing. Caleb pulled a chair close and placed his head on his sister's back taking Emily's hand. "We thought you were dead. We just found you and thought you were gone." Caleb's devastation broke Emily's heart more thoroughly than Mandy's tears.

"Shhhh." Emily held them both and shared her own silent tears.

Brandt sat on the opposite side of the bed allowing them to grieve.

Finally the tears slowed and they lay quietly. Weeks before Brandt explained that wolves needed touch and now she understood.

The door opened and Dmitri stuck his head in. "Brandt, I need to have a word with you."

Brandt looked at Dmitri and reluctantly stood. Placing a soft kiss to the inside of her palm, he followed the vampire from the room.

The three siblings fell asleep.

When Emily opened her eyes the following morning she was alone with Mandy. Her sister was touching her with one hand and hogging the sheet. Emily quietly got out of bed and went into the bathroom. After brushing her teeth and putting on a bathrobe, the only item of clothing she could find, she left the room and walked into the living room area of the suite. No one was there so she made her way out the door and down the hallway following the voices her sensitive ears picked up. She walked into another suite and Brandt rose from the couch walking quickly toward her. Without giving her a chance to protest, he picked her up and carried her to the couch then sat down with her in his lap. She shyly looked at the others but no one seemed to think it strange so she laid still and listened. Brandt gave her a gentle squeeze and he kissed her forehead.

"Everyone will be on their guard now and attacks will be more difficult." Dmitri's voice was strong and direct.

"We had no idea the cats were organized or that they found vampires willing to take them." The anger in Samson's voice was palpable. His wild gaze shot around the room and looked everywhere but at Amy.

Brandt spoke up, "The vampires are the biggest threat. Even with three we are in for a bloody war. And, we have no way of knowing if they only have three. Incorrect assumptions will get us killed. We know they had help from prides across the southern border but confirming their numbers will be almost impossible."

"My bears will have more information in the next few days. I know it's not in our nature to sit still but we need to know what we're facing. Have you heard back from your wolves?" Dmitri looked at Brandt.

"They checked in but don't have new information. Marcus spoke to his military connections and we can have half our men back from their service overseas if it becomes necessary. The government wasn't happy but the last thing they want is for the public to get wind that there is a beastkind war going on. Keeping our existence quiet is their biggest concern." Brandt's hand held Emily's head to his chest and he softly kissed her hair.

A sleepy eyed Mandy entered the room and the meeting broke up. Brandt kept Emily in his arms and began walking back to their suite.

"I can walk."

"I realize that but I've been away from you for the past few hours and I need to hold you. Be quiet."

Mandy giggled; a sound they both appreciated.

When they entered their own rooms, Brand turned to Mandy. "Go find your brother and tell him that food is on its way and if he wants any he had better hurry or Emily will eat it all."

"That wasn't nice."

"If you don't want to share I won't give them any."

"That's going a little too far, don't you think?" She couldn't help her grin.

"Okay, I'll let your sister eat but I doubt Caleb has gone very long without food."

Caleb was shoving a piece of pizza into his mouth when he walked in behind Mandy. Brandt only raised his eyebrows as he sat on the couch with Emily.

"What are we having for lunch?" said Caleb after he swallowed his last bite.

Emily laughed full out this time.

Mandy sat on the couch with Brandt and Emily. She took Emily's hand in hers and held tight. Emily knew they were the same age but Mandy had a sheltered upbringing and had felt safe her entire life. This was the first time she was truly scared and she needed comfort.

They ate spaghetti and Brandt's fork lightly stabbed Caleb's hand when it reached for the last of the bread.

"Ouch, what did I do?"

"My mate is eating the last piece of bread and it is not up for discussion."

Emily took the bread and split it in half. She disregarded the sour look on Brandt's face and offered a piece to her brother. He didn't look at Brandt, just shook his head no, and then smiled and grabbed Mandy's hand. "The bears are playing poker. I need you for a distraction so I can win some of my money back.

"Only because they're good looking and I need some eye candy right now," was Mandy's reply. The two bickered on their way out of the suite causing both Brandt and Emily to smile.

Brandt stood up, ignoring Emily's protest and carried her to their bedroom locking the door behind them. He lowered her legs slowly to the floor and then untied the sash on her bathrobe opening the sides and slipping the material past her shoulders. It slid to the floor at her feet.

Her hands went to the bottom of his shirt and began pulling upward.

He stopped her and he stepped back slightly removing his clothing himself. His hands moved up to her cheeks and he lightly placed his lips on hers kissing her with incredible tenderness.

Emily needed her mate but gentleness was not what she wanted.

Chapter 27

His broad shoulders tightened as Brandt picked her up and gently lay her on the bed. Ignoring her hot gaze, he ran his fingers through her silky straight hair and fanned it out across the sheets. He then stroked down the soft curves of her beautiful face and neck before gliding over her breasts. Dark eyes followed the path of his hands and reveled in the sight and feel of her body. Feather light touch, traveling down the softest thighs on earth, past her calves, and lower to her feet where his teeth nipped the sensitive pad of her toe before giving a soft lick.

Dreamy sighs escaped her lips while she fought against her body's need to move.

The touch of his lips slowed, revisiting every inch of her skin to relearn the taste and scent of her. Gentle bites and moist lips followed his hands, setting off tiny arcs of energy. His exploration slowly continued.

"Brandt, please." Urgent almost begging; her voice quavered with need.

He glanced up, eyes now completely black met passion filled blue, and he released a groan from deep in his throat. "I am kissing and worshiping every inch of your body. Lie back and let me love you."

Emily had never heard such desperation in her mate's tone. Biting her bottom lip did little to keep her anxious sigh from escaping. Closing her eyes she tried to withstand his sensual torture. His mouth moved ever so slowly up and across her sensitive breasts. Finally, her searching fingers were able to grasp his erection and apply pulsing pressure along the thick pliant length.

Again his grip was uncompromising when he pulled her hand away giving a low growl of displeasure.

This time, her growl showed annoyance and matched his. She needed him buried deep inside her. She growled again.

It was her wolf that noticed the change in his scent. What she thought was gentleness and then desperation was Brandt holding tight to his beast. His restraint was at an end and she felt his raw energy charge through the room.

Ice cold rage, barely held in check, edged his words through tightly clenched teeth. His eyes drilled into hers, "I've seen the video. I watched you die. Even knowing you live, your death has imprinted on my mind. This, right now, is for my wolf. He needs to soak your essence into his soul and know you live. I will give you what you want when his needs are met." He breathed in deeply exhaling more aggression. "You will let my wolf do this." Pure male alpha power detonated with his words.

Emily knew she would die. Every nerve ending begged for release but she didn't fight, her wolf acknowledged her mate's need. By the time Brandt's lips reached her brow, her moans were loud and desperate. She inhaled sharply, trying to steady herself. Lifting her arms, she clenched her fingers painfully into his biceps. Past the point of need, alpha she-wolf was taking over.

Without warning, as if she had no hold on him at all, Brandt flipped her to her stomach, his weight pressing into her back.

She instantly began to struggle.

"No, I am not finished." The small amount of control he maintained was ready to snap.

She squeezed her eyes tightly closed feeling the sensual torment scorch through her body.

Brandt struggled with his beast. Breathing in her scent was not helping, and his wolf strained within the man. Finally the path of his mouth, teeth nipping and lips kissing, ended at her calves.

He straightened. Grabbing her legs, he thrust her thighs apart. One hand pressed into her lower back to hold her still. With his other, two fingers touched her moist entrance and then without warning plunged into her heat.

She exploded upward but he applied pressure to her middle back pushing her body into the soft bedding.

His fingers moved. Slowly.

In and out, the sweet torture continued and her hands grabbed fistfuls of cotton sheet. Her need centered on his fingers, her desire unbearable. With no warning, sharp burning fangs entered her neck at the juncture of her shoulder. She screamed and her body bucked uncontrollably. Strong hands lifted and flipped her over.

At last, past the point where she had any control, he thrust forward burying himself deep. Her fingernails dug into his back not caring about the damage. Her body throbbed, desire building, every nerve, every inch of her body, needing release as the heat traveled, centering between her thighs. Blood covered lips found hers and her shattering release screamed past his mouth.

His fingers painfully grabbed her hair at the base of her neck and pulled her head sharply back, his eyes savage. Words, agony to get past his elongated fangs, growled from deep in his throat. "You will never leave me."

She would never leave. Her world centered on him. He was the water that quenched her thirst, the air that filled her lungs.

Unrestrained, his body moved fast and her inner muscles tightened around his erection in wave after wave of pleasure. She screamed again as her sex continued to pulsate.

His mouth came down hard on hers and finally his hot release exploded into her body. His growl ignited from deep in his throat. His seed found home.

Their harsh gasps slowed, becoming even. He gathered her hair into his hand and pulled her head back gently for another soul-shattering kiss.

When he finally released her she looked into his eyes and watched them return to their natural deeper shade of brown. "You never lost me, I could think of nothing but you."

He tightened his hold inhaling her scent while letting his strained muscles ease.

She knew something more was wrong. She continued to smell his uncertainty. The damage caused by the cats had faded and the bullets had not killed her. Her thoughts were troubled but exhaustion took over and she drifted off to sleep.

***

Another day of waiting, Emily felt stronger, almost back to normal. She longed for home. They were all bored so her sister and brother taught her to play poker with a couple of grumpy werebears.

Caleb made introductions, "This is Honey, and he enjoys taking my money by the handful. Korep," He nodded at the other bear, "Gives me a chance every so often but I think they both have a sixth sense when it comes to cards." There was no animosity in Caleb's voice and it was obvious they had all become friends.

Emily's curiosity over the bears was difficult to hide and she took sideways glances while they played. Honey was huge and if she had to guess he was at least six foot six. Nothing about him was sweet and it was hard not to laugh when thinking about his name. His shirt appeared painted on his torso, every inch of corded muscle clearly defined. His hands were the size of sledge hammers but they held cards like delicate crystal. Brown hair kept out of his way in a ponytail fell several inches down his back. The most surprising thing about him was his lips. Belying his strength, they looked soft almost plush and had an unwavering pout.

Emily looked back and forth between her sister and this goliath. Mandy almost drooled while tension sizzled. They needed to get her home, quickly.

The other bear was slightly smaller, though alone no one would dare call him small. His brown eyes were direct, almost cold but he grinned more often than Honey. He also cast glances between his friend and Mandy. Their reaction to one another seemed to bother him the same way it did Emily. Not good.

The cards helped pass the time and also kept her mind off Brandt. Her body continued to tingle from his lovemaking the day before though the intensity of it worried her. She tried to imagine what she would feel if it was him in the video. Her wolf helped to shield the pain but if she watched Brandt beaten and shot, she didn't think she would be thinking of a slight pain adjustment.

In the afternoon Brandt walked in and asked her to accompany him to another meeting.

He lifted his hands in defeat when he bent slightly thinking to pick her up and she growled. They walked into Dmitri's suite and sat side by side on one of the couches though Brandt made sure they were touching.

He started the discussion, "I received word from my wolves that the cats crossed the border into South America. There has been no word on Nicolas' body but a full out search is impossible at the moment." Brandt placed his hand on Emily's thigh and squeezed slightly before continuing, "Zenya disappeared from Marcus' ranch last night. The babies are safe but we're sure now that she was supplying information to the cats."

Emily stood instantly dislodging Brandt's hand. "That is not true. She wouldn't do it." Her voice was angry and her belief in her friend absolute.

Dmitri spoke up his voice tight. "You knew her a short time. The bottom line is that she's a cat and her first loyalty will always lie with her own kind. Marcus made a mistake when he took her in and we all paid for it."

Emily's eyes shot fire staring with deadly intent at the vampire. "What have you lost? Are any of your bears dead? You just said cats stick with cats, if that's true then why do you care? Marcus and Amy protected their young and gave them a nursemaid. She may be a cat but she loves Amy and those children. She would have risked her life to save them." Refusing to back down or lower her eyes she didn't flinch when Dmitri's went amber.

"Brandt, control your mate." His fangs flashed and his gaze never left Emily's.

Brandt's tone remained even, "My mate is alpha. I cannot change her thoughts and she will speak her mind like we all do. However, we are uneasy and stressed; fighting one another will get us nowhere." He looked at Emily. "Dmitri is not your enemy."

She took a deep breath and slowly sat down while gaining control of her anger. She knew Zenya had not betrayed them but this was not the time and they needed the vampire. Her eyes again met his. "I offer apology. I owe you for saving my life. I have few friends and one is now dead. I only wish to protect them."

His ire cooled and his eyes slowly reverted to their previous color. Sorrow reflected in his voice, "Maggie and I had a relationship many years ago and I cared deeply for her. I will avenge her death or die trying. We are all on edge and it is I who should ask your pardon. I have never met a female alpha and sometimes forget that it's ingrained to hold eye contact. It would also help if you were not so beautiful." He quirked the side of his mouth making him even sexier and he knew it.

Emily blushed.

Brandt looked at the vampire, his gaze darkening. "Mine."

Dmitri laughed. "Yes, you have made that perfectly clear with your possessive scent." He then winked at Emily.

The tension dissipated and Samson spoke for the first time. His voice remained tight though he managed to sound unaffected by the vampire's statements in regards to Maggie. "When are we returning home?" His clouded eyes went to Brandt but stayed even with his alpha's chest.

"It could be a few days. I have something private that I must handle first. It does not involve the wolves or bears." His voice left no room for discussion. It was also obvious he remained unhappy with Samson and his anger overrode his second's obvious devastation.

Sam tipped his head down further in acquiescence.

Emily looked back and forth between the two. She could feel the grief surrounding Samson. She turned fully to Brandt, she had no idea what her mate had to do that was more important than going home, but she would not question him while they were with the others.

They discussed a few additional issues and then the meeting broke up.

Emily and Brandt walked back to their suite. He led her straight into their bedroom and again locked the door.

She didn't know who was in control, he or his wolf, but the assault of his hands, mouth, and teeth bordered on desperate. He didn't seem to mind the bloody scratches left on his skin.

They lay without talking until their breathing slowed and she whispered huskily, "Please, talk to me? I know something is wrong."

"You are mine."

"That doesn't answer my question. There is something you are not telling me."

Without a word, Brandt got out of bed, walked into the bathroom, and closed the door behind him.

She heard the shower turn on and she groaned in angry frustration. The damn man could stew for a while by himself. Mandy promised to help her with reading and she needed to get her mind off her exasperating mate.

That night they slept together but for the first time they didn't make love. He was gone when she awoke. Letting out an irritated growl, she put clothes on without brushing her teeth or hair and went in search of her stubborn wolf.

He was in the poker suite talking to Caleb and Mandy. Complete silence descended when she entered. Her siblings looked at her and then nervously glanced away.

"What's going on?"

Brandt didn't give them a chance to speak. "We have company coming in an hour," His voice distant. "You should probably shower and dress accordingly."

"Who?"

"We'll talk about it later." He left the room, casting a stern look at Mandy and Caleb.

Emily regarded her siblings. Neither would meet her gaze which made her angrier. Storming out of the room, she headed to the shower and childishly slammed every door behind her. She prepared herself for company but stayed in her room when ready. She knew it was best if she didn't see her mate before the mysterious person arrived.

Brandt opened the bedroom door. The look on his face completely dissolved her anger. He appeared lost. "Our guest is here."

Emily stood and walked toward him but he stepped back avoiding her touch when she walked past. Dread consumed her when she looked across the room. A human woman dressed in a professional looking skirt and jacket stood waiting. She appeared to be in her fifties though age didn't detract from her beauty and her striking green eyes made her more so. She smiled and laugh lines appeared at the corners of her mouth.

"Emily, this is Doctor Laura Stevens. She needs to speak with you. I'll be in Dmitri's suite." Businesslike, abrupt, and cold, he left the room.

The two women looked at each other both showing their perplexity without speaking for a moment.

Laura's voice was steady, "Do you mind if we sit down. I'm fairly certain you have no idea why I'm here and that is unfair to both of us."

Emily walked to the couch and directed the doctor to a comfortable chair. They both took a seat. "I haven't been told what is going on Doctor Stevens, and Brandt has refused to answer my questions. I would really like an explanation." Emily was proud of her control when what she wanted to do was scream.

"Please, call me Laura. I need you to hear me out and let me finish before you hunt down your mate." She smiled slightly but didn't wait for a response. "I'm a geneticist. I have spent years researching a solution that will allow beastkind to successfully mate and produce children." She looked directly at Emily and continued. "We, my team and I, have discovered that the dominant genes of beastkind kill each other. When mating takes place with a human, the dominant gene accepts the lesser gene and can procreate. We tried artificial insemination, AI for short, with human sperm and beastkind eggs and reversed the process using beastkind sperm and human eggs. We've had no success unless the male and female procreate the old-fashioned way with sexual intercourse. We managed to isolate a hormone that both male and female beastkind create when they have sex thinking this might be the key to allowing AI to work. It didn't. We have managed to discover the reason why beastkind cannot mate but we have failed at finding the solution."

Emily's subconscious prickled and her lungs began to feel constricted. "Why are you giving me a science lesson on the procreation of beastkind?"

"I am here to discuss enabling you to have a child."

"But you just told me it's impossible to have one with my mate."

"I know but I'm still here to discuss the possibility of your having a child."

"With a human?"

"Yes."

"No!" Horror was evident in the one agonizing word.

Laura's voice softened, "Emily, I have done this for many years. My mother married a wolf when I was a baby and Nicolas' pack raised me. It's important for the clans to have children. More than one hundred wolves, including the young, died recently; my entire clan wiped out. You are a rare alpha female. I have met only one other. It has been my life's work to find answers to this problem and make it easier for mated pairs to have offspring. Though I haven't given up, failure has consumed my research." Her professionalism gave way to momentary despair but then she continued, "Brandt will love this child. It's not what you might think. He will embrace the offspring as completely his, it's in his DNA. Getting past the sexual encounter happens quickly and is soon forgotten by both parents."

"You're telling me you are here to arrange for a man to have sex with me, impregnate me, and then I go back to my life with my mate like nothing happened." The horrifying torment in her voice was tangible.

"Brandt asked me to make the arrangements with you but he should have discussed everything and given you time to adjust."

"He didn't discuss it with me because he knows I will kill him." Holding herself in tight control, she stood, turned her back on the doctor, entered her bedroom, and softly closed the door behind her.

Chapter 28

More than an hour passed before Brandt entered their bedroom. Emily was sitting nude against the headboard. Expecting tears he was wary at the undeniable rage shimmering through the room. He stopped, not approaching, giving her time to control herself.

Her ice blue eyes moved inch by inch up his body coming to rest on his eyes. "Get out." Her alpha power detonated with her words.

Brandt made his first mistake. He took a step in her direction.

More than one hundred pounds of growling white she-wolf exploded off the bed with one goal; his jugular.

Completely clothed Brandt couldn't take the time to shift. He could only act. Grabbing his angry mate, he tried to be gentle and used her forward momentum to propel her to the side.

That was his second mistake.

Emily's teeth sank into his thigh. Pain exploded and instead of releasing him she increased the agony by shaking her head furiously. Brandt's fist slammed against the side of her jaw forcing her teeth to loosen.

This time he didn't mess around and grabbing fur and skin he threw her more than eight feet across the room where the side of the bed stopped her flight. While she was scrambling to her feet, he divested himself of his pants. His wolf burst from his skin, ripping his shirt.

Emily charged.

He didn't worry about his injured thigh. She was going for his throat, her powerful jaws seeking arterial blood. His body twisted as he poured alpha power into his internal words, "Emily stop, fucking stop." His dominant growl vibrated through the room.

Rage, hot alpha she-wolf rage was his answer.

Her jaw snapped deeply into his shoulder.

His teeth found her snout giving it a fierce bite.

She released her hold.

His leg and shoulder wounds bled freely, soaking his fur in sticky red. She was bleeding slightly from her nose. Seriously injury was becoming an option. If he knew anything, he knew she was trying to kill him.

The bedroom door slammed back on its hinges and Samson burst through. He stood in shock taking in the scene before him.

"Get the fuck out and make sure everyone stays away," Brandt shouted the order into Samson's mind.

Sam quickly grabbed the door and closed it behind him.

Emily used Brandt's momentary lack of concentration to attack. She hit him in the side with everything she had, using her wolf's body, her snapping teeth going for his neck.

Brandt changed to his human form and slammed his fist upside her head. The force would have killed a normal animal or human.

She hit the floor hard and stayed down.

Brandt slowly gained control of his breathing not taking his eyes off Emily. He didn't approach. Cautiously he sank to the floor from where he stood. He waited, watching her sides heave. Her wolf was crying. His head went between his knees no longer able to look at her.

White bloody fur became human skin and sobs echoed through the room. The sound was heartbreaking. Her arms pulled in tight and her legs came up. Her naked body formed a tight ball, her grief an uncontrolled wave.

He didn't look. He couldn't. It took everything he had to finally speak, "When I woke after being shot, I almost killed Sam. If Dmitri had not been there, I would have. The cats had you and they killed Maggie. I held her when she was a child; I changed her diaper and read her Dr. Seuss. She died saving you and I gladly forfeit her life. Samson saved me, only me." Brandt was silent for a moment, "I am nothing without you. I would not survive. Samson made the wrong decision," his breaths harsh while he gathered his thoughts. "It took twenty-four hours to find your location. I could feel nothing, no connection. Dmitri's people discovered where you were. Then your scream sounded in my head. You were terrified, but at least I knew you were alive. Then I felt your pain. No sound, only pain. We were within a few miles when I went to my knees feeling the bullets enter your body. Each was agony, I wanted to die. I couldn't go on without you." His eyes found hers, they were black pools. One lone tear trailed down his cheek. "I prayed. I prayed to God and the goddess. I begged." His devastation was absolute, haunting. He relived every second of the nightmare. "The one thing, the only thing

I knew I could never give you was a child. It was all I had to bargain with. I made a deal with the gods. If you lived we would have a child. It's my debt for your life. The thought of another man putting his hands on you is torture. It's tormenting me every minute of every day and night. But, the thought of losing you is worse. I will not let you go." His head went down, alpha eyes lowering.

Emily looked at her mate, the man who gave her life, the man who loved her more than life. He was beautiful, powerful, unforgiving, and incredibly stupid. Her throat released a low growl, her body rumbled with the need to strangle him for making such a senseless bargain. But, she loved him more at that moment than anything she previously felt.

The muscles of his back and arms remained tense, frozen in place like chiseled granite. He did not look up. Her body unfolded and she moved to his side.

On her knees, she placed her arms around the broad shoulders that held her, loved her, and cherished her. Inhaling deeply she gathered his scent; blood, sweat, sorrow, wolf and man. Her arms tightened. She took everything her alpha had and poured the power into her mate with her words. "I love you."

His body moved, his arms coming around her, his head sinking into her soft breasts. "I cannot take a chance that the gods will punish me by taking you. I promised them a child. Our child."

Moments passed.

Her voice loving though concise, "But I didn't. You have fulfilled your promise. I made no bargain and another man will never touch me. You are my mate."

He locked his eyes to hers, his tense facial muscles relaxed. "Emily, you need a child. Everything inside you craves a baby. I've seen you with Kinsee and the twins. They fill a place in your heart that Carolynn took from you. You will be an incredible mother and I will be a father who will love our child and thank the gods every day for sparing you and giving us a baby. I can give this to you. I never thought I could but I was wrong. Your life and your happiness are more important to me than anything else in this world. We have time. You can wait but we will have a baby."

Stupid, stupid, man. Tears slowly fell down Emily's cheeks again. She knew it would never happen. His eyes held hope and made promises she couldn't accept. Her body shifted and blood streaked white fur replaced the woman. Using her rough tongue, she began cleaning the blood from her mate's skin. She could not face him but she needed to be close. She let her wolf take over.

Brandt understood. He lay still while she cleaned his wounds and her scent healed his memories. At last he placed his arms around her neck, his tanned naked skin dark against her white fur. He rose and picking her up, lay down on the bed using his fingers to soothe and stroke the silk of her fur. Eventually they both fell into an exhausted sleep.

A soft knock at the door woke him. His arms continued to hold his mate's wolf form. Brandt watched the door open a crack and Samson stuck his head slightly inside. He then stood back out of sight not closing the door, just waiting.

Carefully Brandt released her and got up gathering his pants from the floor. The injury on his thigh was painful and the pants made it worse. He left the room quietly closing the door behind him. He followed Sam to Dmitri's suite then sat down while looking closely at the vampire. It was obvious he should still be sleeping.

His churlish words let Brandt know his displeasure. "You and your mate had a disagreement?"

"Hmmm, if you mean the fact she tried to kill me, I guess we did. I'm assuming for some reason Samson thought it necessary to wake you." His irritated gaze sliced to the wolf in question and then returned to Dmitri. "It was a private domestic situation between me and my she-wolf."

Dmitri let his angst go with a laugh. "He woke me because he thought you might have need of medical attention that only a vampire can provide. The bite on your shoulder is fairly deep and you were favoring your left leg when you walked in. I am at your service."

Brandt gave a slight grimace. "I think these wounds need to heal on their own. Neither is life threatening, and my mate might be more forgiving if I show a bit of pain."

This time Dmitri's laughter resonated through the room. "Then I will leave for my bed while you and Sam clear the air. I don't think my bears would tolerate a wolf in our clan and I'm tired of Samson's moping. Do something about it." With that the vampire walked out.

Samson didn't look at Brandt while he spoke. "I should have gone for Emily and died in place of Maggie. My body should be awaiting a funeral pyre. But, in the split second that a decision was required, I didn't hesitate. I protected my alpha. I don't know if I could ever do differently."

Brandt held on to his temper and let his wolf soothe him before he spoke. "She is your alpha too. If you had gone for her and I died, she would have killed you, make no mistake. If she died because of your choice I would kill you. Maggie did her job and so did you. Both of us need to move on." This time he let his calming essence reach Samson.

Samson continued to look down.

"Emily is not happy with me and I need you to make nice. She needs a friend and I'm afraid her anger is not yet over. Home is calling and our wild needs to run, we're leaving." Brandt got up and rested his hand on Samson's shoulder for a moment. He gave one last clench of his hand and left.

When he walked into the suite, Mandy and Caleb glared daggers at him while they ran their hands through Emily's fur. She hadn't changed to her human form. Before the doctor arrived, he had informed them of the reason she was coming and gave them no opportunity to talk him out of it. He could smell their anger but ignored it. His only concern was for his mate. He tried linking with her mind but she shut him out.

"We are leaving for home within the hour, be ready." Brandt went to his room and began gathering his and Emily's clothing. The plane was on standby. He had given instructions at the last moment because he knew they had more than one traitor within the clans and was not taking any chances. Emily remained in the other room with her siblings. Her sadness was like a thick haze filling the entire suite. Brandt spoke with the bears so they could relay his last instructions to Dmitri. He wanted Dmitri safe and with no way of knowing the number of vampires they were dealing with he worried. If the shit hit the fan his friend along with his bear clan had a home with the northern pack.

When he was notified the vehicle waited, Brandt went to collect his unhappy group.

Samson stood outside the door to the suite. His eyes remained downcast. "She's not communicating with anyone."

"I'm sending Mandy and Caleb out here." Brandt turned and entered his suite.

The young wolves weren't happy but they trudged out of the room casting worried looks at Emily.

The door closed quietly behind them leaving Brandt alone with his mate. He sighed having no idea what else he could do or say he just knew they needed to be home. "We're leaving. I know I hurt you but we have more immediate problems right now." Maybe if he pissed her off she would respond.

Emily walked past him and nudged the door with her nose unable to get it open.

"Fine." He snapped grabbing their bags and turning the knob with his human hands.

Two bears walked with them through the lobby and out to the waiting vehicle. People stared at the large white dog with no leash or collar. Emily ignored them and kept her head up while walking through the luxurious foyer between her brother and sister.

The bears went back into the hotel when the SUV pulled away. The ride to the airport and the flight home were silent except for necessary instructions to the chauffeur and pilot. Security was high when they stepped off the plane. Emily remained silent. When their vehicle pulled up in front of the main house and the SUV's door opened she jumped from the vehicle and ran.

Thomas came out front to greet them and gave Brandt an inquiring look. Mandy and Caleb walked away without a farewell. Brandt continued past his father without saying a word and entered the chateau. He went straight to the liquor and filled a large glass to the brim with Scotch.

Thomas arched an eyebrow. "Is there something I need to know?"

"Emily is not happy with me and is refusing to communicate or change form. I brought Doctor Stevens to our hotel to speak with her and I don't wish to discuss it." His tone was final. "Funerals?"

"All is prepared and tonight will work if that is your wish."

"It will do."

Chapter 29

Emily ran. She ran away from her mate and tried to outrun her confusion. The trees flew past. Her paws sank into the familiar black earth and pine needles while she ran. Time passed. Subconsciously she veered her direction finding herself at Patricia's house; winded and lonely.

Wolfred walked outside with Kinsee by his side.

Emily's wolf smiled.

The child's cry of joy and then the feel of the little girl's small arms wrapping around her neck, finally opened a warm place in Emily's heart.

"Patricia is taking a nap. The cats killed her brother Leeland and she's taking it hard. She's chosen to remain in wolf form so the baby arrives earlier, but she's struggling." Exhaustion plagued his eyes. Before he continued Kinsee began speaking.

"Can I play with Emily? Please, I want to run."

Telepathically Emily spoke, "She can come with me and we won't go far, but I'll keep her occupied for an hour or two." She needed something to take her mind off the problems weighing her down and Kinsee offered a needed diversion.

"Give me your dress and off with you. Don't cause any trouble." His voice was lovingly gruff.

The dress flew over her head with a tiny splitting sound.

"Thank you my alpha," he said with an exasperating smile and shake of his head. "I need some sleep and I'll take advantage of your offer. Kinsee has done nothing but ask when you were coming home."

"Let's go Kinsee, I bet I can find the first rabbit."

The two were off. They romped for an hour and Emily managed to keep Kinsee from killing more than one rabbit though they chased several. The two finally lay down on a bed of pine needles to rest. Kinsee was asleep in a manner of minutes. Emily groomed the child's soft fur and breathed in the unique aroma of fledgling wolf. It was fresh and light without the stronger odor of adult beastkind.

Emily quickly turned her head when she heard paws slowly moving through the trees in their direction. It was Patricia.

She went down beside Emily and Kinsee speaking quietly with her mind. "Wolfred is sleeping, thank you for giving us a short time of peace."

Emily sank further into the soft earth. "Brandt wants me to have a child."

"Ahhh. I'm surprised."

"Shocked is more of what I feel. He had a doctor come and speak with me."

"That would be Doctor Stevens?"

"Yes. She explained what she was there for but Brandt hadn't said a word."

"For an alpha to allow another man to touch his mate so soon is--- umm, unusual. He's so possessive of you. I'm not sure what to say."

"When I was shot he made a deal with his god." Anger laced her words, "I don't mean to be rude, but no other man will ever touch me."

"Kinsee is lying with you now because a man other than Wolfred touched me. It is probably the hardest thing we must live with being beastkind. I believe it's the price we pay for existing hundreds of years. I know that doesn't help or make it easier. Brandt will not force you."

"That he would allow a man to touch me is causing too much anger and resentment inside my head and heart. I would kill any woman he took to his bed." Emily finally laughed slightly, "Well, maybe only remove her nipple and then kill him."

Patricia's voice held a smile. "I think maybe the greater love is that he would allow another man to touch you. Babies are the most precious thing we have. Right now I carry a child for our pack's future. It will be the fourth cub born in the last ten years." Her voice softened and she continued, "Tonight is the funeral for our dead. Even if you don't want to speak with Brandt right now, the pack needs you. We all felt Brandt's anguish while you suffered. Even from such a great distance his pain was unbearable. We are facing a war and instability will cause problems that we cannot afford. With our scenting abilities, we notice when troubling problems are worrying our alpha… sorry, alphas. Anger is okay. We are all angry right now. We need strong leaders and no doubts about our future.

Every wolf will die to avenge our fallen and the loss of Nicolas' pack, but we need you."

"I know and I will be okay but if you don't mind I'll lie here with Kinsee a little longer while I gain control of my emotions. I'm so very sorry about your brother."

"He was my only brother. He died protecting Kinsee and me. If he hadn't been here it might have been Wolfred that we lost but more likely, all three of us. Losing my brother is incredibly hard but I don't think I could go on without Wolfred and Kinsee. I would make the same deal Brandt made." She took a deep breath. "We must do our grieving tonight and then put melancholy behind us."

"Thank you for being so wise. I needed to speak with another woman and Maggie is gone too."

"She was special but we have you now. Yours and Brandt's strength will carry us. He needed you long before you came into his life. We are so happy you found us."

"He found me but thank you."

"I will head home and begin cooking dinner. Enjoy your time."

After another hour, Emily used her nose to nudge the sleeping child. Kinsee was up and ready to run after her nap. They took a roundabout jaunt and slowly made their way back to her parent's home. Patricia greeted them and Emily realized it was impossible to see even a small bulge while the mother to be was in wolf form.

"Thank you Emily, would you like to stay for dinner?"

"No, I need to get back to my mate and prepare for this evening. I will see you tonight." Emily kissed the top of Kinsee's head with a swift lick and then turned and disappeared into the trees.

The cabin door was open and she figured Brandt left it that way for her. Sorrowful music came from inside. Entering she saw Brandt lying on the couch with his arm over his eyes. He didn't move. She walked further into the room shifting to human. She knelt by the couch raising her fingers to his chest, her palm going flat over his heart. The arm not covering his eyes took hold of her fingers and brought them to his lips. "I love you Emily. I don't have the words to bring you comfort."

Emily placed her head on his stomach while he began trailing his fingers through her hair. "I'm still angry, but that doesn't matter for now." She breathed deeply of his scent. It was more her home than the forest and earth, the scent more comforting. "What will happen tonight?"

Sitting up, Brandt drew her onto the couch so he could hold her. "We will mourn and celebrate the lives of those lost. The pack will sing the song of passing. Tomorrow we will meet again at the ring and speak of vengeance for our fallen." His arms were strong, reassuring, and loving. "Parts of our combined military forces have followed the cats beyond the Mexico border and into South America. We are not prepared for a full out battle yet but we will be. We also have people checking out the cat clans to the north. We have never had difficulties with them but need to know that they will stay out of the fight. If not, we have a bigger problem on our hands. I need you to keep this last bit of information to yourself. There are leaks coming from somewhere, one or both mine, and Columbus's pack. We don't know."

"Why are you telling me this?"

"Emily, if something happens to me you will be alpha. You are strong enough to lead our pack even if you don't realize it yet. Every beastkind who meets you feels your growing power. That is another reason I think the cats tried to kill you. You give us strength."

"I'm only strong with you beside me. I don't think one of us would survive without the other."

"I know for my part you're right but the clan needs to follow us both. Tomorrow night I want you to call the pack. When our meeting is over, I want you to call them to change. It's important that you be aware of your strength and your wolf needs to know how to use it. Only an alpha can call the wolves to change. You will be a strong leader when I am not with you."

Her tone was angry when she answered. "You are not leaving me. I don't care how strong I am or if I could lead. I will not do it without you."

"We plan on attacking the cats in South America. Not today and not tomorrow but eventually it will happen. Having an alpha here gives us added protection. I don't plan on dying but we need to fight this war and we will be stronger if we are able to separate when needed."

"We will see."

Brandt laughed. It felt good and he squeezed her tightly holding her until the sun set.

He woke Emily from a fitful nap. "Cheri is coming." Disentangling himself from her arms, he walked to the door.

Emily went to their room to put on clothes. When she came out Cheri voice was irritated, Amber beginning to show in her eyes.

"The northern cats are staying quiet. That in itself worries me. When the true war begins, we will be watching both borders. I am asking the European clans to send us warriors. We need more in numbers and extra muscle. If we must, we will call our entire military force home and the government can be damned."

"I agree. The next issue is that we still have no word on Nicolas."

"Do you think there is a chance he is alive?"

"No, not after what they did to Emily." Brandt took Emily's hand and brought her closer. "They would be fools to keep him alive."

"They are fools for starting this war. Nothing but their annihilation will be the outcome. We should have taken then out months ago after they attacked Marcus."

There was so much fury in the statement that it was hard for Emily to feel anything but assurance.

"I will see you both at the funerals tonight. I am sorry you are part of this Emily. We've had many years of peace and the young should not have to suffer this sorrow."

Emily blinked and Cheri was gone.

Hours later they made their way deeply into the woods, miles beyond the last cabin. Brandt explained about the area during her earlier explorations. She avoided it when she ran and had never been close. Now, there were wolves everywhere. The only werewolves not in attendance were those left behind to guard the perimeters of their territory. Even the children were present.

With ten wolves to mourn, one person from each family spoke on behalf of the fallen.

Emily stood quietly by her mate's side.

Each fallen pack brother and sister received their final farewell. Maggie's father told stories of her when she was a child and muffled sobs sounded throughout the clearing.

Emily allowed her tears to fall and reached her hand for Samson applying brief pressure. She could feel his grief. It had a heavier feel and was more devastating than hers.

Cheri finally spoke and talked of the bravery of the ones taken. When she finished her short speech, it was Brandt's turn.

Alpha power flowed through the air. "No wolf lives without a price. Protecting our brothers, sisters, and children is that price. The time for mourning ends tonight. We will sing the last song for the dead and pull their strength inside us. We are never alone, their souls forever remain intertwined with ours, and their memories will bring joy. Tonight our grieving ends. Tomorrow vengeance begins."

The wolves quickly disrobed and fur replaced skin. Brandt's was the first howl to ring out with Emily's a split second behind. Cheri lit the pyres and the night filled with the cry of the pack.

The heart wrenching melody pierced the tree tops and echoed through the surrounding hills. The cry of wolves on guard for miles around rang with theirs. Pain resonated into the night.

When Brandt and Emily finally made their way back to the cabin they were both exhausted, but Emily needed Brandt's touch.

Their love making was gentle at times and fierce at others. They finally slept when the sunrise began peeking through the windows.

Chapter 30

Brandt remained on the phone most of the following day. Emily, Thomas, and Samson worked with the information Brandt relayed to them. They were fed numbers and locations. The cats were splitting up. It was obvious they planned carefully and tracking them became almost impossible. Their spies found no information on the vampires leading them and they could be anywhere including across the ocean. There were rumors that the cats disposed of Nicolas' body before crossing into Mexico. Several teams continued searching.

In the late afternoon, Cheri woke and let them know she would be down shortly. When the last rays of sun left the horizon she joined them and immediately caught up on the latest news.

"You know Nicolas would not want anyone in additional danger to bring his body home." Cheri directed her words to Brandt.

"It doesn't matter, he's not around to give orders, and he deserves to rest with his pack. The soldiers searching know this could be a setup and they are to clear out immediately if something doesn't smell right. They volunteered. Some are the only survivors from the eastern clan. They are only alive because they were away in the military. If they have nothing to do I'm afraid they will seek vengeance on their own and not wait for us. They are young and have no alpha. Controlling them is difficult at best. We are trying to locate Ivan to see if he will help with the immediate problems and lead their pack. If not we will send his son Asia."

The discussion continued for several hours. Finally Brandt took Emily's hand and pulled her up. "It's time. We'll go outside."

Samson and Dominique knew the pack was meeting but didn't know what else to expect.

The moon was high and the night clear. Bright stars were visible throughout the night sky and twinkled between the trees. The earth's magic was everywhere, waiting.

Cheri and Thomas were aware of the situation. The vampire took Dominique's hand and she asked Thomas to take her other.

They walked a mile to the arena. Their surroundings seemed unnaturally quiet.

Brandt released Emily's hand whispering in her ear, "It's there inside you. Find it. Gather it and feel your power. When it peaks, let it go."

Emily removed her clothing and took a deep breath. She felt the energy and pushed it up from within. It wasn't painful but different. Unsure, she let it grow.

"You have it now my love. Focus, allow it to build. Your wolf will control it. You need to feel your wild side, the part of you that runs. Hold it until the feeling consumes your entire body."

The power grew. Her insides clenched and vibrated. She could almost see the physical aspect of the energy. Electrical tingles spiked through her nerve endings. Her skin felt hot and she wanted to change to wolf but she held back and gathered more energy. At last it was time, her wolf knew. She severed her hold.

Dominique screamed as her knees gave out.

Cheri could feel Emily's power explode as Thomas released her hand and dropped under the weight of the call.

"Oh shit!" Samson tried to resist but finally he hit his knees, releasing a loud groan.

Brandt remained standing and placed a hand on Emily arm. She pulled the power back slightly and took a breath.

Dominique, Thomas, and Samson struggled to stand.

Wolves appeared through the trees. Their eyes locked with hers until she acknowledged them and they quickly looked down.

Samson directed his question quietly to Brandt, "How did you know she could do this?"

Brandt didn't look at his friend. "Why did you think she couldn't?"

"She may be an alpha but she's young and the ability to call the pack is usually transferred to an alpha after they win a challenge to the death."

"She did win a challenge to the death. She killed her mother the only alpha she ever knew. She's lived her entire life controlling her power and staying sane. She could be the strongest beastkind we've ever seen. When I bit her that first night and tasted her blood it was pure energy. I've never been around anything like it." He then turned, drilling his eyes into those of his friend, "And she's mine."

Emily took her mate's hand. She overheard his statement. "No, you're mine." Her eyes held a raging ocean. A hurricane swelled in their depths.

Brandt pulled her in front of him and placed his hands on her upper arms. He continued to feel the electrical charge release from her body. His hands absorbed some of it and then, finally, he combined his power with hers.

The wolves dropped to their knees, pressed down, unable to rise.

Her hot whisper released on a power filled breath, "Can you do this in bed?"

He didn't answer but let a wicked grin escape.

Brandt and Emily's wolves knew what to do, and the power gradually dispersed allowing the wolves to rise.

Brandt spoke, giving the updated information he could share with the pack. There was no grumbling, no challenges, and no fear, only combined unity radiated. He gave them orders to double the guards. Revolving rotations and also switching watch locations would start tonight. Their territory needed protection but the wolves also required rest. Being ready at a moment's notice could be the difference between life and death. Samson would handle the schedules. When the wolves weren't on shift they were to be resting or working out in the gym. If you weren't a fighter you would be providing meals for wolves on duty. Everyone had a job to do.

Brandt continued, "We have information about the traitor who risked our lives and killed many of our friends and family members."

Furious anger flowed out from the pack.

Brandt looked at Emily. It was her turn to speak.

This was hard but they had discussed her words. She didn't hesitate. "The she-cat Zenya who lived with Marcus and Amy betrayed their trust and helped plan the attack. We have ordered her immediate capture." Slow deep breaths allowed her to continue, "If it's not possible I want her head, removed from her body, and delivered to me. Betrayal it met with death. We don't know who else is responsible but we will discover the truth. They will meet the same fate."

Emily let her words sink in and then inhaled deeply. She drew on the power of all the clan wolves. Feeling their combined energy, she drew it into her body. Pain lanced her nerve endings. This was more than her and Brandt's combined power, it was everything the pack held. The energy was thick, it scorched her insides, but she continued to take more.

Finally, release. A hot and punishing wind swirled, slamming through the trees, and encircling the wolves in lava.

When done naturally, shifting from human to beast was painless. When pulled forth by an Alpha, agony ruled. The stronger more dominant wolves resisted. The lesser wolves dropped, skin exploding to fur. But eventually none could deny Emily's call and they each surrendered to their beast.

Cheri was gone, Thomas left behind. This was the time for the pack's magic.

Brandt immersed himself in the energy coming from her body. Her power had a different feel. It wasn't like that of other alphas. She survived where others would not. She earned the right to stand by his side and lead the pack.

When the air was thick with her power, his hand sought hers. He was withstanding the change like she had done the last time he had demanded this from his wolves. The energy now flowed between them and it was time to join the pack.

They shifted.

Emily threw her head back and began the cry of the wolves. The clearing filled and echoed as every wolf gave voice to their beast. It wasn't the haunting cry to mourn death; it was the cry of war.

***

Hours later Brandt and Emily returned to the cabin. Once inside, he held her tight and let her cry.

She cried for Maggie, her mother and Zenya.

He hoped no one delivered Zenya's head. After her tears, he made love to her. Their power was still high and they needed to merge as one body. Their release soothed the energy and finally, they slept.

Chapter 31

Three months later…

The days, weeks, and months brought wartime changes to the clan. The pack remained on constant guard. There were small skirmishes over the border but revenge was not yet within reach and the delay was difficult for the wolves. Columbus had similar problems.

Nicolas' body was still missing and the clans had called off the official search.

Two weeks after Emily called the wolves, Patricia came to the cabin. She requested Emily place her hand on her barely visible stomach bump. The baby rolled beneath Emily's startled fingers. Her soul began to melt.

Patricia gave birth to another girl. Sheeann was a miracle. Emily watched when the small cub opened her eyes for the first time and then again when she first shifted to wolf. The child brought joy to everyone. The wall around Emily's heart crumbled slowly and the pull of motherhood put her on constant edge.

It took her another month to speak with Brandt even though he already knew. He only waited for Emily to make peace with the decision. This would be the single hardest thing either of them had ever done.

Brandt kept his hand wrapped securely around Emily's. During the past few days, he refused to let her leave his sight. Cheri planned to meet them in Dallas and stay at their hotel. Emily would go to a different location with Dr. Stevens.

Patricia would accompany Emily while Cheri controlled Brandt. When the doctor arrived at the hotel, his fists pumped tight as he fought his rage. His ferocious scent filled the room.

Cheri did her job. Brandt knew what she planned but his cry of anguish echoed through the room and he resisted. It didn't matter. She was vampire and he couldn't win. Finally, she lowered his unconscious body to the floor.

Amber eyes looked to Emily. "Go, I will make sure he is okay and won't let him suffer while you are gone."

Frozen, Emily's tears ran freely. She couldn't take her eyes from Brandt.

Dr. Stevens spoke. "It will be easier once you are separated from him. You will be away no longer than three days. We will discuss the specifics once we are at the clinic. It's time for us to go."

Emily walked to Brandt and knelt by his side. Her tears fell on his face and she softly kissed his lips. "I love you." She rose to her feet and didn't look back. Patricia and the doctor followed.

When Brandt woke he unsuccessfully tried to fight Cheri again. Oblivion took him into the black hole, Emily's name on his lips.

Two days later, Patricia entered Cheri's suite.

"She's in their room and barely speaks. She's asked that I leave her alone."

"Brandt should awaken soon."

A crash from the bedroom stopped her next sentence. She pulled Patricia back from the path to the door.

More beast than human, Brandt tore the door behind Cheri from its hinges. The door to his and Emily's suite was propped open. Against every demand from his wolf he stopped. His sensitive ears easily heard the gut-wrenching sobs coming from within. Taking deep breaths for control, he finally entered. She lay curled on her side, facing away from the door. Her entire body shook with her cries. Her grief carried him to the bed.

Her scent, the scent a she-wolf with child released his pain in wave after wave of protectiveness. He gathered her into his arms and held her while her sobs continued. This was the moment that scared him the most. He had worried his fury would explode but now that he was here, he only felt love and overwhelming peace. He let it go. His alpha power ignited and traveled through her body. After several minutes he carried her to the bathroom. She didn't resist but she wouldn't look at him. He put her on her feet and removed her clothing. After adjusting the water temperature he cradled her body and stepped beneath the spray; the same spray that once brought pain and terror. He let the water cascade over them keeping her head pressed against the crook of his neck. Her crying subsided but her body continued to tremble. Finally, he set her on her feet and began to wash each inch of her beautiful flesh. She kept her eyes closed allowing him to remove the lingering scent of Dr. Stevens and Patricia from her body. They bathed her before their return.

He placed Emily's arms around his neck and then used his powerful muscles to lift her placing her backed her against the shower wall. His hands went to her thighs, placing her legs around his waist. In one swift move his body sank deeply into hers.

Shocked blue eyes opened and stared into his. He clenched his jaw but kept his body motionless, buried deep inside hers. At last his mouth came down, demanding her lips part. He poured every ounce of passion into the kiss.

For two days, grief had crushed Emily's spirit. When the doctor said she was pregnant it meant nothing. She was isolated and trapped inside a cage like the one which held her for nineteen years. The only difference being this cage was in her mind.

Brandt's touch did not break the bars of the misery. The water did nothing. The soap could not wash away her shame. She could not meet his eyes.

Then his erection entered her in one hot and burning stroke. The shock caused her eyes to open. Obsidian black looked back, no hatred, or revulsion but pure infinite love.

His body moved, stroking her cold depth warming her heart. Slow methodical pressure inward and then out. His mouth traveled from her lips, down her neck and then closed around a nipple adoring it with his tongue. He sucked gently then moved to her other breast repeating the caress. His hips suddenly stopped their steady pressure and his eyes again captured hers.

"My lips are worshiping the breasts that our child will suckle." He gently moved a wet lock of hair from her eyes. "Look at me Emily. You are my world and this child is ours. Our cub will never suffer like his mother did for nineteen years. We will raise our child in love and gentleness. I demand everything from you, right now. Love me and don't ever let go."

Her arms tightened and her body responded to his words. They broke through the ice and pain surrounding her heart. Soft luscious lips met his.

He sank deeper into her body, taking everything. His hips rocked slow and steady until she answered his call. When her mate scent finally ignited, his gentleness gave way to his beast. His hips flexed faster and faster, his teeth sought her shoulder and once more he staked his claim on the beautiful woman that now carried his child.

When the water finally grew cold they went to bed. He wrapped his body around hers and sought her breast, cupping it gently with one hand. His other hand found her flat stomach where their child now rested and he splayed his fingers over the warm flesh. His voice was husky in her ear, "Mine."

***

The scent of the forest surrounded them. They sprang over broken limbs and ducked beneath low hanging branches. A not so gentle nip at her flank caused her to turn sharply and extend her teeth in Brandt's direction while she tried to grab his front leg. He was able to twist and tackle her. They rolled in the pine needles and he shifted to human. Her blue wolf eyes stared appreciating his muscled biceps and powerful legs holding her in place.

"Change my love."

It was a command she couldn't resist. Human arms closed around him becoming the perfect match for his. "I love you."

He tightened his hold and he sniffed her neck, inhaling her scent. He could feel wetness on his chest and looked down at her beautiful breasts. Milk leaked and dampened his skin causing him to rub sensually against her. "Our son will need his mother soon but I need her more right now.

"Then stop talking and do your worst."

His laugh was a husky growl. "My worst will make you scream and your moans will echo through the trees."

Blue challenged black, "I'm waiting."

"Mine." he said before his lips claimed hers.

***

South America

The room was dark only a small sliver showed through the solid door that kept him imprisoned. Chains, attached to his arms and legs, also secured him to the wall. He was barely able to lie on the floor.

A putrid bucket for waste sat next to him but he had not eaten in weeks or drank water in days. He no longer needed the bucket. His body filthy, with lice skittering through his shaggy hair, and blood crusted on his skin, he no longer cared.

He was dying. Lack of food and water---torture, and the loss of his pack had finally taken away his will to live. The next beating would be his last.

When he arrived in hell, he swore he would take cats with him before he died but that was no longer possible. Revenge couldn't hold back his pain; grief was no longer important. He gave up but knew his friends would take retribution for the murder of his family. Darkness descended, he hoped this was death.

Light entered his cell then shadows quickly replaced it as the door closed. His mind was cloudy but he knew this was his last moment on earth.

Did he have a burst of energy to fight one last time? He didn't think so.

The steps approached. They were soft, coming closer than usual. Maybe they thought him so near death it no longer mattered. A body knelt beside him. The cat was inches from his hands.

Fuck yes; he would finally take one with him in death.

Every last bit of alpha's power roared through his body. Coming to his knees he wrapped his hands around the throat of his enemy.

So weak, where once he could twist off a head, this death would take longer. He swore he would squeeze every breath of air from the cat's body.

He wanted to see the eyes that would precede him in death. His wolf gaze took over and through the darkness he pulled the dying man closer.

Panic filled green spheres with black cat irises stared back. Small hands came up to clasp his, Zenya.

A female cat he met once before he landed in hell. Shock loosened his grip.

Terror stared back and she sucked air sharply into her lungs. Her throaty words barely made it past her lips. "Amy sent me."

His fingers loosened more. His rasping words growled into her ear. "Helping me won't save you. I will kill every cat alive."

She was now taking deep long breaths but her eyes never wavered. "Fine Nicolas, but kill me when you don't need me anymore."

"That can be arranged."

Author's Note

As with all my books there is a team of people who are with me during my publishing journey. Special thanks to my mom and Linda, you always make me better than I really am. Fantasia Frog Design is responsible for my amazing cover. You are simply incredible and it's my favorite though I haven't seen the cover for book III yet. To the wonderful tribe I belong to on Triberr "Steamy Sexy Sensual Romance" You ladies rock. To everyone who read Amy's Story, left a comment on my blog, review on Barnes & Noble, Amazon, or All Romance Ebooks thank you for inspiring me to write. Denise at BlogHer; you always making me feel special and you are an awesome lady.

I invite readers to visit me at http://fangchronicles.wordpress.com for the latest news on my world of fangs or email delenmcclain@gmail.com. If you are willing to take a chance and read something different by me, I also write under the name Suzie Ivy about my day job as a midlife police officer.

Don't miss

Fang Chronicles: Amy's Story

Book I - Marcus & Amy

Amy is hot on a story as she tries to discover what life is like for teenage girls living on the street. When her disguise almost gets her killed, she's saved by one of New York's most eligible bachelors.

His private life is filled with secrets and his story sparks Amy's interest. Discovering the truth lands her in a world of vampires and werewolves that she never dreamed existed. She also never dreamed she could truly love a man or vampire but Marcus shows her the light. Now the two must fight the one person who can destroy their chance at love. With the help of Marcus' clan of werewolves the war begins.

~

Fang Chronicles: Zenya's Story

Book III Nicolas & Zenya

With a beastkind war on the horizon, and his entire pack wiped out by the southern lion pride, Nicolas longs for death after months of daily torture at the hands of his enemies.

Zenya, a werecat, rescued by wolves, places herself in danger's way because Nicolas's dark eyes haunt her dreams. They're natural enemies but their beasts have other ideas.

Add in a one-armed teenage hellion, a blind female with a heart of gold, and a deadly vampire with a boyish face, and Nicolas just might have a new clan.

Misfit cats, crazy wolves, and a special miracle combine with danger, love, and revenge in Zenya's Story.

~

Fang Chronicles: Mandy's Story

Book IV Honey & Mandy

Every beastkind knows you don't mess with a Kodiak bear—everyone that is except Mandy, the wolf-pack Alpha's sister. When Mandy hears whispers that the bad attitude bear, Honey, has chosen a mate, she takes matters into her own hands because her wolf decided months before that Honey was hers. If drugging, kidnapping, and making him live in a feral cage won't work she's planning to give Honey a little bad attitude of her own.

The bear clan is ferocious, deadly, and their fighting skills coveted by other beastkind. With war on the horizon, Honey has little time for games or courting much less more than a few grunts of acknowledgement to a young she-wolf who seems to be everywhere he looks. When he wakes up in a feral cage at the hands of that same exasperating she-wolf… all bets are off.

If anyone thought bears and wolves don't mix, they've never seen Mandy on a mission. She refuses to give into the sexy he-bear when he tries to seduce her out of her tight little assets and himself out of the cage she's locked him in. Two can play that game and in the end Honey will learn, they both need to win, or else.

~

Fang Chronicles goes back to the vamps!
Book V
Fang Chronicles: Dmitri
2014

Want some more D'Elen humor?

Read Bad Luck Cadet and Bad Luck Officer by Suzie Ivy, D'Elen's other pen name!

Available in e-edition at your favorite online bookstore

Made in the USA
Middletown, DE
24 March 2017